The last thing Tess wanted was to work with a man she'd slept with.

"But don't you ever think about that night?" Slaid asked.

She forced her voice to sound steady, cool. "Just so you know, I don't mix up my personal and professional lives."

"After what we shared, you couldn't at least leave a note? I didn't even know your name."

Tess wasn't used to feeling guilt. She swallowed it. "Well, now you know it. And if you insist I stay, that is still all that you'll know about me. Clear?"

Mayor Slaid Jacobs laughed, but it was a bleak sound. "Clear as day."

"Okay," she agreed. "Tomorrow, then. But I hope by then you'll have reconsidered your choice."

"Oh, no." He sat back down in his chair, crossing his long legs with his boots up on the desk. "I choose you, Tess."

Dear Reader,

Tess Cole, the heroine of this book, appeared fully formed in my imagination while I was writing my first novel, *A Ranch to Keep*. Unapologetically sexy and completely independent, Tess sat down next to my heroine in a bar and advised her to put on a trench coat and nothing else, and go seduce the man she desired.

I knew immediately that I wanted to write Tess's story, but I realized it would be challenging. Tess never had relationships, just the occasional one-night stand, and I had to try to understand why. What made her the way she is? And what kind of man could possibly be strong enough to stand up to her, and soulful enough to soften her?

Enter Slaid Jacobs, rancher, single dad and respected small-town mayor. Slaid believes in tradition and family and he takes his personal responsibilities and relationships very seriously. So what happens when he falls in love with Tess, who tries to avoid relationships altogether?

I hope you enjoy their story.

Wishing you joy,

Claire McEwen

CLAIRE McEWEN

—

Convincing the Rancher

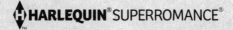
HARLEQUIN® SUPERROMANCE®

Recycling programs
for this product may
not exist in your area.

ISBN-13: 978-0-373-60894-2

Convincing the Rancher

Copyright © 2015 by Claire Haiken

Printed in U.S.A.

Claire McEwen lives by the ocean in Northern California with her husband, son and a scruffy, mischievous terrier. When not dreaming up new stories, she can be found digging in her garden with a lot of enthusiasm but, unfortunately, no green thumb. She loves discovering flea-market treasures, walking on the beach, dancing, traveling and reading, of course! Visit her online at clairemcewen.com.

Books by Claire McEwen

HARLEQUIN SUPERROMANCE

A Ranch to Keep
More Than a Rancher

Visit the Author Profile page
at Harlequin.com for more titles

This book is dedicated to every reader who has overcome a difficult childhood and found a way to live and love despite the scars.

And to my husband and son, who teach me more about love every day.

Heartfelt thanks to my sister Beth, who works in public relations and generously shared her knowledge and experience while I was writing this book. And thank you to James Allen of Allterra Solar, who kindly answered all my questions about solar power. Any mistakes, detours from fact and embellishments are all mine!

And a special thank-you to Danny Click, for his guest appearance.

CHAPTER ONE

THE HIGH DESERT air nipped her skin with icy teeth. Tess hunched her shoulders and used her free hand to haul her collar up higher, but the frigid wind worked its way between the seams of her coat, stealing her warmth inch by inch. Clutching her phone, she paced the sidewalk, raising her voice as the wind tried to whip it away. "Ed, just because my friend moved out to this backwoods cow town, that doesn't make me qualified for this!"

"We've been over this, Tess. You already know the area." Ed's voice was calm, and she pictured her boss, comfortable and snug in his San Francisco office, probably sipping excellent coffee. She'd had to endure vile convenience-store slop on the drive down, and she was pretty sure there wasn't an espresso to be found in Benson, California.

"I've been here *once*." She could swear the formidable peaks of the Sierra Nevada were glaring at her. She still couldn't believe her best friend had left San Francisco behind for *this*.

"Come on, where is the Tess Cole I know and love? The one who enjoys a good challenge?"

"You mean the one who doesn't want to spend the next month in a town whose population wouldn't even fill our conference room?" Tess looked around at the white clapboard buildings, weathered by the fierce gusts that made this area so perfect for the wind farm she'd been sent here to sell. Down the street she saw a few ancient brick storefronts. It would be picturesque if Tess were a fan of the Wild West. She'd never cared much for history.

"Tess, did you call me just to complain? We've been having this same conversation for weeks. It's not going to be easy convincing that town to accept a wind farm, and you're the best community-relations person we've got. Anyway, don't you have a meeting with the mayor soon?" Ed didn't often get angry, but she could tell he was frustrated now.

Tess took a deep breath of the icy air, then another, calming herself. Silently counting to ten, she watched a semitruck trundle past, headed down Highway 395 toward Los Angeles. For a split second she imagined flagging down the driver and begging a ride to Southern California. She'd readily leave Ed and his windmills far behind for some sunshine, shopping and fine dining. That was her world. Not snow-topped mountains, cattle and a wind farm no one wanted.

But she also didn't want to get fired. If she ever left Ed's public relations firm, it would be on her own terms. "You're right, Ed. I'd better get started."

She made her voice contrite, but in her mind's eye she gave him a kick in the shin. It felt good.

"You can do this. Sell them on this wind project. The sooner you do, the sooner you can come home." Ed hung up and Tess listened to the silence a moment, his absence still her closest link to home.

Shoving her phone into her coat pocket, Tess stretched, cramped after the long drive from San Francisco. She looked around, coming to terms with her exile. Benson was located on the edge of a huge flat valley that seemed to come in two forms, brown pasture and brown desert. It would all be incredibly boring except for one thing. Just beyond the town, the abrupt peaks of the Sierra Nevada jutted straight up. Their jagged cliffs seemed to roll on endlessly, one granite slab piled behind another. It was only October, but there was already snow on the mountaintops.

It was pretty if you liked your nature freezing and intimidating. Tess had never given nature much thought, but walking up Main Street, she decided that this was definitely not her kind of nature. If she had to pick a favorite, it would be tropical, with beaches and fruity drinks.

Benson town hall towered over all the other buildings, built of granite cut from the surrounding mountains. Luckily, Tess found a restroom just beyond the creaky double doors. She stood in front of the mirror, inventorying the damage to her carefully assembled look.

The mirror's vintage glass provided only a wavy reflection, but one thing was clear—she was a mess. Her long blond hair, once slicked into a neat chignon, was now poking out in every direction. Her mascara had fragmented into ebony dust. And her pink cheeks and cold-reddened nose completed the havoc wreaked by the Benson wind.

Tess reached into her leather tote for her voluminous makeup bag. The sight of the colorful tubes and jars lifted her spirits a fraction. The Benson climate might challenge her skills, but she had no doubt she'd soon figure out the right products for the harsh conditions.

Her hair back in place, her face perfected once again, Tess plucked a piece of lint from her suit jacket and pulled the skirt down. It hadn't looked nearly this short in San Francisco, but something about this historic granite building made her outfit choice seem frivolous. It would have been better, and a whole lot warmer, to wear a pantsuit. *No regrets,* she reminded herself. *No regrets, ever.*

Briefcase in hand, she left the restroom and stepped lightly up the stairs into the marble-floored reception area. A wholesome-looking young woman sat at the desk, and her eyes widened in surprise when she saw Tess.

"I have an appointment with the mayor," Tess informed her. "Please tell him that Tess Cole is here." She kept her voice firm and polite, no trailing questions at the end of her sentences. It was best to take charge up front.

"Um…yes, I'll get him right away." Her old wooden chair screeched on the marble floor as the young woman stood up. She clumped down a hallway to the right of the desk. Tess watched as the girl poked her head through the third doorway on the left, and then returned, self-consciously straightening the hem of her dress. "Go ahead, Ms. Cole," she told Tess, and sat down at her desk again to shuffle papers.

Tess walked down the hall toward the open door of the mayor's office. As she drew closer, she heard a deep, clear voice saying, "Gus, we have always closed down Main Street for the holiday parade." Tess paused outside the door, annoyance creeping in. If he was expecting her, why was he on the phone? The voice was momentarily silent, as its owner, presumably Benson's mayor, listened to someone on the other end of the line. "I would disagree," the masculine voice continued. "I think the parade is good for business, and if I remember correctly, your shop is always packed on parade day. Are you sure this doesn't have something to do with the fact that we asked Wyatt Silver to be the grand marshal this year?"

Gus? Wyatt Silver? These were names straight out of some old Western. What had she gotten herself into? She felt ridiculous standing in the hallway like this. He might be the mayor of the middle of nowhere, but courtesy was courtesy. Tess took a few quiet steps backward, cleared her throat and then stepped heavily, clicking her heels on the floor.

She heard the mayor say, "Gus, I'll need to call you back," just as she'd hoped. She knocked lightly and moved into the open doorway, plastering a confident smile on her face. Then she stopped, momentarily stunned.

The man sitting with cowboy-booted feet crossed on the desk was gorgeous. His light brown hair was cut short, almost military in style, and exposed his features, none of them perfect, but all together creating masculine beauty. Below his dark gray eyes was the outline of strong cheekbones, his skin clean-shaven and tanned. His nose was just slightly crooked, as if he'd broken it at some point.

Something about him looked familiar—she could swear she'd seen him before. Or did he just resemble a celebrity? Either way, she could think about it later. Right now she had to make a good first impression.

She stuck out her hand and strode toward the desk. "Mayor Jacobs, I'm Tess Cole, public relations consultant." As he stood slowly and reached for her hand, she realized he was staring, the surprise on his face turning into a slow smile that creased the weathered lines at the corners of his intense eyes. In that instant he shook her hand, it was clear that he recognized her, too. *But from where?*

His hand was huge and enveloped hers—there

was something familiar in that, as well. It could be just because Tess had a thing for big guys. And Mayor Jacobs was big. His six-foot-something frame towered over her five-eight. She was having a hard time not staring at his broad chest and his thick muscled arms under his sleeves. She'd never much cared for men in flannel and plaid, but Mayor Jacobs could probably change her mind about that.

What was wrong with her? She'd worked with all kinds of handsome men and always kept her cool. Maybe it was the way he was smiling so broadly now, his wide mouth open in a grin that revealed a single dimple in his cheek and even, white teeth.

"Why are you here?"

His abrupt question brought her back to earth— it was such a strange way to start a conversation. "I believe I explained that when I made this appointment? My firm is representing an alternative energy development company called Renewable Reliance."

"I remember. But I meant, why are *you* here?"

Now she was totally confused. Did they speak a different language in Benson? What was this cowboy talking about? "I'm sorry… I'm not following…" She kept her voice neutral.

"You don't remember me, do you?"

Tess froze. She was at a disadvantage. Something she absolutely hated. She scanned her brain for some situation where she might have met the mayor before. Then it hit her, and tension turned to relief. "Oh, yes! It was when Samantha married Jack, right?" The mayor looked puzzled, so she tried again. "Samantha Rylant? She married Jack Baron about six months ago. She's a good friend and they live in Benson. We must have met at their wedding."

The mayor gave a short laugh, studying her face with an expression of disbelief on his own. "I know them pretty well. But I was out of town for that happy occasion. I…" He paused as if catching himself. "I'm sorry, why don't you have a seat." He indicated the chair opposite his desk and she sat down reluctantly. He sat down as well, moving with surprising grace for such a big man. He leaned back and regarded her bemusedly over the vast mahogany expanse. "I guess I would have hoped our previous meeting was a little more memorable for you."

Now she really was at a loss. "I'm really not…"

"Phoenix, Arizona? The Fairway Resort?"

She'd been there, as a guest speaker at a convention a couple years ago. "Oh, were you attending the PR conference?"

"No, I wasn't." He watched her carefully.

"Then where did we…" The realization hit her in the stomach and chest, and her heart started pounding. This couldn't really be happening. Tess kept her work life and personal life separate—completely separate—until now. A one-night stand. She'd had a one-night stand with the mayor of Benson.

Recollections of that one night trickled in and she felt her face warm. Memories of his huge hands roaming her body, the way he'd felt surrounding her, inside of her. How had she not recognized him? She felt hot for the first time since she'd arrived in Benson. She was blushing—and she never blushed.

She tilted her chin up. No way was she letting him know she was this rattled. The smile she gave him was one she'd practiced for a long time—slow, confident and just a bit seductive. "You know, it *is* coming back to me now."

"You left." He steepled his fingers and looked at her over them. "You walked out before dawn. I never got your name."

"It's simpler that way."

His expression darkened. "Simpler for you."

Tess looked up at the old stamped-tin ceiling. If there was some kind of patron saint for sinners like her, she could really use some intervention right now. This was way too uncomfortable, and certainly not the first impression she'd hoped to make.

She stood. "Mayor Jacobs…"

"Slaid." His eyes were deep and dark and troubled. "Or did you forget my name, too?"

She had. Though in her defense, they'd been drinking whiskey neat—a lot of it. She might not remember his name, but she remembered the headache she'd had when she'd crept out of his room after he'd fallen asleep. After the most amazing sex she'd ever had. The mayor of Benson might have been a one-night stand, but the raging chemistry between them had meant there'd been no boundaries, no embarrassment, just an insane heat. That night had haunted her, had become the standard by which she judged the men she slept with since. None of them had ever measured up. How had she not recognized him?

Her hands went to her burning cheeks. "Slaid, I apologize if my memory is faulty. It was a while ago."

"Two years," he said.

"Okay. Two years." He obviously had a great memory, and Tess didn't want to think about what else he might be remembering. "It's very strange to meet you again in this way."

"Yes," he agreed. He was standing now as well, one hand fiddling with a pen he'd picked up, betraying that he, too, was uncomfortable.

This situation was a disaster. But there was a silver lining. This could be her ticket out of Benson. "I'll tell you what. I'm going to call my boss and we'll put a different consultant on this job, so it doesn't have to be awkward for you. Okay?" She started backing away, wondering how she would explain this situation to Ed. By laying out the mortifying truth, probably. He wouldn't replace her for any other reason. Her past relationship with Benson's mayor would jeopardize their success here—that much was clear.

"No." Slaid's voice was firm.

"No?" Tess echoed. How could he not see how messy this would be?

"It's not okay with me. Of course you can go, but be sure to mention to your boss that if he puts anyone else on this project, I won't be cooperative."

"But that makes no sense." Tess was practically pleading. The last thing she wanted was to try to work with a man she'd slept with. A man who was making her feel so unsettled right now that she could barely think.

"It makes sense to me and I'm the mayor. Any PR consultant working for an energy firm will need a decent relationship with me to get their job done, and I don't want a replacement. You're the consultant I want to work with."

Tess stared at him in horror and growing concern. "Why?"

His voice softened. "Don't you ever think about that night?"

He wanted sex. How disappointingly predictable. Although somewhat tempting... She forced her voice to be steady and cool. "Just so you know, I don't mix up my personal and professional lives. Ever."

"Seems as though in this situation you already have." His voice was soft but his jaw was set. He wasn't backing down, that was clear.

"I'm not responsible for this bizarre coincidence, Mayor Jacobs."

He didn't answer, just raised an accusatory eyebrow. The jerk. It wasn't as though she'd taken advantage of him. He'd been an extremely enthusiastic participant that night. "If you insist that I stay, it's a hundred percent professional between us. Is that very clear?"

Mayor Slaid Jacobs laughed, but it was a bleak sound. "Clear as day. We're adults. And if you're here to discuss energy development, we'll likely have a rocky road ahead. It won't be a problem to keep things professional."

"What do you mean, 'a rocky road ahead'?" Tess was angry now. "This is exactly why we need to get someone else on this job, Mayor Jacobs. You don't know anything about the project, yet you're already making assumptions that we'll be on opposite sides."

"People constantly show up here trying to get their hands on our resources. In the eighteen hundreds the prospectors came for the gold. In the twentieth century Los Angeles took most of our water. Nowadays everyone's after the minerals in our hills and the gas underneath. So what are *you* after?"

"You mean, what is *Renewable Reliance* interested in? They're investigating wind-energy production in this area. And, as I've experienced since arriving in Benson, you definitely have enough wind."

"Yes we do. And it's not for sale."

"You have no information. How can you say that?" This was ridiculous. Was he out for some kind of revenge?

"I don't need information to imagine what a bunch of windmills will do to the economy of my town."

She'd said she'd keep this professional and she would, no matter what. The key was to be patient. "I think if you keep an open mind, you'll find that the wind project can benefit Benson in many ways."

"Maybe." But there was no maybe in his tone.

"I'm sorry, but it feels like you are making this personal," she ventured.

"I'm the mayor and I've lived here all my life. Of course I take anyone trying to put a large energy project in our area a bit personally." He paused, his voice more neutral when he spoke again. "Where is this company hoping to site these windmills?"

"East of town," Tess replied. "But I don't have the exact location yet. They promised to send me maps within the next couple days. As soon as I know, I'll inform you, of course."

"And I assume they'll be providing environmental impact reports, a public comment period, et cetera?"

"Of course. My job is to present all the relevant information to the community."

"And you'll be in town for…"

"About a month, I think."

"A month." She watched his face for some clue as to how he felt about that. But his jaw was set, and it was hard to read more than stubbornness in his expression.

"Well, I look forward to hearing what you have to say, Tess." There was a touch of sarcasm in his tone.

"I think you need to reconsider my offer to get a replacement." Tess tried again. "Clearly you have a problem with me."

"I don't." He didn't elaborate, just glanced at the old clock hanging on the wall. Its ticking was suddenly loud in the silence between them. "Listen—" he looked frustrated, as if the confidence he'd been projecting was wavering a touch "—can I suggest we reschedule this meeting for tomorrow morning? Say nine-thirty? It will give us both a little time to regroup."

Tess bit back the words that wanted to spill out— words containing all the arguments she'd been studying up on over the past few weeks. He was right about one thing. Now wasn't the time to make them. She needed to step back, regain composure and strategize on how she would present the details of this project to him in the most positive light. "You're right, Mayor Jacobs. I'm tired from the drive and I'm sure you have a lot to do." She motioned vaguely to the stack of papers on his desk.

"We'll meet tomorrow morning. Perhaps by then you will have reconsidered your decision. I have some extremely competent colleagues who could take over for me."

"Oh, no." He sat back down in his chair and crossed his long legs with his boots up on the desk once more. "I choose you, Tess. So get used to it."

She noticed how thick and muscular his thighs looked under his jeans, and instantly a searing memory of what they'd felt like in Phoenix surfaced. Muscles, ropey and taut, so big her hands had felt dwarfed as they moved along them.

Tess jerked her gaze from his legs and glared at his face instead. "I may have to stay here and work, but I don't work for you. So please don't tell me what to get used to."

He raised his hands in mock defense. "Point taken."

"Thank you." There was nothing more to say. Tess turned and walked sharply out of his office. Her shoulders ached, muscles taut as if already gearing up for the fight ahead. Her stilettos hit heavily on the marble floor, the sound echoing in the empty hall. She wondered what Slaid was thinking as he listened to her walk away.

CHAPTER TWO

THE SUITCASE SLIPPED out of her hand and landed on her foot. Tess gasped, tears welling in her eyes. She was not going to cry. No matter what life threw at her—and it had thrown a lot worse than a resentful mayor and a painful suitcase—she never gave it the satisfaction of her tears. She waited for the pain to pass, pushing it away until it subsided into a minor, throbbing inconvenience. Slamming the hatchback of her rental Jeep, she studied the house Samantha had found for her to rent. It was three blocks off Benson's main street, putting it right on the edge of town.

When she'd been a kid, growing up in the despair of public housing and the chaos of foster homes, Tess had dreamed of living in a house like this—a classic, clapboard, turn-of-the-century cottage with a white picket fence. She'd never have dared to hope, back then, that her dreams would come true. An odd lump formed in her throat as she stared at the evidence to the contrary. Though nowadays, a country cottage wasn't really her style.

"Tess!" Her name was accompanied by the roar

of an engine and Samantha pulled up to the curb, looking surprisingly at home at the wheel of a huge silver SUV. Her friend cut the engine and tumbled out to fling her arms around Tess. "I'm so glad you're here!"

"Look at you in your mom-mobile! You are the cutest pregnant lady ever, Sam!" Tess tried to hug Samantha back but it was hard to get close enough with a baby bump between them. Her friend was in the third trimester, and on her tiny frame, her pregnancy was really showing. "This isn't working!" Tess pulled back laughing and put one arm around Samantha's shoulders instead. She'd missed this closeness. For the first time since she'd arrived in Benson she felt a glimmer of hope. At least she'd have a chance to reconnect with her friend. "How'd the meeting with the mayor go?" Samantha asked.

Tess had no idea how to answer that. "Fine," she lied. Samantha picked up one of her suitcases, but Tess grabbed it back. "*You* are pregnant! I've got the bags."

Samantha sighed and opened the rickety gate. "It's so weird to have everyone trying to look after me."

"Get used to it. You've got a couple more months to go." Tess yanked her unwieldy suitcase roughly over the flagstone path.

"You know what else is weird and kind of terrifying?" Samantha asked as she pulled out a key for the door. "Trying to choose a house for you.

You live in a beautiful, modern apartment with a view of the entire city! There's nothing like that out here."

"I'm sure it's great," Tess reassured her.

She was lying again. Nothing was going to be *great* for her in Benson, especially with her and Slaid's history getting in the way, but that wasn't Samantha's problem.

"I think you'll like it, though I still wish you'd stay with us. We have our house, *and* we have my grandmother's old farmhouse furnished and ready."

Tess felt a pang of guilt. "That's so kind of you, but I think if I stay in town it will be easier to make contacts in the community." She didn't want to hurt her friend's feelings, but the last thing Tess wanted was to stay in Samantha's house, or anywhere on Samantha's ranch, where life revolved around her friend's pregnancy. She wished her memories didn't hurt so much, but they did. "Besides, aren't you turning Grandma Ruth's house into a bed-and-breakfast? You don't need me getting in the way while you're working on it."

Samantha smiled sheepishly. "I don't know… Maybe I'm too sentimental… I can't seem to change anything about it. So for now it's my office and a guesthouse. Perfect for friends…like you!"

Tess realized her excuses weren't satisfying her friend, and there was no way she could tell Samantha the real reason. Because despite a decade of friendship, Tess had never explained that she'd had a baby—or that she'd placed it with an adoptive family. Or that she'd never been able to forget those few moments she'd held her son, and the complete devastation she'd felt saying goodbye to him. There were a lot of things she'd never told anyone, and it was way too late to start now. So she shrugged and plastered a smile on her face. "Unfortunately, my friend, I am here to work, and being near you would be too tempting. I'd want to hang around your gorgeous ranch and gossip all day."

That seemed to appease Samantha. She pushed open the front door, revealing a small entryway, the whitewashed wood panels punctuated by a line of iron coat hooks. "Welcome home, then," she said with a tentative smile.

Inside, Tess left her bags by the door and followed Samantha on a tour of the cottage. Her friend had been careful in her choice, and it showed. The old plank floors were polished and the walls were a clean white. The tall windows and high ceilings let sunlight flood the rooms. It was soothing. There was a front bedroom that had been turned into an office, and Tess appreciated the old scarred pine table that served as a desk—there was a lot of space to spread out and work.

The shabby-chic decor was the exact opposite of the sleek modern pieces Tess had chosen at home, but she had to admit that it perfectly suited this place. There was a cozy kitchen with a giant gas stove and a comfortable living room with overstuffed armchairs in front of a fireplace. The tiny bedroom was dominated by a scrolled iron bed frame. Tess noted with relief that two extra duvets were stacked on top. She would need them for the cold fall weather out here.

"Tea?" Samantha walked down the tiny hallway toward the kitchen.

After her meeting with the mayor, Tess would have preferred a brandy. "Sure," she answered, and hauled her suitcases into the bedroom. She sat on the edge of the bed for a moment, pulling the pins from her hair, letting it fall around her face. She took a deep breath and exhaled. Her heart hadn't slowed down since she left the mayor's office and her mind was whirling, asking the same question over and over. How was it possible that she'd slept with the mayor of Benson?

She heaved herself up and walked into the kitchen on leaden legs, gratefully accepting the steaming tea Samantha handed her. Its warmth was somewhat comforting. There was a small table by the back window of the kitchen, and Samantha lowered herself carefully onto one of the chairs. Tess sat down opposite her because that was what was expected. And if she just did what was expected, then she wouldn't do what she really wanted, which was to call Ed and threaten to quit if he didn't let her go home.

She looked out the window. On this side of the house, they had a view of the rear garden with its small flagstone patio. There was a fire pit in the center of it surrounded by a few old, wooden Adirondack chairs painted in festive colors. It was a cheery scene until she looked beyond the picket fence, where there was only high desert. The dry ground was speckled with scrubby bushes until the hills got high enough to be speckled in granite. Then they sloped abruptly and turned into mountains.

"This is a great spot!" Samantha enthused.

"It's beautiful." Beautiful in a rugged, formidable way that made Tess want to jump in her car and race home. "I appreciate all of your help. The house is perfect."

"You'll be able to sit here and see all kinds of animals—jackrabbits, deer. And that fire pit will be a lovely place to sit at night and watch the stars."

The enthusiasm in Samantha's tone left Tess bewildered. Lonely contemplation had to be one of her least favorite activities. She looked at her friend instead of the window—there was way too much open space out there, too much quiet. "I'm not much of a stargazer."

"Maybe you'll become one now. Just wait until it gets dark. You'll be amazed at how clear the sky is here in the fall."

Tess made a mental note to stay inside and close the curtains at dusk. Time to change the subject. "How are you feeling anyway?" she asked Samantha, knowing she should.

"Hungry. And sleepy. I just want to nap, then sleep, then nap some more."

"Of course." Tess remembered her pregnancy, how her body had craved sleep so badly there were days she couldn't keep her eyes open. Her uneasiness morphed into full-blown anxiety. The long drive today, with so much wilderness all around, had cracked open the closed doors of her mind, the ones that usually kept memories like this at bay.

"So what did you think of our mayor?" Samantha asked.

Her meeting with Slaid was another life event she'd like to shove behind a closed door. "He seems nice enough." She tried her best to sound disinterested. "But I couldn't really tell—we only met for a few minutes. What's he like?"

"Well, handsome, for one thing. But you're probably already aware of that."

Oh, boy, was she ever. She could instantly picture what he'd looked like in that hotel room in Phoenix, skin bronzed over the toned muscles of his abs, his thick erection pressing against her thigh as he leaned on one elbow, trailing a hand across her breasts.

"Tess!" Samantha's laugh brought her out of her reverie. "Where did you go? He must have made quite an impression!"

Her face got hot.

"I don't think I've ever seen you blush! What's

going on?" Samantha's extraordinary green eyes were wide and full of confusion.

Tess couldn't look at her friend and confess at the same time, so she looked out at the intimidating view instead. "I slept with the mayor." It was a relief to just say it.

"What?" Samantha gasped. "Today?"

"Not today! I'm not *that* crazy." She looked back at her friend and had to laugh at the arched brows. "Okay, maybe I *am* that crazy sometimes. But it was about two years ago. On a business trip to Phoenix."

"You've got to be kidding me."

"Unfortunately not," Tess said weakly.

"And let me guess. You did the Tess Cole tiptoe of shame."

Tess laughed at her friend's skewering look. "Yes, of course. But it's not shame—it's practicality. I don't want to get involved, and neither do they, so it's best just to get out of there before anyone has to make any awkward, meaningless, morning-after conversation."

Samantha sighed. "And how did it go, then, when the mayor discovered who you were?"

"Not well," Tess admitted. "It didn't help that it took me a while to recognize him. He seemed kind of upset."

"Yes." Samantha nodded, and Tess glanced over. Her friend was staring out the window now, with a slightly sad expression on her face. "I imagine he was."

"What is it?"

Samantha looked at her, biting her lower lip as if considering how to answer.

"Please tell me, Sam. I'm in a mess here."

"Slaid's a great guy. A really good mayor and very well liked around here." Samantha paused.

"But?" Tess prompted.

"He's sort of a model citizen. His father was mayor, and his grandfather…and he was a big high school football star. He goes to church every Sunday. And even though he keeps really busy with his own ranch and running our town, he always seems to have time for whoever needs him…" Her voice trailed off.

"So you're saying…"

"I don't see him as the one-night-stand kind of guy."

"Yeah, I kind of got that impression today." Tess sighed.

"There's more," Samantha said. "Personally, he's had a rough time of it. A couple years ago, his wife left him and their son. She moved away and hasn't been back. It was hard on Slaid, and his son has had a tough time, too. Lately it seems as if they've both been doing a lot better. As if they're healing."

Tess looked back at the view over the desolate plains and the mountains beyond, putting the pieces of Slaid's history together. She'd met him two years ago. Obviously, Mr. Perfect had had a bad moment after his wife left him and slept with a strange woman in Phoenix. That would be her. Tess. Who had then walked out on him and made him feel even worse. "I don't know how I'm going to work with him," she confessed.

"So the meeting *really* didn't go well," Samantha clarified.

"No."

"Tess," Samantha said quietly, and put a soft hand on her arm. "I hate to suggest it, or even think about it because I want you here in Benson, but professionally, the right thing to do might be to excuse yourself from this project."

"I tried!" Tess sat up straighter as the confusion of their meeting returned. "I told him right away that I would get someone else to take over for me and he said no! And when I insisted, he told me he'd…" She thought of Slaid's gilded reputation in this town. She couldn't share the threat he'd made in such a bad moment. She owed him that much. "Well, he just insisted that I stay on. He doesn't want anyone else on the project. It makes no sense. Shouldn't he want me to go? I could ruin his reputation if I told people about Phoenix!"

Her friend didn't answer for a moment and they just sat, leaning on their elbows, staring at each other. Finally Samantha spoke. "That's just weird."

And there it was, summed up perfectly. Tess was

surprised by her own laughter. "It is! Do you think he wants to keep me here just to torture me?"

"Maybe it's a case of the devil you know," Samantha said. "Maybe he's nervous about having a consultant around and he figures that at least he knows you."

"But he doesn't!" Tess said. "Not at all… Well, only in a naked and sweaty kind of way, but other than that, we're strangers!"

"A naked and sweaty kind of way…" Samantha giggled. "Tess, you are the only person I know who would end up in this predicament. It could be a sign that it's time to mend your wild ways."

"To be honest, my ways have been a lot less wild the past couple of years," Tess confided. "It all gets kind of boring after a while."

"Boring?" Samantha repeated. "You have definitely been sleeping with the wrong men. Perhaps it's time for something new. Like getting to know the guys first for a change."

"That is *far* too much work," Tess countered. "No, I'm pretty sure vibrators were invented for people like me. They don't ask for much, just a few new batteries every now and then."

"Tess!" Samantha exclaimed in shock. And then the laughter started again and Tess put her head down on the table, resting it on her folded arms, laughing until her hands were wet with tears. When she looked up, Samantha was wiping her own eyes and grinning at her. Tess suddenly felt a deep gratitude. Even if Mayor Slaid Jacobs came to his senses and ran her out of town tomorrow, she was glad she got to have this laugh with her friend today. She hadn't realized just how much she'd missed her.

"So how was that night with the mayor two years ago, if you don't mind me asking?"

"Incredible." Tess sighed, remembering how much she'd wanted him then. How much she could still want him now if she let herself. "Truly amazing."

"What are you going to do?"

"Just try to pretend it never happened, I guess. And keep out of his way whenever possible. Hopefully he'll realize how much better it would be to have someone else on this job."

"I know you'd like to get back to the city," Samantha said softly, "but I kind of hope you stay."

"You know I could never move out here like you did."

The teasing light was back in her friend's eyes. "Never say never. This place has a way of growing on you. Stay too long and it might even get under *your* skin."

Tess glanced back out the window, at the vast mountains filling the horizon, and the enormous empty sky graying with the dusk. She shivered. It wouldn't grow on her. She'd be lucky if she survived a month of all this cold solitude and silence.

SLAID SAT DOWN heavily on the rock and twisted the top off his beer. The cold bitterness was exactly what he needed after his visit from Tess today. He looked up at the nearby peaks, noticing the way the setting sun lit up the granite. Something he'd seen almost every day of his life, yet had never taken for granted.

He liked this rock. His son called it The Thinking Rock because Slaid had come out here a lot after Jeannette had left them, to brood and try to figure out where it had all gone wrong. Now that Devin was a teenager, they came up here together for the occasional heart-to-heart.

It was up on the edge of their property, where the hills started to give way to the mountains, and it had a good view. He could see his house in miniature below—a low rancher his father had built in classic '50s style. It wasn't picturesque like some of the old farmhouses in the area, but big glass doors gave way to all kinds of patios and he liked that mix of inside and out. He never felt removed from the land he loved.

A motion beyond the house caught his eye. Devin was leading Orlando out of the barn. His son tied the horse to a fence and started brushing the gelding's smooth gray coat. Slaid knew he should be the one doing that task. Devin had plenty of his own chores to finish and then homework to start. It was just one example of how Tess Cole was already throwing him off his game.

Tess. The name suited her. Sleek and strong, just like the woman. He'd wondered about her name for the past two years. Wondered, sometimes, if there was any way to find her.

And now she was here, in Benson, more beautiful than he'd remembered and more unsettling than he could have imagined. Seeing her long, thick, blond hair wound up in that tidy bun today made him remember how it had curtained them as she'd straddled him on the bed, kissing him as if she was ravenous. Her curves in that sexy business suit reminded him of how her breasts had filled his hands, how her hips had moved when she'd ridden him.

"Hell." He said it aloud, and the sound evaporated into the empty sky. He took another gulp of beer and felt a twinge of regret when he realized it was almost empty. He probably should have stashed a few more bottles in his pockets before he left the house. If he were a less-responsible guy he would have gone for it. But he was *very* responsible, usually. Just not that night in Phoenix.

That night he'd been lonely, recently dumped, and just drunk enough to step out of the confines of his normal behavior and proposition the unbelievably sexy woman draped on the bar stool next to him. For one night he hadn't been the guy whose wife had walked out on him, or the dad whose kid was tearing up the town with his seemingly infinite reserves of anger. For one night he hadn't been the dutiful son, responsible for the hopes and dreams of the generations of ranchers who'd left him their legacy. He'd just been an anonymous man, making love to an anonymous woman in an anonymous hotel room, and it had been the hottest night of his life.

But she wasn't anonymous anymore.

What he'd done in their meeting earlier came back to him garnished with a twist of guilt. He'd pressured her to stay—hell, he'd *made* her stay.

Maybe he'd done it out of anger. It confounded him that she didn't remember him. How was it possible that one night could mean so much to one person and so little to another? He'd thought about her countless times, and she'd walked into his office today with no clue who he was. She'd looked at him as if he was a total stranger while she was etched so clearly in his memory. Well, she'd remember him now, all right. Not for their night together—apparently that had been totally forgettable—but for the way he'd been an asshole and had selfishly pressured her to stay in Benson.

And then it hit him. He didn't hold all the cards here. She could chat to whomever she wanted about their one-night stand. And it could certainly change his life if she did. He wondered what his constituents would think if they knew what he'd done in Phoenix with Tess—*and* how much he'd enjoyed it.

The good people of Benson had elected him mayor almost unanimously. And why not? He was a pretty upstanding kind of guy. A high school football hero, college scholarship kid. Head of the Cattlemen's Association, a city council member and now, mayor of the town. People thought of him as an up-front, what-you-see-is-what-you-get kind of guy. And he was—except for that one night.

He should have agreed when she'd offered to leave town. It would have ensured that his reputation was never tarnished. Because it wasn't just his reputation he had to worry about. Being a leader in Benson was family tradition. His grandfather and his dad had both been mayor, and his great-grandfather had pretty much founded the town.

Maybe he owed his ancestors an apology because he hadn't been able to let her go. In some bizarre miracle, after two years as a ghost in his fantasies, she was here in Benson. And that had to mean something.

The problem was, he had no idea how he was going to handle having her in town. He'd promised her it would be easy to keep things professional, but he'd pretended a confidence he didn't have. All the attraction he'd felt that night in Phoenix was still there, sharpening his senses the moment she'd walked into his office, making him hyperaware of every one of her movements, every seductive curve under that power suit she wore.

Which made the reason she was here even worse. Windmills. Looking out to the plains beyond his ranch, he tried to imagine them speckled with huge, white turbines and instantly all the wild emptiness was domesticated and destroyed. It was awful enough to imagine—he couldn't allow it to happen.

Slaid drained the bottle and stuck it back in his pocket, taking one last look at the view. There was dinner to cook, dishes to clean, homework to help with and a few rounds of a video game to play before Devin went to bed. Then he needed to rewrite the agenda for next week's city council meeting to make sure the wind farm was on it—there'd be a lot to discuss.

It would be a busy night, but he kind of liked it that way. Staying busy kept him from thinking too much. He'd learned that trick after Jeannette had left Benson, and it seemed as though he would need it again now that Tess Cole had arrived.

CHAPTER THREE

TESS WASN'T PREPARED for a Jeep that looked like an ice sculpture. With a pang of longing, she pictured her underground parking space in San Francisco, where even on the rare frosty morning she never had to worry about a frozen car. Reluctantly she opened her wallet and stared at her rainbow assortment of credit cards, wondering which one she could sacrifice as an ice scraper. The Saks Fifth Avenue card was nice and thick and would work the best, but she didn't want to risk ruining it. Same with Bloomingdale's. And there was no way she'd sacrifice Nordstrom—their annual shoe sale was coming up.

She finally settled for Talbots and started scraping at the frosted windshield. The ice came off in a spray coating her bare skin. "Ow!" she exclaimed and pulled her hand away abruptly, shaking it to try to get the frost off and the heat back in.

"Don't tell me you didn't bring gloves?" The deep voice had her whirling to confront the mayor. He looked warm and comfortable, his thick parka advertising the fact that *he* was prepared for the weather. The battered leather cowboy hat on his head was one more reminder that she'd left San Francisco far behind.

"It's probably seventy degrees at home today," she said by way of an answer.

"It's seventy degrees in San Francisco most days. Didn't you check the weather report before you drove out here?"

She hadn't. She'd been in denial until she'd pulled into town yesterday. Despite all the arguments with Ed and the cramming she'd done to understand wind power, she'd ignored the fact that she'd be living in this tiny town in the middle of nowhere for the next month or so. Tess could safely say that denial was one of her strongest abilities.

But now there was no denying two things: she was totally unprepared for the weather in Benson, and Slaid Jacobs was one of the most attractive men she'd ever laid eyes on. The navy blue of his parka somehow made his gray eyes even more vibrant, and his broad shoulders filled out the jacket well. He'd tucked his dark denim jeans into brown suede work boots, laced up casually over the cuffs. He was perfectly at home in the cold, in comparison to her shivering self.

She wouldn't be here shivering if he was chivalrous. If he hadn't insisted that she stay in town. He might be good-looking, but right now she kind of hated him.

If he noticed, he gave no sign. "Tess, an idea.

We've got a shop here that sells all kinds of outdoor gear. Let's leave the car and walk over there. We can have our meeting as we go and you can get set up with the right clothing. You can't survive out here in that thin wool coat."

His voice was smooth and rich, like coffee. Like the espresso she couldn't have this morning because she was stuck in Benson.

"Is this your idea of a peace offering?"

He gave that slow, widening smile she'd noticed right away when she'd first seen him at the bar in Phoenix. It had done things to her then and it was having the same effect now. "Maybe it is. I don't know you too well, but you seem like someone who might like to shop. Plus, you look really cold."

Tess glanced down at her beloved gray Burberry, with the nipped-in waist and shiny black buttons, and sighed. The last thing she wanted was a shopping trip with Slaid, or a parka like his, but he was right about one thing—she was freezing. "Fine," she agreed. "Lead the way."

He held out his hand, and to her horror she almost took it. Slaid jerked his hand back before she could and shoved it in his pocket, obviously embarrassed, too. This was ridiculous. How were they supposed to work together?

She stumbled along next to him, her brain a chaotic mélange of feeling. Anger that he'd pressured her to stay in Benson, horror that her past had come back to haunt her and her natural appreciation of a gorgeous guy. Memories of what had happened between them that night in Phoenix scrambled her thoughts further. The images and sensations showed up like random jolts of electricity, leaving her nerve endings sizzling and frayed.

If she could just turn off those memories and focus on work and only work, she might be able to think coherently.

She tried to keep up with his long strides in her stiletto boots and keep an eye on the sidewalk, stepping over anything that looked like ice. She could endure a lot, but falling in front of Slaid might be her breaking point.

She didn't know what to do, so she did what she was best at. She went into business mode. "So thank you for taking his meeting with me...again. As I told you yesterday, I'm in town because I work for a public relations firm that has been hired by Renewable Reliance."

"Yes, the wind project," he said, his voice as dry as the desert. "I remember."

She plowed on. "I'm in charge of community relations."

"Well, you're off to a great start. Considering that you've already had relations with the town mayor."

Tess stopped abruptly as the initial hurt turned to fury. "Is this how you're going to handle this? Did you want me to stay so you can be self-righteous and hold that night over my head? Because I seem to remember that I wasn't alone in that hotel room. In fact, *you* invited me back to *your* room."

Slaid stared at the ground, and they walked a few steps in awkward silence. Then he broke it. "I was rude. It was a stupid thing to say. We agreed to keep things professional and I dropped the ball. It won't happen again."

She was momentarily disarmed by his apology. "Well, it was a fumble, but maybe you can recover."

He looked at her in surprise. "You know football?"

She needed a cordial relationship with him to make any progress with the community, which is how she justified her little white lie. "Sure. Some. I'm a San Franciscan. We love our Forty-Niners."

"So much that you ran 'em out of town."

Tess stared at him a moment, racking her brain for what she knew about the football team— something to explain his comment. A lightbulb lit in some dim corner of her mind. San Franciscans hadn't been able to agree on replacing foggy and crumbling Candlestick Park, and a neighboring city had happily jumped in to build the football team a new stadium. She gave a little laugh of relief. "Oh, yes. They're the Santa Clara Forty-Niners now. It doesn't have quite the same ring."

"But they're keeping their old name, right?"

"Oh, right. Of course." She was the one fumbling here. Hoping he'd attribute her red cheeks to the wind, she switched back to the topic she actually knew something about. "About the windmills—My job will be to interface with the community and make sure you, and the people of Benson, have up-to-date information about the project. I'll be responsible for presenting the environmental impact reports and creating opportunities for public input."

"And if I tell you that the only input the people of Benson will give you is a resounding *no*?"

"Then my job is to tell you that you're putting the cart in front of the horse. Renewable Reliance has a right to perform this exploratory process. They've already been granted the necessary permits from the Bureau of Land Management. And there will be plenty of opportunities for you and the citizens here to weigh in."

"But personally, you think this project is bogus."

"There is no *personally*. I'm here to do my job—to present information about the project to the public. I don't weigh in on the projects I represent."

"But, I take it, the information you present will be your client's side of the story."

"Of course. But it will be a true story. Just the facts."

"Facts can be bent."

"By *everyone* involved," she argued, "including you." She wanted to kick herself as soon as she said it. What was it about Slaid that made her lose her cool? She should be buttering him up right now, making him and his town feel special, lucky to be chosen as the site of a wind farm. Instead she was trading insult for insult.

They'd reached the door for Benson Wilderness Outfitters, and Slaid grasped the handle and pulled it open for her, but his expression was far from chivalrous. "I don't bend facts," he said.

"Well, neither do I." He waited and she waited, hands on her hips. Finally a slight smile of dawning understanding curved one corner of his full mouth. "You're not going to let me open this door for you, are you?"

"You go ahead," she answered. "I can get my own doors." She didn't want his bogus chivalry, but if he waited any longer she'd have to give in. She was rapidly going numb, and she craved the warmth she knew would be inside the shop.

"Stubborn much?"

"It's considered an asset in my field."

"I'll bet." Slaid went in first, letting the door swing shut behind him. Tess grabbed the handle and jerked it open again, relieved to feel the warm air on her frozen face.

Slaid walked partway across the shop, then turned to face her. "So you're pretty good at your job? That's why they sent you out here?"

"That's what my boss told me, but I think he was just desperate to get someone out here to this godforsaken place."

"Oh, no, not godforsaken." Slaid's smile was suddenly gentle. "Spend some time out here in these hills and mountains, and you'll know we're right in the heart of God's country."

"I may have to pass on that opportunity, Mr. Mayor. Trekking the great outdoors is not my style. Plus, I doubt that God would welcome a poor sinner like me strolling around his chosen land."

Slaid laughed and pointed to a wall of outdoorsy-looking boots, similar to his own. "Why don't you get some more practical shoes anyway, just in case God's a little more welcoming than you give him credit for?"

Despite all the tension between them, Tess had to laugh at that. She went over to study the boots, wondering which ones were the least ugly. This was strange. She'd never had a business meeting that involved shopping before. And she'd never have guessed Slaid would be so helpful. He quickly pointed out the most feminine and classy looking of all the hiking boots on the wall, and also found her some wool socks to try them on with. Then he came back with another pair of boots for wearing around town—knee-high black leather with a sturdy rubber sole and low heel. The kind of boots a lot of women were wearing to stride around San Francisco these days, though so far Tess had passed on the trend. But once she slid them on over the wool socks, she knew her style was going to change, at least for now. They were comfortable and, more important, warm.

Then Slaid wandered over with a knee-length

down coat in a rich, dark teal blue with fake fur lining a generous hood. Tess slid it on and was pleased to see that it was actually cut in a feminine line, not too thick and bulky. He handed her a sweet, matching teal wool hat and another one in black. He had her choose two kinds of gloves—black fleece for everyday and another pair, more like ski gloves, for when it snowed. Tess hoped she'd be long gone from Benson before *that* happened. After a couple of turtleneck sweaters were added to the pile, Tess stared at Slaid in awe. "You are a way better shopper than most of my girlfriends!"

He grinned. "I have a teenage son. I'm used to shopping quickly, before he gets too mopey."

She kept forgetting he had a son. Of course she did. She knew almost nothing about Slaid, except what Samantha had told her and what he looked like naked...and wanting. Tess quickly pushed that image from her mind, but not before it heated her face. She turned to a rack of scarves and studied them intently.

"How about that eggplant color," Slaid suggested. "Or the dark blue, to match your eyes. They really are so blue they're almost purple, aren't they?"

"The eggplant might go best with the teal coat."

He picked up the scarf and gently wrapped it around her neck. His fingers brushed the skin there and she shivered, fighting the sudden urge to lean into them. "Yep. Your eyes *are* almost purple."

She looked up then. His expression had grown

serious, his voice soft. "You're even more beautiful than I remembered." He was so close she could kiss him if she just leaned forward a few inches.

"And *that* is totally inappropriate," she reminded him, and herself, pulling away abruptly. But some strange fragment of her heart fluttered at his words. And she realized that by never sticking around to get to know the men she slept with, she'd missed out on little compliments like this. And another thought flickered. What else had she missed out on? She turned away and went to the front of the store, loading her items on the counter.

The clerk was on a ladder, hanging up climbing ropes on a high rack near the door. Slaid wandered up next to her and called, "Harris, this is Tess Cole. She's in town for a while and needed some warmer clothes."

Harris turned and grinned. "Hey, Slaid." The man climbed down and surveyed the pile of clothes. "Gotta make sure you're layered up for the mountains. You be careful out here, Tess. The weather can change on a dime, and you can count on some pretty cold nights this time of year."

"It's hard to believe I'm just a day's drive from San Francisco."

"A day's drive but a world away." Harris smiled as he loaded the clothes into a big paper bag.

"You're not kidding." Tess handed him her credit card, feeling hollow at his words. A world away and not the world she wanted to be in.

She sighed, unbuttoning her beloved wool coat and folding it carefully for Harris to put in the shopping bag. She slid her arms into the new parka, vowing to smack Slaid if he tried to help her into it, and ignoring the tiny twinge of disappointment that winged through her when he didn't. Zipped into the fluffy down, she was incredibly cozy, but all that puffiness felt a bit like she was wearing a spacesuit—as if she needed another reminder that she was in an alien environment.

But as soon as she stepped outside she was grateful for the down barrier between her and that crisp cold. They started along Main Street, back toward Tess's little cottage.

"I'm a little apprehensive to continue our meeting," Slaid said. "It seems as though when I'm around you, my foot goes in my mouth and I say the wrong thing. I'm sorry."

"Let just focus on work," Tess said. "Let's forget about that night two years ago. It doesn't matter, it's irrelevant."

"Right." Slaid nodded, but he gave her a slightly quizzical look. "Completely irrelevant."

"Yes." She hoped she could follow her own advice. His moments of kindness and humor had her a little worried, too. She couldn't afford any complications. Succeeding at this job required all her focus. And she could already tell that Slaid had the ability to make things a lot blurrier.

"So—" Slaid slowed his stride to match hers

"—to sum up our meeting, strictly business now, Renewable Reliance wants to put a wind farm here. And you get to be their spokesperson. What happens next?"

"I'll get all the informational materials together," she answered. "Make some pamphlets, translate the environmental impact report into clear talking points and make a video that we'll have available for people to download or watch at the library."

"All in a month?"

"If I'm lucky. I think a month of exile in Benson is all I can handle."

Slaid laughed. "Is that how you think of this? Exile?"

"Pretty much," she answered, glancing at him. When he really laughed it was low and deep, as if he was truly enjoying himself.

"You know," he said, his eyes still crinkled with humor. "A lot of people would consider you in paradise, not exile. We get tons of tourists out here to hike, mountain bike, camp, fish, rock climb, horseback ride…"

"None of which I have the slightest interest in."

"What *are* you interested in?"

Tess opened her mouth to answer and shut it abruptly. She thought quickly, mentally trying to pick apart her life in San Francisco. "Work, mostly. I shop. Go to the gym. Spend some time with friends." She suddenly wished she'd made time to take up a hobby.

"Huh." That was all he said—but it said a lot. When she looked at her answer from Slaid's point of view, her life, which she always tried hard to portray as glamorous and fascinating, actually seemed pretty boring.

Then he spoke. "How about you try a few of those things I mentioned while you're here?"

"You mean fishing? Hiking?"

"Why not? If your boss sent you out to live in the middle of nowhere, why not use a little of the time to try something different? I'd be happy to show you around, strictly as professional colleagues, of course. Maybe I could teach you a few new skills."

She flushed at his choice of words. He actually had taught her a few things during their night together. She was pretty sure she'd taught him a few, as well.

"Not like that." How had he read her mind? "Not to be crude, but I don't think you need much tutoring in that area."

Heat flooded her veins and lit up every nerve. "Slaid, I think it's best that we agree not to talk about *that* topic. We need to pretend that Phoenix never happened."

"Maybe." There was a pause and she glanced at his profile as they walked, trying to read what that *maybe* meant. He didn't elaborate.

"I'm here to work," she reminded him. "I have to be professional or I could compromise my credibility. And I'd hate to do anything to damage your image as mayor."

"And how might you do that?" He was looking down at her with a half smile. "You don't really strike me as the kiss-and-tell type. More like kiss and leave."

"Trust me, Mayor Jacobs. I was doing you a favor by stepping quietly out of your life—I won't apologize for that. And I told you yesterday, if you insist I stay on this project, I will, but that's the *only* thing I'm here for."

"Work isn't everything, Tess. And if you get to know the area, you might think twice about destroying it."

So that was his motivation. She shouldn't care, but for a moment she'd thought he really wanted to spend more time with her. And even if it was out of the question, it had been an enticing thought. "I don't know how else to explain it to you. I represent this project, but it's not *mine.* I have nothing to do with it and *I'm* not destroying anything—I'm simply here to interface with the public."

"But you just agreed that the project will destroy the area."

Tess wasn't sure if it was humor or malice that she saw in his eyes. "I agreed to no such thing! Stop trying to box me into a corner or make me feel guilty. I'm here to do my job and I intend to do it well. I assume you'll do your job to the best of your abilities, also. Just two civilized adults doing what we're being paid to do." They'd reached the gate in her picket fence. "I appreciate your time this morning, Slaid. I'll keep you informed as the project progresses. And thank you for the shopping trip."

"Are you warmer now?" he asked, and there was a softness in his voice that surprised her.

"Yes. Not my usual attire for the office, but it will have to do."

He looked her up and down. She could almost feel his gaze under her layers of warm clothing.

"I think it's an improvement. They have business casual clothing, why not business country? Business wilderness?"

"I'll ask my boss about it." She couldn't stand there with him any longer. Not with the strange wanting, that couldn't, *shouldn't* be rushing through her.

"Goodbye," she told him, and fled past the gate and through her front door, shutting it gratefully against the chill of the air and the heat that was Slaid. Maybe she was a coward, but she was ready to hide out in the temperate climate of her little cabin.

CHAPTER FOUR

TESS SAVORED THE rich taste of her cappuccino as it rolled across her tongue. After five days in Benson she'd fled to Samantha and Jack's house this morning and begged for espresso. She'd been as desperate for her fix as any addict. She swallowed blissfully and leaned back in her chair in Samantha's sunny kitchen. "Slaid deiced my car."

Samantha stopped stirring her coffee. "When?"

"Every single morning this week. I don't know when he does it because I never see him, but every morning someone has scraped the ice off my car. It has to be him!"

"Well, he is known for keeping early office hours," Samantha said. "Maybe he's doing it after dropping off Devin, his son, at school."

"He's making it hard to stay mad at him."

"I know you didn't appreciate him pressuring you to stay here. But can't you see that it's a little sexy, too? Maybe the guy is really happy that you're in town."

"But why?" Tess asked. "We've met twice since I arrived and all we did was argue! He thinks I'm an evil developer and wilderness destroyer and I think he's close minded and full of himself."

"They say there's a thin line between love and hate." Samantha's smile was so obviously hopeful that Tess laughed.

"We are not talking about love here! Quite the opposite."

"Okay, lust, then. Lust isn't logical. And admit it, you've thought about him over the past couple years, haven't you?"

"Once in a while." A lot. Way too often.

"Maybe you should just go out with him," Samantha suggested tentatively.

"Like on a date?" Tess repressed a shudder.

"Yes, a date. Like regular people do."

"Honey, I am not regular people when it comes to that stuff. I can't stand it."

"Even when there are perks like not having to scrape the ice off your car?" Samantha raised an eyebrow.

"Well, that is the one temptation."

"Now I know you're lying. *He's* a temptation. Half the women in this town are in love with the guy! Just his shoulders alone melt knees. In the summer they did a dunk tank for charity and he was in it and I don't think the female population talked about anything but his abs for months afterward."

"Okay, fine," Tess admitted. "Two temptations—he deices my car and he's good-looking. But it's irrelevant. I'm here for work, and even if I liked him, which I don't, or he liked me, which he doesn't, we couldn't get involved. Our relationship has to remain strictly professional."

Samantha sighed. "Well, you can't blame me for dreaming."

Tess laughed at that. "I know you're happy here in Benson, Sam, but don't get any ideas about being my matchmaker."

"But if you lived here, we'd see each other all the time. You could be in your godson's life almost every day!"

Tess stared at her friend in shock, then realized that the expression of horror on her face probably hurt Samantha's feelings. "Um...that would be great!" It hadn't occurred to her that she'd be asked to be a godmother.

"You'll do it, right?" Samantha asked. "Be godmother to our baby boy?"

Tess tried to suppress the flutter of panic in her stomach. "I'm so honored that you'd ask me." She took a deep breath and tried to wrap her mind around the idea. *Godmother.* So far she'd mostly managed to pretend that this baby wasn't really happening. Obviously she knew Samantha was pregnant, but Tess didn't like looking too far ahead. Soon the baby would be here, and she'd be expected to adore it, and she just wasn't sure she could handle that. Not after living through the pain of giving up her own child. "Absolutely. How exciting!"

The corners of her mouth ached with the effort behind her smile.

"Anyway, back to your situation." Apparently Samantha wouldn't be easily distracted from her matchmaking. "Slaid is a really good guy. And I bet deep down, he's crazy about you. Just give him a chance. You're here in Benson for a few weeks. Try something new—go on a date!"

"I'd rather try something *else* new."

"How about learning to ride?" Jack walked into the kitchen and poured coffee into a to-go mug. "I'm heading out to the barn right now. Apple needs exercise."

"My horse," Samantha explained. "She's getting fat right along with me."

"You're not fat. You're more beautiful than ever." Jack kissed his wife with such tenderness that Tess had to look away. It felt as though she was intruding. Jack put his hand on Samantha's belly, and his blue eyes shone with hope and happiness. "I can't wait to meet this little guy you're growing for us," he said softly, then kissed his wife once more and grinned at Tess. "I hope you're up for some baby-sitting duty, Aunt Tess."

Tess inhaled her coffee and spluttered out, "Of course." She needed to finish this project and get out of here before her friend's due date—that much was clear. "Well, it's been great to see you both," she said brightly. "But the windmills call."

The mood in the room shifted. It was subtle,

but Tess was good at sensing subtleties. There was nothing like growing up with drug-addled, abusive parents to hone a person's people-reading skills. She'd learned early on to identify any signs of trouble.

"About the windmills…" Samantha said quietly.

"You know we don't support them," Jack finished for her.

Tension coiled in Tess's stomach. She'd figured they'd have doubts or questions, but she wasn't expecting them to come out against the project immediately. "I don't get it. Don't you want clean energy?"

"Of course we do," Samantha said. "But windmills would be a huge change for Benson. We wouldn't be surrounded by nature anymore."

"We love the wilderness, and it's what brings tourists here," Jack added.

"So I've heard." Tess sighed.

Samantha looked relieved that Tess understood. "So many of the tourist businesses are my clients. I can't be their public relations consultant if there is no public to relate to. They—*we*—need this place to stay pristine."

"And there's also the issue with the birds," Jack added.

"What do you mean?" Tess asked.

"We're a pit stop on one of the biggest migratory routes in the world. Windmills kill birds, Tess. By the hundreds of thousands."

"I know they can, but there is a lot of new technology to mitigate that," Tess defended.

"*Mitigate* just means there will be slightly fewer birds killed."

"I'll get you the actual figures as soon as they send the environmental impact report," Tess told him. "I think you'll be amazed at what they can do to protect wildlife these days."

"Thanks, Tess." Jack took his hat from the hook by the kitchen door and clapped it on his head. "Though I don't think your statistic will change my mind. Sorry." There was an awkward pause. "Well, I've got a couple horses to take a look at. I'll see you gorgeous women later."

They were silent for another moment after he left. Tess thought about the birds she'd seen outside her window this morning. Big, black, noisy ones—crows or ravens. They'd woken her up and she'd been upset at the time, but that didn't mean she wanted them shredded in a wind turbine.

"So you support the project?" Samantha asked.

"Sam, I keep telling you, I don't have an opinion."

"How can you not have an opinion?" her friend asked. "This is important stuff."

Tess wouldn't let herself be drawn in. "I have all kinds of opinions about a lot of things. But I don't get to pick and choose my work assignments and I'm not paid to have an opinion about them. In fact,

I'm paid to remain as neutral as possible and just present the facts."

"Let's be honest," Samantha said, "your job is to put a spin on the truth so the project that you're representing sounds fantastic."

"Well, yes, I'm expected to present the facts in the best possible light—"

"I just don't know how you do it," Samantha interrupted. "How you can represent a project like this one."

That stung. "Well, you're in PR. And I'm sure in your old job especially, you didn't always believe in what you were selling," Tess said, trying to mask the hurt. "You know what it's like."

"Yes, but I just represented beauty products."

"And were all of those products organic?" Tess challenged. "And free of any animal testing?"

Samantha looked troubled. "No, not all of them…"

"You see?" Tess asked. "You don't have to believe in your product in order to sell it."

"But this *product*, as you call it, affects a group of people who have lived here a long time. Who have built a life here over generations. And it isn't fair that some outside company is coming in to change all that without their consent."

"They'll have a chance to voice their concerns," Tess reminded her, trying to ignore the lump of guilt that was forming in her stomach.

"Fine, but will their concerns really be heard?" Samantha asked.

"I have no idea," Tess admitted. "But if they aren't, they can always file a lawsuit."

"Which is costly."

This conversation was starting to feel extremely *un*fair. "Sam, are you blaming *me* for all the flaws in our democracy?"

"No!" Samantha looked away, contemplating something out the window for a moment. "I'm sorry, Tess. I'm not trying to make you feel bad. I just want you to think more about what you're doing. About *who* you're working for. And about the consequences that it could have for our town."

Tess made a point of rarely thinking deeply about *what* she was doing. And the guilt she was feeling now was exactly why she preferred to bury her head in the sand. "Look, I'm sorry. I understand that you don't support the wind farm. And I understand why. But I'm here to do my job, and that's what I have to do."

"I know." Samantha attempted a smile but looked forlorn instead. "And can you understand why I'm going to take the other side in this fight?"

"I do." Tess hid her distress by taking a last gulp of coffee. "And speaking of the fight, I'd better get to work. It was great seeing you and Jack. Thanks for the breakfast."

"I'm sorry if I upset you, Tess." Samantha stood up. "I don't want this to come between us. Can we hang out later in the weekend? I'm decorating the baby room, and I could use your style advice."

Ugh. Maybe she was a terrible friend, but it sounded like torture. "Honey, you know my style is just about as un–baby friendly as it gets. If you listen to me you'll have some kind of brushed stainless-steel crib and minimalist wall art."

Samantha smiled at her joke, just as Tess had hoped she would. She wanted things to be okay between them, but right now all the ease of their old friendship seemed to have disappeared. Maybe their lives were just too different. She blew Samantha a kiss and put her cup in the sink. Then she was out the door, into the thin mountain air.

Her shoulders didn't relax, the tension in her jaw didn't stop aching, until she was in her car and safely back on the road into town. The one thing she'd been looking forward to in Benson was spending time with Samantha. But she hadn't thought it through, hadn't realized that Samantha would be opposed to the windmills and entirely focused on her soon-to-arrive baby.

There wasn't much she could do about the windmills, but Tess wished she could muster up some excitement, some love and joy at the prospect of her godson. But that door in her heart was rusted shut by her own deeds and regrets. Tess rolled down the car window and let the cold air flow over her.

She'd just have to do what she'd done for so long now that it had become a habit. She'd fake it. She was good at that.

CHAPTER FIVE

TESS UNDERSTOOD WHY Renewable Reliance wanted to put windmills in this valley. From inside her Jeep she could hear the wind roaring. She wasn't looking forward to stepping outside the shelter of the vehicle.

But she had to brave the gale because Allen Tate, the CEO of Renewable Reliance, was arriving in Benson next week for a video shoot. The footage would be used in a promotional video for the windmill project, and also for advertising the company. The CEO considered himself a pioneer of alternative energy and he'd decided that Benson was a good place to foster that image. And actually, his judgment wasn't bad. These jagged hills east of Benson absolutely fit the definition of the word *rugged*.

They looked like teeth, Tess decided. Teeth from some strange monster with bad oral hygiene. The brown rock had been pushed up abruptly by long-ago geologic forces and didn't seem to belong in the same region as the surrounding fields. As if to underscore the contrast, cows grazed placidly right below the rocky hills, seemingly oblivious to the dramatic cliffs looming above them.

Tess took a sip from her water bottle, wishing it were coffee or brandy or something warm. Maybe when all this was over she'd write a book—a city girl's survival guide for tiny cow towns. First on her list of tips would be to invest in a small espresso machine. Her second tip would be to always have a flask of something stronger on hand, for moments like this one.

And her third tip, unrelated to beverages, would be to make sure, before agreeing to go, that you'd never slept with any of the tiny-cow-town officials.

She sighed and zipped up her parka, wrapped her scarf tightly around her neck and pulled her wool cap over her head. Taking the small camera from her purse, she opened the door, only to have the wind slam it shut in her face. She shook her head in awe. There was certainly wind power in this area. She tried again, this time shoving the door with her shoulder. She burst out into the chill afternoon, her senses immediately overwhelmed. All she could hear, smell and feel was wind.

Holding on to her hat, she trudged into the gusts, scanning the side of the road for places where a few cars could park at the same time. To her relief there was another large turnout beyond the one she'd parked in. Perfect for the film crew. Across the road from it was a gravel driveway and a rustic wooden gate, which led to the fields below the rocky teeth.

She walked over to take a closer look. If they all hopped the gate they could shoot footage of the CEO right here, with the twisted hills behind him. They could get some pretty light if they filmed in the morning, and she knew the wind would be quieter at that time of day, as well. She took a few pictures and stood staring at the view, trying to make sure she hadn't forgotten anything else she needed to do while she was here.

The sound of an engine approaching distracted her, and she looked up to see a white pickup pull up behind her rental Jeep and stop. A man jumped out and started running toward her. She had an instant of panic before realizing it was Slaid.

"Tess, are you okay?" He was shouting as he ran across the road and over to the gate where she stood.

No, she wasn't okay. Slaid wore faded jeans, a shearling jacket and cowboy boots—and they all suited him perfectly. She suddenly wished he'd gained weight in the past two years, or gone bald or gotten married. Anything that would make him less attractive.

"I'm fine. How are you, Slaid?"

He stopped in front of her and she noted that he wasn't even out of breath. "I saw your Jeep and thought maybe you had some car trouble and needed help."

The idea that he'd assumed she was some kind of damsel in distress was a little irritating. "Thanks. I'm good. Just taking a few pictures. We're doing a video shoot out here next week."

His brows rose. "A video here? Why?"

"This is where they're siting the windmills." Tess shoved her hands in her pockets, wishing they could have this chat somewhere warmer.

"You're kidding me." His voice was suddenly rough and low. "And when were you going to tell me about this?"

"Actually I was planning on keeping it a big secret," she snapped back. Slaid scowled, evidently not amused by her sarcastic humor. "I was going to stop by on my way back to town. The email with the map and directions just came an hour ago."

His expression grew even more contorted as he looked over at the hills. "Well, the directions must be wrong. They can't site their project here. This is my land."

"No, that can't be right." She looked around at the desolate landscape, wondering if she'd made a mistake. She didn't think so.

"I think I know my own pasture, Tess. And those are definitely my cattle over there."

His attitude wasn't helping their situation, or her mood, which was rapidly deteriorating. She was cold, and a dull ache drummed in her temples, probably from all this wind. "Well, I suppose it's possible I read the map wrong. Why don't you take a look at it with me? It's in my car."

They walked in troubled silence back across the road and wrestled the doors open. Slaid sat in the passenger seat and Tess pulled her hat off and ran her fingers through her tangled hair. "I don't know how you live with this wind."

Slaid didn't answer, just reached for the folded map on her dashboard.

Tess sensed the distress radiating off him and figured she'd steer clear of any more small talk. She fished in her bag for her file of documents and found the page she'd been looking at previously. She handed the directions to Slaid. "Look, it says mile marker twenty-three." She pointed ahead of them, where a small white sign had been placed close to the ground, the number twenty-three clearly visible. "So that's it, right?"

Slaid was quiet, looking at the map before folding it carefully and setting it back on the dashboard. He handed Tess the directions. He didn't look at her, just kept his eyes on the landscape in front of them. "That's my land," he said again, his voice heavy.

"Well, if you own it, then the company has made a mistake. I'll give them a call and get this cleared up."

"No, I don't own it," he said. "It belongs to the Bureau of Land Management. My family has leased it for years. Since I was a little kid and my dad wanted to expand our business."

"So it's not your land."

The look he shot her was full of angst. "It's land we've held the rights to. It's land we've been promised we can count on for our business."

"Well, windmills and cattle can coexist." Tess tried to sound encouraging. "It doesn't mean your business is ruined."

"What do you know about that, Tess?" He turned to her then and his expression was hard, his eyes piercing. "You come out here from the city with your files and your computer and you want to tell me what my business needs? Well, I'll tell you what it needs. Consistent access to good pasture."

"Which I'm sure you can work out."

"Really? And are you speaking from your vast knowledge of raising cattle? And constructing windmills?"

"There's no need to be rude." Her knuckles were white on the file. What she'd give to just shove him and his misdirected anger right out the door of her Jeep.

He went on as if she hadn't spoken. "Your project is a threat to my livelihood. A threat to my family's business—our heritage. A heritage we created with hard work, good ranching practices and sticking up for ourselves when someone tries to push us around."

She'd make one more attempt at rationalization,

and then she really would kick him out of this car. "I think you're seeing things in black-and-white, Slaid. It can work. It works all over Texas. It works at Altamont Pass just a few hours west of here. There are hundreds of cows grazing perfectly happily under those windmills."

"You make it seem so simple, but you have no idea what you're talking about."

She bristled all over but remained calm. "You are making this too personal, Slaid. The world is changing and we all have to adjust or get left behind. It's basic economics. It's Business 101."

"Okay, so here are some economics for you. *If* they let me keep my lease, they'll still kick my cattle off while they're building the windmills. Which means I have to bring them all back to my ranch, and buy extra feed because I won't have enough pasture. And since we're in a massive drought and I'm already buying extra hay and water, the expense could quite possibly destroy my ranch. *That's* Business 101, Tess. Now, I've got to get going. I have a lawyer to call."

He opened the door and got out, letting the fierce wind slam it behind him. He was reflected in her rearview mirror as he stalked back to his truck, jerked open the door and got in. His engine revved and he pulled the big vehicle into a quick U-turn. It got smaller and smaller as she watched him drive away, heading back to Benson to fight the windmills.

His anger seemed to linger in the cab. Maybe the wind would blow it all away, because she didn't want it and certainly didn't deserve it. She rolled down the window for a quick blast of fresh air. Ugh. She'd known this gig would be a hard sell, but she hadn't expected to end up in a personal battle with the mayor.

The anger and worry she'd seen in his face were understandable, but it didn't give him the right to be such a condescending jerk and lash out at her. And now *she* was angry. Angry enough to work harder on this project than she'd ever worked on anything before.

The setting sun colored the jagged rocks on the hillsides a pinkish hue and cast deep shadows behind them. It was dramatic in a moonscape kind of way. She could see how windmills would change that forever. Doubt pricked at her, and she shoved it down. It wasn't her job to care, she reminded herself. She had no opinion in this fight. She was hired to outline the various benefits to the project. And there *were* real benefits. Big ones like reliable jobs and clean energy. She'd keep her focus on those positive outcomes and work hard. If she did, Slaid would see all of his outdated arguments blown away by her own. Obliterated in a blast of high desert wind.

She rolled up the window and drove back to Benson, making a mental list of talking points that would support the wind project. It would be a big challenge, but she'd been through tough work situations before and come out on top. She'd get through this one, too.

After parking in front of the cottage, she grabbed a notebook and listed all of her ideas. Staring at the bullet points, it occurred to her that the skills she used in this job—the thick skin, the tenacity, the ability to work alone in a hostile environment— were all skills she'd honed during her disastrous childhood. They were coping skills she wished she'd never had to develop, but they certainly served her well on days like this.

Suddenly she felt tired. It had been a rough first week in Benson. Watching the last rays of sun turn the town pink and gold, she wondered what it would be like to have a different job, one that was less combative, that didn't require her to be so tough all the time. Because on days like this, she grew weary of fighting so many battles.

Tess hit the steering wheel with her palm, jolting herself out of her self-pity. She jumped out of the car and stormed into the cottage, angrier with herself than Slaid now. Life threw all kinds of crap at people every day—she was living proof. And sitting around moaning about it didn't help. She was lucky to have a job she was so good at. Pity parties could lead to horrible choices. Choices like the ones her parents had made when they'd decided drugs were more important than keeping custody of her. Choices like she'd made when she was sixteen and discovered drugs herself, emerging from her self-inflicted haze pregnant and more alone than ever.

She would not fall into self-pity just because the mayor of Benson was rude. Slaid Jacobs and his soon-to-be-homeless cows weren't worth it. Tess shed clothes as she walked through the house, and by the time she was in the bedroom, all she had to do was throw on her running gear and grab her iPod. Then she was back out the front door.

She welcomed the freezing wind now. It was invigorating and cleansing, and it scoured any remaining wisps of self-pity from the hidden corners of her soul. Her mind cleared, her confidence flooded back and soon she was charging forward in the growing darkness, trusting herself to navigate the bumpy back roads of Benson. She was moving fast and on her own—just the way she liked it.

CHAPTER SIX

SLAID STARED AT the letter through a fog of sleep-deprived disgust. It was from the Bureau of Land Management—official notice that his grazing lease would be temporarily suspended due to the impending construction of windmills on the property. Perfect timing. He'd tossed and turned all night, emotions jumping from anger about the windmills to guilt at the way he'd laid into Tess yesterday. And now this. He slammed the mailbox and threw the letter into the cab of his truck.

Adding insult to injury, his lawyer was out of town for a few days. He knew that shouldn't upset him; Matt was down in Los Angeles at a funeral and it just wasn't right to be angry with someone for honoring their deceased aunt.

With the morning to himself and fury to spare, Slaid got behind the wheel and pulled his truck up to a pile of fence posts he'd purchased a few months ago. It was a good day for a sledgehammer, a post-hole digger and a bunch of barbed wire. Loading the heavy wooden posts into the truck felt good. Pounding them into the ground would feel even better.

A noise had him glancing at the road that led from his ranch over a slight rise and back down to Benson. Jack Baron's old truck appeared, rattling down the hill. Why such a rich guy drove such a beat-up old farm truck, vintage 1950s, was a mystery to Slaid, but Jack was a little quirky in his taste.

"Thanks for coming out here," Slaid said as Jack descended from the creaky vehicle. He'd called his friend late last night, cross-eyed from staring at websites, trying to figure out how to stop the windmills. A few years ago, Jack had led a successful fight to stop a real estate development company from turning one of the most beautiful mountains outside of Benson into an enormous resort. Slaid wanted his opinion on fighting the wind farm. He just hoped that Jack's marriage to Tess's friend, Samantha, wouldn't complicate things.

"Sounds as if we've got a problem on our hands." Jack glanced toward the truck Slaid had been loading. "And a project. You want some help?"

"If you've got the time to spare, sure." Slaid went around to the driver's side and Jack swung up into the passenger seat.

"These windmills are going to be worse than I thought," Jack said as they started up the gravel road that led out to Slaid's farthest pasture. "I knew Tess was here to represent Renewable Reliance, but I had no idea their site was so close to town, or on your land."

"Yeah, apparently she forgot to mention that."

"She didn't know either, Slaid. Look, I know you're pissed. I am, too. But you've gotta be pissed at the right people. Tess doesn't own that company and she doesn't even want this job. Samantha told me her boss had to twist her arm to get her out here."

His gut-churning guilt grew tenfold. Jack didn't even know the worst of it—that Slaid had pressured Tess to stay in Benson when she'd wanted to go. He let out a long breath. "Yeah, I got that feeling. And I'll bet Tess said something to Samantha about our argument yesterday. You must think I was pretty hard on her."

"Well, she and Samantha talked on the phone a little last night. Tess mentioned that you were pretty angry, but if she was truly upset by what you said, she'd never admit it. Tess doesn't let on much about her troubles to anyone."

Shame combined with the guilt. "Maybe I did take things out on her." They'd reached the old fence, its posts leaning and rotting, the wire rusted and sagging. Slaid parked the truck and cut the engine. They got out, and he tossed Jack a pair of heavy leather gloves, then pulled on a pair of his own. Once Jack unlatched the tailgate, they started pulling the posts from the back.

The talk turned to the fence for a few minutes. They pulled the most rotten section out entirely, loading the rusty wire into the truck and carrying the new posts over. Then they set to work digging out a few old posts that were still firmly cemented in the ground.

"This is crap work, you know." Jack grinned at him over the shovel. "Don't you usually pay someone to do this?"

Slaid slammed his shovel into the hard earth. "Just felt like a little manual labor. When I've got a problem to solve, a little sweat and dirt sometimes helps."

Jack's laugh echoed over the quiet hillside. "I know the feeling. I don't think my ranch was ever in better shape than when Samantha showed up next door. I must have replaced half my fence line that fall. Then I got myself sucked into helping Todd with his crazy wild mustangs, and I even painted Jed and Betty's barn for them."

It was Slaid's turn to laugh. "Man, you had it bad."

They were silent for a moment, chipping away at the unyielding ground. Then Jack spoke. "So if you really want to fight this thing, we could use some outside help. Environmental groups for one. They want green energy but without migrating birds getting injured. They definitely don't want the Sierras and the wild lands nearby covered in wind turbines."

"Okay." Slaid grunted as he dislodged a chunk of the old concrete with his pickax, the accomplishment giving him a flicker of satisfaction.

"And we should get the historical society on board. They can make the connection to what's happened around here in the past."

"You mean the water?"

"Yeah. It makes sense if we spin it right." Jack jabbed his shovel into the loose dirt left by Slaid's efforts. "First Southern California steals the water out of the Owens River and just about destroys the Eastern Sierra towns and ranches. Now they're back, threatening to destroy our last untainted resource—the natural beauty that supports our tourist industry. Just so they can have more power down south."

"How do we prove the power is going to Southern California?" Slaid asked, wiping sweat off his forehead with his sleeve.

"Because I bet when we get a good look at what this project entails, there's gonna be a lot more power generated than they can sell around here. Trust me, most of it will be going down to LA."

"But Renewable Reliance will just say that's all speculation."

Jack's brows drew together as he considered Slaid's point. "Well. They'll have to answer our questions, at any rate. We'll just hope they'll answer them somewhat honestly."

"Seem as if you're saying our success might be rooted in how well we tell the story. We've got to get the media interested." Slaid slammed his pickax back into the dirt. "But what if it backfires? I mean, this country needs clean energy. So how do we avoid looking like a bunch of ignorant, backward-looking people who don't want to do our part?"

"I'm not sure." Jack tried to wedge his shovel under the old post. "The thing is, I want wind power—in theory. I want my energy coming from a cleaner source. But do I want those windmills here in Benson? Nope."

"I feel the same."

"Samantha and I had an idea the other night. I don't know if it would work for everyone, but we're thinking of installing solar panels on our roof. Maybe this is a crazy idea, but what if everyone in town did it? We could prove that we're not just saying no to wind power because we're selfish. We'd be saying no because we already have our own source of clean energy."

"Not a bad idea. It would add to that story you're talking about spinning. A solar-powered town, threatened by windmills." Slaid felt more hopeful than he had since Tess had shown up in his office. "What if we worked with the state for some rebates, or even a solar company for a bulk price on panels and installation?"

"It's worth looking into," Jack agreed.

"I really think it could be a good strategy." Already Slaid's thoughts were sifting through memories of everyone he'd met over the years, trying to remember if he knew anyone involved in the solar industry.

"And it might get us a win." Jack grinned at him. "If that's what you want."

"It's what I want. I can't let this wind project happen on my watch." Slaid set his ax down and reached into the truck bed for a shovel, using his boot to push it deep into the soil. "I think we should bring it up tonight at the city council meeting. You going?"

"Yeah, I'll be there. Can't shirk my duties as an elected official. Even if I only got a council seat because no one else wanted it."

"Hey, plenty of people wanted that seat!" Slaid assured him. "I just wanted you around to save my ass with good ideas like this solar-power plan. I think it could work, though I'm not looking forward to going head-to-head with Tess."

"Neither are we." Jack leaned on his shovel. "I'm sure this whole situation is really awkward for Samantha and Tess. They've been such close friends, and for the first time they're on opposite sides of something."

Slaid nodded. "Yeah, well, if it makes you feel any better, awkward is a hell of a lot better than how I handled things yesterday. I made it personal. I can't make that mistake again."

"I guess we can't help it being kind of personal," Jack said. "But if the council likes our idea, I think someone should tell Tess about the plan. It's best to be up front."

"That someone being me, I guess," Slaid said.

"The dirty work goes along with being the mayor. But I doubt that'll be an enjoyable conversation."

Jack jabbed his shovel under the post again, managing to tip it partway over. Slaid reached for it and wrestled the old wood out of the ground. "You know, Samantha mentioned that you and Tess…"

"Yep." No way was Slaid talking about sex, even with a guy as easygoing as Jack. He grabbed his pickax and walked over to the next post, putting his full attention on loosening the dirt around it. "I'd appreciate if you and Samantha don't pass that along to anyone else. It's not a night I'm proud of."

"Hell, Slaid, we've all done things we're not proud of."

"But you're not the mayor."

"Or the son and grandson of previous mayors," Jack added. He dug his shovel into the dusty soil. "I get that you've got a heavy legacy to carry around, but that doesn't mean you have to be perfect *every* moment of your life. That's impossible."

Slaid's laugh came out more like a humorless bark. "I've got a divorce to prove that I'm not perfect *every* moment."

Jack grinned. "I've got one, too, so I guess that means we both have our flaws."

They worked in silence for a few minutes, deepening the hole around the post. Slaid didn't want to ask, but something inside him wouldn't let the opportunity slide. "So since the cat's out of the bag, what do you know about Tess?"

Jack scooped up a couple more shovelfuls before he answered, "I can understand why you had that night a couple years ago, but I hope for your sake you're not interested in dating her."

"I honestly don't know what I'm interested in." But the truth was, he hadn't stopped thinking about her since she'd walked into his office.

Jack sighed. "Well, she's pretty, obviously, and funny and smart and a great friend to my wife— loyal as anything. But you'd be half-crazy to get involved with her. She's got a wall a mile thick between her and the world. Samantha's known her since college and says she barely knows anything about her."

Slaid paused. "Really? I just figured it was me she was skittish around."

"Next time you're with her, watch how she does it. The minute the conversation gets personal about her, she'll ask about you. Or make a joke. Or find a new topic. Or leave. Anything but talk about herself."

There was a clank as Jack's shovel hit what must be a pretty big rock. Slaid dropped the ax and picked up his shovel, driving it into the hard soil with his boot, trying to get under it. "Maybe she just hasn't met the right guy." He got the shovel under the rock and started prying. The wooden handle snapped like a twig, sending him staggering backward, broken stub in hand.

Jack just stood there, his shoulders shaking in

laughter. "Oh, man, if that's not an omen for your future with Tess, I don't know what is. I give you my condolences."

Slaid picked up the broken pieces and threw them in the truck. He grabbed another shovel out of the back. "You never know. Why don't you hold off on those condolences for a few more weeks?"

Jack had the pickax now, crouching down to loosen the soil under the rock. When he looked at Slaid, he was still grinning. "Will do. And good luck. You'll surely need it if you're going to try to get anywhere with Tess Cole."

USUALLY SLAID WAS restless during meetings. He was a big, active guy and sitting around talking didn't suit him that well. But this evening he was so tired after setting posts with Jack all day that it actually felt good to be sedentary. At least, it felt good while the city council members brainstormed fund-raising ideas for new holiday decorations. This part was easy. It was the windmill discussion, next on the agenda, that could be tricky. Looking around at the weathered faces of the older ranchers and respected Benson citizens who made up the council, Slaid realized he had no idea what they'd think of Jack's ideas. Most of these folks were fairly traditional. But regardless of how they felt about any kind of alternative energy, the future of power had showed up uninvited at their doorstep. They would have to deal with it.

Gus Jackson, owner of the largest market in town, was chairing the meeting. "Next on the agenda is windmills," he said. "Slaid, you want to talk about this?"

Slaid cleared his throat and jumped in. "Some of you may have heard that there's a company looking to put a wind farm on the grazing land I lease east of town."

About half the folks on his council nodded, while the other half looked stunned. Apparently the Benson gossip mill hadn't had quite enough time to work its magic. "Now, I don't know how you all feel about that, but I think we'll have to come together and take a stand on it, one way or the other."

"I don't want to look at them all day, that's for sure," Sue Emory said, tapping her pencil anxiously. She ran Jeep tours in the summer and snowshoe hikes in winter. "And the tourists won't like it much, either."

"I don't get it. A private company can just come out here and do that? How?" Gus asked.

"They can get a lease from the Bureau of Land Management, just like we do for grazing," Jack answered. And it's easy for them to do it, because the federal government is all about developing domestic sources of energy right now,"

"But here? It's going to mess with this whole area," Bob Allen said worriedly. "It'll change everything."

"Well, I'm new at this," Slaid told him. "But it seems to me that if the feds are allowing fracking all over BLM land, a wind-energy project must be a no-brainer for them. It's a lot less invasive and damaging."

Jed Watkins leaned forward. "I just don't get it. We're a small town. We don't need that much energy. Why us?"

"We've got the wind," Slaid answered. "And it's a straight shot down Highway 395 to Southern California."

"We're pretty sure they'll just sell the extra power to LA," Jack explained. "Or run it across the desert to Las Vegas or some other big city."

The quaver in Gus's voice betrayed his distress, "What do we do? No way can we let this happen."

"Well, we've got to run a campaign." Jack glanced around the table. "Try to get some outside support for our cause. Involve the media and environmental groups."

"Jack thinks we'll get a lot of public sympathy on this," Slaid added. "Especially if we remind people of the struggles folks in this area have endured since LA got its hands on our water."

"Sounds like a good idea overall," Sue said.

"Well, there's another part to this idea," Slaid's nervousness was gone now. So far not one person had protested, or extolled the economic benefits of windmills. "Jack and I were talking earlier." Slaid nodded in his friend's direction. "He had this idea about using solar energy to fight this thing. If we got solar panels installed all over town, we'd be making most of our own power. Then we can prove that *we* have no need for a wind farm."

"But how will we afford all these solar panels?" Jed asked. "Those things are pricey."

"Well, there are rebates from the federal government, and we'll try to work with the state for a grant, too. Plus, I was thinking we could try to find a big solar installation company that might consider a group discount."

The ideas started flying. One of the benefits of a small town was that the council knew every homeowner in it. They made a list of who would be on board, who might get on board with some convincing and the few people who probably never would. Then they made a list of people who might need a little financial assistance.

The council members got so fired up about the solar-power idea that they decided to forego the new holiday decorations this year, and instead use the income from the fund-raisers they'd just planned for "solar scholarships" to help people get their panels installed. Slaid felt a rush of pride. An issue that he'd feared might divide his town was actually going to bring its citizens closer than ever.

His worry about Tess nagged at him, though. If the town came together, they would hand her a big defeat on this thing. And even though he knew that this wasn't *her* project, and it wasn't *her* defeat, as the project spokesperson, this would be a blow to her career. It might even jeopardize her job.

He'd promised Jack he'd let Tess know their plans and give her a chance to come up with a counter-strategy. But he'd done a little researching on the internet these past few days and learned that Tess was considered one of the best in her field. With a heads-up she might still find a way to kick his butt.

"Slaid, are you on board with all these fund-raisers?" Gus asked.

He looked around the table, embarrassed that he'd been caught with his mind wandering. Luckily his assistant, Erica, had made a chart with all additional fund-raising plans on it, and he was a fast reader. He nodded. They were going to be busy, but it would be worth it. "We'll need to schedule a few extra meetings, folks, if you want to make all this happen. And I would call in all the favors you can with friends and family, because we will have to form some new committees. Fund-raising, out-reach, technology… It's gonna take the expertise of everyone we know to make this plan a reality."

An hour later, they all stumbled down the steps of the town hall and out into the dusk. The sun set early these days, earlier still because it went be-hind the mountains so quickly. Waving goodbye to the council members, Slaid relished a sense of accomplishment. This was why he was mayor—for moments like this. When people worked together to make something happen that was way beyond what any one individual could do.

And now it was just a matter of getting it done. They had their plans in place, meetings on the calendar, and if everyone did their part, they could win this fight.

If they did, he might even end up grateful to Renewable Reliance. Earlier today he and Jack had spoken about his legacy—all that inherited family expectation that sometimes felt like a burden. Well, right now it felt like an opportunity. He had the chance to turn Benson into America's first solar-powered town. That could be his own legacy—one he could be proud of.

CHAPTER SEVEN

WALKING TO HIS truck, Slaid's mind went straight back to Tess. He needed to apologize for the way he'd treated her out by his pasture yesterday. He figured he'd bring some flowers. At least they might keep her from slamming the door in his face. Maybe they'd also soften the blow he was about to deliver—that Benson was trying to go solar powered.

Late fall wasn't the ideal time to find fresh flowers, but he headed to the grocery store and managed to grab a few of the least-wilted bunches. The hardware store was just closing but he begged his way in and, though they didn't have a vase, he found a large mason jar—it would have to do. Once he'd wrestled the flowers into some kind of decent-looking arrangement, he drove to Tess's cottage, wondering what kind of reception he would get. Part of him couldn't wait to see her again. The naive, optimistic part that was still excited that the woman he'd dreamed about was right here in Benson. Another part of him kind of hoped she wasn't home. He wasn't looking forward to their conversation. If she was gone, he'd simply write a note of apology, leave the flowers on her doorstep and make his escape. He could deal with delivering the news about the solar panels another day.

When she answered his knock, he knew the easy way out wasn't an option. But suddenly it didn't matter, because she took his breath away. Without makeup, her face had a softness he'd never imagined. Her wide blue eyes were rimmed with soft gold lashes that he realized now were usually covered in black mascara. A smattering of freckles decorated her translucent skin. Her hair hung past her shoulders in soft waves. Dressed in a plum-colored sweater and black knit pants, she looked relaxed, much younger and way more beautiful than ever.

Her eyes widened at the sight of him. "Slaid, what are you doing here?"

"Apologizing," he said softly. "May I come in for a moment?"

Her expression was guarded, and she glanced down with evident regret at her casual clothing, pushing a lock of hair behind her ear in a self-conscious gesture that was out of sync with the Tess he knew. "Okay."

She opened the door wider for him and he stepped into the entry, feeling like a fool standing there with flowers in his hands. But after the way he'd acted, he knew he deserved to feel like a fool. And worse.

"These are for you." He handed her the bouquet.

"Why?" she asked sharply, taking the jar.

"Because I was an idiot. I took that whole wind-mill thing out on you when I know it's not your fault. Hell. You wouldn't even still be here if I hadn't put pressure on you to stay. I had no right to act like that, Tess. And I'm sorry."

He waited for her smile, wanting to see the corners of her lush mouth tilt up. But it didn't come. Instead she looked troubled.

"I don't need flowers. We're professionals, Slaid. You were just reacting to some bad news. I'm a big girl. I can take it. I definitely don't need an apology."

Her words and tone jarred him out of his thoughts, which had been stuck on her mouth and the realization that he wanted to kiss her. He yanked his eyes away.

"Maybe you don't need to hear it, but I need to give it. I messed up and I know better."

"You really are a Boy Scout, aren't you?" She set the flowers down on an end table next to a white armchair.

"Eagle," he said automatically before realizing how stupid that sounded.

"Right. Well, Scout, apologies are for personal relationships, and we're not personal. We're business. So you do what you need to do, and I'll do what I need to do, and we'll just try our best to keep it civil. How's that?"

Scout. Her nickname had him feeling like a little kid. It didn't help that she sounded as if she was explaining the ways of the world to a child. He'd come here with flowers, stood on her doorstep struck speechless by her beauty, and that was how she saw him. Some Boy Scout country boy who needed her to school him in being professional. Irritation ran up his spine and he stiffened. "That's fine. And since we're being civil, I think I owe you a heads-up."

"About?"

"The city council just voted to pursue a plan to make Benson the first one-hundred-percent solar town in the country." He waited for her reaction, but if she was worried, he couldn't tell—she was that good. She just stood a little straighter, tipped her chin up a little more proudly.

"Well, I appreciate you telling me. I'll need to let my client know, as well… You understand?"

Hell, he hadn't thought of that and neither had Jack. Renewable Reliance might be able to pull strings and put obstacles in their way that Tess on her own could not. "Of course," he said, trying to play it as cool as she did.

"Is there anything else?"

"Um. A thank-you? For the flowers?"

"I didn't realize I had to say thank you for an apology."

Damn. If there had ever been anything between them after their night in Phoenix, she was mak-

ing sure it was buried under about a mile of ice…
and he was slipping and sliding like a fool without
skates. He tried one last time. "Look, if you want
to go back to San Francisco and get someone else
to take your place in Benson, I'll be okay with it. I
should never have tried to make you stay."

"I can see why you'd rather I was gone now, but
I don't back away from a fight, Slaid."

"I don't want you gone." There, he'd said it, and
the shock on her face might well be worth the embarrassment of putting his feelings right out there.
"That's not my intention. Tess, I'm *apologizing*—
for forcing you to stay in the first place and for my
behavior since. I'm trying to correct my wrongs."

She stared at him warily. "That's nice of you. But
like I said before, I don't need apologies. We're on
opposite sides of this issue—that's just the way it
is. We have to agree to do our work and not take
anything personally."

He'd have to remember those last few words next
time he was distracted by her beauty or memories
of what they'd shared. None of this was personal.
Even the sex hadn't been personal for her. "I'll just
say good-night, then."

"Good night," she said calmly, and went to the
door, opening it for him, signaling that their conversation was over.

Slaid clapped his hat on his head and walked out,
the shreds of his dignity trailing behind him. He
thought back to Jack's warning earlier today. His

friend had cautioned that Tess was hard to get to know, but he hadn't mentioned that she was a cat, with sharp claws hidden beneath her sleek form. Claws that could softly and easily slice a man's confidence into bits.

TESS CLOSED THE door behind Slaid and leaned against it, letting out the breath she'd been holding. She prided herself on anticipating all obstacles, but she couldn't have predicted this one. An entire town going solar? It was brilliant. She had no idea if they'd be able to pull it off, but it was a truly inspired move.

Unfortunately, she was on the receiving end of their inspiration. She would call Ed tomorrow and tell him about this new development, and then wait to hear what Renewable Reliance wanted to do about it. And in the meantime, she would have to come up with something good, something fabulous, to convince the people of Benson that solar wasn't the way to go.

I don't want you gone. His words were pulsing neon in her brain, emanating fear and desire that sent a shiver up her spine. He made her crazy, angry and frustrated. He was her enemy in what was going to be a very tough fight. But in those few moments since she'd arrived when they hadn't been arguing, when they'd shared a spark of humor or a smile, she hadn't wanted to be gone, either. And those moments troubled her.

She wandered over to the flowers Slaid had brought—white roses, some pink carnations and a whole bunch of baby's breath. A standard supermarket offering. She trailed her fingers over the soft rose petals anyway. No guy had ever brought her flowers before. Probably because she rarely told them her name or where she lived. And because women like her, who were so clearly out for just a one-night stand, didn't inspire the traditional thank-you bouquet after a night of sex, no matter how good.

It was kind of sweet that he'd brought them. Totally inappropriate, of course, but sweet. And yet she'd been hard on him—she'd had to be. Seeing him at her door, totally gorgeous and all hopeful, flowers in one hand, his leather cowboy hat in the other, had just about taken her legs out from under her. And there was no way she could let that happen. She needed them strong and steady and completely reliable if she hoped to win this fight.

She picked up the flower-filled mason jar and carried it back to the kitchen, setting it on the table. Opening a cabinet, she pulled out a glass and the bottle of single malt she'd brought with her. She poured herself a small amount and stood sipping the fiery liquid, its heat the only thing she could think of that would calm her nerves.

Staring out the window into the thick darkness beyond, she let the alcohol do its work. She'd figure out a way to deal with Slaid's solar plans. They were just one more challenge in a challenging job. It was the personal stuff she was really worried about—the mixed-up way he'd made her feel tonight.

Something on the table caught her eye, a local newsletter that had shown up in the mail today, presumably meant for the owner of this cottage. Pumpkins and fall leaves decorated the front and framed the words *Fall Harvest Festival*. It was on Saturday, only four days from now.

Inspiration hit her and brought hope with it. It would to take a lot of work—a crazy amount of work—but if she could book a spot at that festival she knew she'd have a chance to meet most of the people who lived in and around Benson. And with the right literature, the perfect festive booth and the chance to talk with people face-to-face, she'd have a good shot at convincing at least some of them to support the wind farm. And if she undermined Slaid's solar strategy in the process, well, all was fair in love and war. And though he'd shown up with flowers tonight, he'd clearly declared war.

"SAMANTHA?" TESS KNOCKED on the wooden frame of the screen door. "Are you there?"

"Come on back!" Her friend's voice echoed through the rooms of the old farmhouse.

Tess pushed open the door and followed the sound across the old worn floorboards of the living room. It was filled with slightly shabby furniture that had belonged to Samantha's grandmother—a big contrast to the stylish, modern home her friend now shared with Jack. Off a hall behind the living room was the office.

"Hey!" Samantha greeted her, getting up slowly from her chair to offer up a hug. "So glad you wanted to stop by."

"Thanks for making time for me," Tess said, returning Samantha's embrace and giving her a brief kiss on the cheek. She took in the built-in shelves, the huge antique desk and the framed bulletin boards. "I forgot you have such a nice office. So this is where the local PR magic happens."

"I'm not sure it's magic," Samantha said. "But it's nice to have this place to work in. It keeps me from getting distracted by all the stuff I need to do at home. I mean—" she waved vaguely up the hill "—home is right next door, but it's nice to have my own quiet space."

Tess took a slow breath, trying to calm her stomach. She hated asking for help, but she was desperate. "I have a favor to ask you. Kind of a big one."

"Sure. Sit down." Samantha lowered herself gingerly back into her desk chair. "Oof! Once I'm sitting or standing I'm fine, but getting from one position to the other is a challenge."

"Well, you look great," Tess assured her. "You've got that pregnancy glow." She took a seat on the chair next to Samantha's desk. "Okay, here's my request. Can you get me a couple of booths at the harvest festival?"

"A couple?" Samantha pushed her cat's-eye glasses further up her nose and peered at Tess. "It's this weekend!"

"Yes, but Ellen who works at the market told me that you're the head of the planning committee."

"You talked to Ellen at the market?"

"Yes. I'm getting to be a regular fixture around town. Why do you look so surprised?"

"I don't know. Because you're Tess! You love San Francisco, you hate it here and yet you're chatting up Ellen at the market. It's just strange."

"Well, believe me, it feels strange to me, too. So can you help?"

"Why do you want booths?" Samantha asked.

"Because the city council wants to put solar panels everywhere to prove they don't need wind power. It's a crazy idea, it will never work, but I need to step up my game regardless. So I've decided to have my very own mini wind-power expo at the festival."

Samantha was quiet for a moment, looking anywhere but at Tess. Finally she sighed. "Tess, that crazy idea… It was Jack's. And mine."

"Oh. Really?" Tess stared at Samantha—the urban PR expert she thought she knew so well. When had her friend morphed into an environmentalist? Slowly hurt trickled in. She hadn't thought Samantha would work directly against her.

"I'm sorry," Samantha said quietly. "I know it's awkward between us right now. It was just an idea we came up with, and Jack ran it by Slaid, who took it to the city council. They liked it."

Tess sighed. "Well, thanks for telling me. I guess I'll get going." There was no reason to stay—no way Samantha would help her now. She was just embarrassed that she'd even asked.

"Tess." Samantha's plea was quiet. "I don't want this to change us."

"I think it already has," Tess said. "Look, right now we're on opposite sides, but let's just agree that when this is all over, no matter who wins, we'll still be friends." She stood up.

"Wait." Samantha held up a hand to stop her. "I can get you the booths."

"Really?" Tess sat down again. "Are you sure?"

"You're my friend. You deserve the chance to do your job, to present your side of this debate. You can have the three booths on the east end of the fair." Samantha picked up a file folder and pulled out a photocopy of a crude hand-drawn map. She pointed to a pair of crossed wavy lines. "This is the corner of Third and Main. See? You'll be here."

"And can I put up a stage?"

"Excuse me?"

"A stage," Tess repeated. "And a dance floor. I'd like to bring a band. I know there's one scheduled for later in the day, but I'll have mine play earlier."

"Where are you going to get a band?"

Tess couldn't tell her that Renewable Reliance was giving her an unlimited budget for this event. Ed had called her this morning with the news. "Connections, of course! I've booked the finest Texas blues band in California."

Samantha's eyes got wide. "You got Danny Click? To come here?" She and Tess and their friend Jenna had gone to hear him many times in San Francisco, joining his fanatical followers in dancing until the early hours of the morning.

"With his band. The Hell Yeahs."

"How did you do that?"

"Danny and I actually go way back."

"Did you sleep with him?" Samantha asked.

"No! Of course not! He has a girlfriend and she's become a good friend of mine...now that one of my best friends left me to live in a small backwater town."

Samantha smiled. "I didn't leave *you*..."

"I know, I know." Tess grinned, glad that some of the tension between them had faded for now. "The truth is I just promised Danny a lot of good barbecue and a chance to support clean energy. I'm calling it Brunch with the Blues."

"You're serving food?" Samantha asked. "Tess, how are you going to organize all this in the next few days?"

"No problem," Tess assured her, mentally saying goodbye to any sleep she might have gotten this week.

"Well—" Samantha reached into the folder again "—here's the form for the food permit. Just read it carefully and sign the bottom. I don't know what to say about the band. I can run it by the committee, but I doubt…"

"Pretend I didn't even mention the band. Once people hear him play they won't send him away. I'll take all the blame for not having a permit. I'll even pay the fine if there is one."

"But—"

"Please, Sam? I know you don't agree with the project, but I have to try my best to make it happen. Please don't say anything about the band?" She couldn't believe she was begging. Ed had better have a huge bonus for her when this was over.

"I feel bad doing it, but okay."

Tess tried to suppress her sigh of relief. She had a shot at winning now. Great music and good food could make anything sexy, even wind power.

"I'm sorry I can't be more supportive."

Tess was already reviewing the food form. She scrawled her name on the bottom once she'd finished. "Don't worry. We're both professionals. We can handle this." She gave the form back to Samantha. "I feel like I've been saying that a lot lately."

"To Slaid?" her friend asked, smiling.

"He came over last night and apologized for everything. He even brought flowers."

"Oh, that is so nice!" The worried look that had

sobered Samantha's features was replaced by a grin. "He likes you."

"He likes to win. He said he won't pressure me to stay anymore. I think it was his way of trying to run me out of town."

"Well, I can't blame him. Especially after he finds out what you have planned for the Fall Harvest Festival."

"Please don't say anything to him, either? Or Jack?"

Samantha sighed, looking troubled again. "Tess…"

"Fine." She had to remember that Samantha was married now. Her first loyalty was to Jack. Tess was glad that her friend was happily married, but sometimes she missed the days when it was just her, Samantha and Jenna against the world. "Forget I asked. It will all be fine, even if they know."

She stood, glancing over to the windows that looked across the hills and valleys rolling out below the house that Samantha had inherited.

"I love my view," Samantha said. "Isn't it pretty?"

"Well, you know me." Tess sighed. "Give me the San Francisco skyline any day." And suddenly she wanted, more than anything, to go home.

CHAPTER EIGHT

"HEY, THANKS FOR helping me fold these last night." Slaid grabbed a pile of flyers and handed them to Devin. "Will you help me pass them out?"

"Dad, that is so uncool."

"I'd say preventing this area from being covered in windmills is about as cool as it gets. C'mon, Dev. Just hand out the flyers to everyone you know. I'll do the same, and between us we'll get this done in a half hour."

"Okay," Devin said. "But if I help with this, can we talk about raising my allowance?"

"Ha-ha." Slaid grinned at his son. "I've always loved your sense of humor."

"Dad, please?"

"We'll talk about what chores you want to take on to raise your allowance, sure. But I don't think a few minutes of community service warrants a raise. Fair?"

"Yeah. I guess so."

Slaid ignored the unenthusiastic tone in his son's voice. He'd learned early on that one of the keys to successful parenting was to know what to react to, because with Devin there was usually a lot to choose from. "Meet back here around noon?"

"Sure." Devin wandered off in the direction of the food booths, probably looking for hot dogs and friends. Slaid shoved extra flyers into his back pocket and grabbed a stack to carry, then shut the door of his truck. He heard music—really good music. Someone must have a sound system at their booth.

The Fall Harvest Festival lined Main Street and ran from one end of town to the other. Making his way slowly toward the music, Slaid passed out flyers. They were simple and informative, letting residents know about the proposed wind farm and inviting them to a meeting to learn more about putting solar panels on their homes. Pretty much everyone he ran into wanted to stop and talk and was willing to take a flyer, but he was surprised by how empty the fair seemed. Families with small children were at the arts and crafts booths and the pumpkin carving station, but even the food booths were sparsely populated.

As he made his way down Main Street the music got louder. It was just his style, some insane combination of country, Texas blues and a few ripping rock and roll guitar solos. The louder the music got, the more people he saw. He was quickly running out of flyers. It seemed like most of the population of Benson had ended up at this end of the fair. And then he realized why.

The raised stage shouldn't be there. He was certain he'd never signed a permit for it. Nonetheless, it blocked the entire street, capped by a huge blue banner that read Danny Click and The Hell Yeahs, Brought to You by Renewable Reliance. On either side of the stage, a replica of a windmill rose, blades turning slowly.

A lean, long-haired guitarist was fronting the band responsible for the awesome music. They were far more together and professional than any of the local groups scheduled to play that afternoon. A wooden floor had been laid down in front of the stage, and even at eleven in the morning it was packed with people dancing.

But it wasn't just that. One side of the stage was lined with food booths emblazoned with signs that said, Free Brunch, Brought to You by Renewable Reliance. A hissing sound had him looking more closely and he saw that one booth was actually an espresso bar. Another served a full hot breakfast and the third booth was loaded with delectable baked goods. A barbecue area was being set up next to the booths, complete with picnic tables topped in red-checked cloths.

The other side of the stage was lined with information booths, decorated with catchy slogans like Wind Energy—The Power of the Future. People were walking away from those booths with handfuls of glossy flyers, booklets and even toy windmills for all the kids. Slaid glanced down at the

black-and-white, photocopied flyer in his hand. It
looked homegrown and pathetic.

A flash of orange caught his eye. It was another
banner, emblazoned with bold black letters that
spelled out Solar Power—Not Such a Sunny Outlook. Underneath it stood Tess, smiling and nod-
ding as she talked with one of the teachers from
the local elementary school.

As Slaid stared, a young woman he didn't recognize approached him. She was very pretty, probably
in her midtwenties, and she wore a tight blue T-shirt
with the words Renewable Reliance, The Power to
Change Lives written across the bust.

"May I offer you some literature on the potential
for wind energy in this area?" she asked politely,
smiling sweetly.

"No, thank you, I'm good," Slaid answered, turning away and bumping right into Jed and Betty
Watkins. His city council wingman and his wife
had lattes in their hands and a plate filled with
scones and croissants.

"Slaid!" Jed said heartily. "Grab some breakfast and take a minute to enjoy this band. They're
something else."

Slaid glared at him and Betty spoke up. "I saw
that look, Slaid Jacobs! We can enjoy this and still
not support the windmills. It's fun to dance first
thing in the morning. You should try it! It's such a
great idea! You and the council should have thought
of something like this."

"Well, even if we had, we wouldn't have been able to fund it."

"Don't be bitter," Betty admonished. "Just go get some breakfast and enjoy yourself."

"The information booths are pretty good," Jed added. "And I was a little concerned after talking to Tess. There's a possibility that if we all get solar panels like we talked about, we'll crash the grid."

"Can you imagine?" Betty asked. "We could blow up our own power system. I think we all need to think carefully before we make any decisions about solar."

The muscles in Slaid's shoulders tightened, and his jaw ached. No way could he compete with the kind of money Renewable Reliance was throwing at this today. He couldn't imagine how much it had cost to get this all done at the last minute. And how much time it would cost *him* to combat all the misinformation that would be out there by the end of the day.

Betty and Jed said goodbye and went off to find a spot to eat their free breakfast. Slaid stood silently, feeling like an idiot with his simple flyer in his hands, staring at the band and figuring out what to do next. A hand clapped him on the shoulder, startling him. It was Jack, who moved to stand beside him. "Well, we knew Tess was great at what she did. But I think we might have underestimated her," he said, a sheepish grin on his face.

"How did she get this into the festival?" Slaid asked. "Who approved it?"

"Samantha let her have the booths. She swears she had no idea Tess was bringing a band. Or that the whole thing would be so elaborate."

The lead guitarist—Slaid figured he must be Danny Click himself—was saying something to the audience. Suddenly he got them cheering. "Do we want clean energy?" he asked. A roar of "Hell yeah!" rose from the crowd in response. Slaid pulled one of his amateur flyers out of his back pocket and handed it to Jack. "I made a flyer," he said.

Jack let out a bark of derisive laughter. "Oh, man, we suck at this."

"Don't I know it." Slaid gestured around him helplessly. "I'm a cattle rancher. I know cows and a little bit about being mayor. I don't know how to put together something like this."

"Maybe today we need to just sit back and observe Tess—learn at the feet of the master. Then we can figure out our next steps."

"Can Samantha help us?" Slaid asked. "She's a public relations person, as well."

"I'll ask her. But I think whatever she does, she'd prefer to do it behind the scenes. She doesn't want to lose her friendship with Tess."

"And Tess doesn't want to lose her friendship with Samantha." The low voice had them both turning and Slaid gaped. Tess had on jeans that accentuated her long, slim legs, and a retro, blue-checked shirt tied at the waist. She wore minimal makeup and looked as fresh and pretty as a 1950s housewife. "Can I interest you gentlemen in some literature explaining the benefits of wind energy?" She smiled engagingly and waggled a colorful flyer at him, holding it right at cleavage level.

"No, thanks, I'm good," Slaid answered shortly.

"I'm gonna go look for Samantha," Jack said, backing away at Slaid's sharp tone. "Nice work here today, Tess."

Slaid continued staring at the band, and Tess turned to walk away. "Wait," he called, and she stopped, turning to face him, one eyebrow raised in inquiry. "You said you wouldn't bend the truth."

She took a step closer and brought her voice lower. "Are you accusing me of lying?"

"Solar is going to crash the grid? C'mon, Tess, you know that's just a rumor made up by power companies that want to keep the status quo."

Tess shook her head. "It's not. The fact is, no one knows how many distributed generation assets the grid can handle."

"How many *what*?"

"Slaid," she said with mock patience. "If you're going to push solar on this town, you'd better learn something about it. The term for solar panels on residences and businesses is *distributed generation assets*. You see, a wind farm provides one source of energy that feeds the grid. It's basically like a clean-energy power plant. That's what our power system, our grid, was designed for. Input from a few big power sources."

"I am aware of that," Slaid said grimly. He didn't appreciate feeling like a schoolboy around her, and he was getting schooled.

"The grid *wasn't* designed to receive energy from all over," Tess went on, "which is what will happen if you have solar panels all over town. The grid wasn't built to be bidirectional. No one knows if, at some point, the power from all the solar panels on peoples' homes will crash the grid by sending so much energy back out into it."

He didn't know what to say. She was right. He hadn't done his homework, and evidently she had. He watched bemusedly as she turned away to hand out a few slick packets of information and encourage people to visit the various booths and exhibits. She'd kicked his butt today, and he didn't know if he should be humiliated or awestruck. He felt a little of both. "You know this band is illegal. You have no permits. And I'm pretty sure they have their amps turned way past the decibel level allowed by city noise ordinances."

"Are you going to shut it down, Mr. Mayor?" Her slow smile went straight through him, leaving heat behind. "I don't know politics well, but I do know that people are having a great time. It seems to me that shutting it down might not be the best political maneuver."

She was right, and it pissed him off. Her upper hand in this conversation was so solid, he couldn't pry it away. He tried again.

"Speaking of maneuvers, what's up with taking over our Fall Harvest Festival and turning it into a wind-energy fair? This is a community event. It's tradition. And now, instead of sack races and pumpkin carving, people are over here drinking and dancing."

"People seem pretty happy. Maybe the Fall Harvest Festival wasn't really as fun as you thought?"

"It *was* fun. It was tradition…what we've always done."

"Looks as if people are ready for something new." Another cheer rose from the crowd as Danny Click finished an especially complicated guitar solo. "It sure seems as though they're enjoying the change."

"It's good music. Of course they like it. Even *I* like it. But it doesn't mean you can just show up here and mess with our traditions."

Tess stepped closer, tilting her chin so she was looking right up into his eyes. For a split second, all he could think was how easy it would be to lean down and kiss her. How much he wanted to. And then she reached behind him and briskly plucked one of his flyers from his back pocket. "Can I take one of these?" she murmured. And then she stepped back.

"Sure," he croaked, trying to recover from her

proximity, and her absence. He tried not to show any of the embarrassment he felt for his flimsy flyer while she examined it.

She opened it, glancing briefly at the contents before looking up and smiling, a teasing light in her eyes. "How cute!" she said. "It's so…um…rustic."

"Tess, be kind. This isn't what I do. And I don't have the infinite dollars of Renewable Reliance stacked behind me."

"You're right, Slaid. I didn't mean to be rude, but I guess I'm pointing out that times are changing. People don't want a photocopied flyer. They want flash, color and pizzazz. Maybe they're ready for the opportunities that Renewable Reliance can bring to this town."

"No, Tess, they just like the band and the free food that Renewable Reliance brought to the town."

She took a long, deliberate look at the growing crowd around the stage. "I guess we'll just have to see."

"I guess we will." It was his turn to step closer, using his height to tower over her. Two could play her flirty game, and since she'd started it, he wouldn't feel guilty about finishing it. "You're pretty proud of yourself, aren't you?"

She laughed softly, and despite his frustration he wanted to taste the mirth of her laughing mouth. "I'm good at what I do, remember?"

Victory suited her. If one good thing came out of today it was that he got to see Tess at her finest, confident and happy with her success. "Well, there are things I'm good at, too."

"I'm sure there are," she said, just the perfect amount of barely detectable boredom in her voice. "It's great to see you, Slaid, but I need to get back to my booth. Why don't you grab some food and enjoy the band."

He might accept his defeat today, but he wouldn't let her dismiss him like that. "Don't get too confident, Tess. This was just one battle. You haven't won the war. Not by a long shot. But by all means, enjoy your victory. It might be the only one you have. I'll see you later. I've got some more *rustic* flyers to hand out."

Slaid turned to go, but the day had lost its magic for him. Glancing back, he saw Tess still frozen in place, staring after him through the shifting crowd. For the briefest moment, he could swear she looked lost. But before he could even finish the thought, her shoulders were squared, her head was held high and she was sauntering back to her booth, the picture of confidence.

All around him in the growing crowd were happy families eating Renewable Reliance's food, carrying their colorful information packets and listening to the music they'd provided. It would take even more work than he'd originally thought to keep Benson pristine and windmill-free. But he'd figure out a way to do it. He had to. Behind him, Danny Click had the crowd on their feet. At the singer's suggestion the audience shouted out another deafening "Hell yeah!" Slaid decided to take the cheer as his own much-needed message of encouragement. He would see his plan through. Somehow. *Hell yeah.*

CHAPTER NINE

THE VIDEO SHOOT was not going well. First of all, it was freezing. Literally. And since Slaid, the ice-scraping fairy, had stopped coming by after learning that the windmills would be sited in his pasture, Tess had been forced to sacrifice another credit card to get the thick frost off her windshield this morning. Then she'd had to rush to pick up the CEO of Renewable Reliance, who obviously wasn't impressed with her late arrival.

Second, the CEO, Allen Tate, proved to be an unhappy guy in general. As he rattled on to her and his unfortunate assistant, a fresh-faced young man named Ben, about the shortcomings of his hotel room and its minibar, Tess fought the urge to yell, "Get used to it!" After all, he and his company had chosen Benson for their project—Benson certainly had not chosen them.

But she had a job to do. A job that today would require all her patience and people skills. Somehow, by focusing on the road and the work ahead of her, Tess managed to hold her tongue and sound sympathetic about the CEO's woes.

She made a mental note to find a decent bottle of wine or Scotch at the grocery store. She'd send it up to his room tonight to lessen his minibar troubles. For a moment she envied him—if only her troubles were that simple. Tomorrow he'd leave here and fly back to Chicago—and the comforts of his suburban mansion—while she would carry on in Benson, at odds with her best friend and the most attractive man she'd ever met, toiling on a project that she already knew the town didn't want.

Tess pulled the car over to the gravel shoulder of the road, across from the gate leading into Slaid's pasture. *The Bureau of Land Management's* pasture, she reminded herself quickly.

There were no other cars, even though the camera crew had left the hotel well before she'd picked up Allen and Ben. She put the Jeep in Park and reached for her cell phone, but there was no signal. Of course.

"We'll have to head back to town," she told her passengers. "We'll see if we can locate the camera crew, or at least a signal so we can call and find out what happened." Allen sighed audibly and Tess sighed inwardly. This day wasn't getting much better.

She U-turned back toward Benson and Ben held up her phone, waving it wildly around, searching for the elusive signal.

"Reception!" he crowed triumphantly.

They pulled over so she could call, but as she was

dialing the camera crew zoomed by, heading in the direction of the video-shoot location. Either they'd been lost and now were found or they'd stopped for breakfast somewhere. Silently cursing them for making her look like an idiot, Tess pulled another U-turn and followed the crew back to mile marker twenty-three.

The coffee Tess served everyone from a thermos on her tailgate steamed furiously in the frigid morning air. Coffee she'd had to brew herself at four o'clock this morning and then pour into the giant thermos that Samantha's friend Betty had borrowed from her church. There was no catering company to be found in Benson.

But thank goodness there was Betty, a woman who had been instrumental, apparently, in helping bring Samantha and Jack together. In addition to her matchmaking talents, Betty was an incredible baker, and Tess had paid her to make a few dozen of her locally famous blueberry muffins. They were a big hit with the crew. At least one thing had gone right this morning, even if it was Betty's triumph, not her own.

Sugar and coffee distributed, Tess breathed in relief. Miraculously, the CEO was chatting happily with Ben while one of the crew members applied makeup to his aggressively preserved face. The camera crew was starting on the scenery footage, filming the road disappearing into the sky shining pink with the last smears of sunrise.

Tess sipped her own coffee, grateful for a couple seconds of calm. There'd been a few mishaps this morning, but maybe this day was getting a bit better. Her conscience pricked. As better as it could get, considering she was about to film a promotional spot for a wind farm on the land Slaid's family had worked and loved for so long. What a mess.

"What were you thinking we should use for the backdrop of his little speech?" asked Will, the youngest and funniest member of the camera crew, as he poured himself more coffee.

"Those wild-looking cliffs," Tess answered. "It doesn't get more rugged than that, and the cows are all the way on the other side of the pasture."

"Perfect," Will said, giving her a glance that was full of admiration. "You look great in that color, by the way."

A couple of weeks ago, she might have flirted back. Maybe even have met up with him tonight. But she was surprised to find that she didn't have the heart for it. "Thanks," she said shortly, and crossed the street to where the CEO and the rest of the camera crew were climbing the gate into the cow pasture. She pointed to where she thought they should set up, relieved to find that the head cameraman agreed with her.

She leaned on the rough wood and watched. The cameras were set up and Allen pulled off his parka, revealing a down vest and plaid shirt—a folksy outfit that Tess knew had been carefully chosen to help promote his pioneering image. Unfortunately, Allen hadn't factored in the autumn cold. Rather than looking outdoorsy and confident, the CEO looked like someone who was freezing and trying not to show it.

Ben helped Allen position himself in front of the hills. "Action!" the lead cameraman called, and the CEO launched into his speech about the importance of the windmills. A speech Tess had written just for him.

He got about three sentences in before the first cow showed up. The big beige animal strolled calmly over to the camera and gave it a sniff. The cameraman yelped in surprise and tried to push the enormous beast away, but evidently Slaid's cattle were curious creatures. A few more lumbered over to snuffle at the camera and introduce themselves to the video crew.

Tess heard a shrill "Shoo!" and looked over to see that one cow was nuzzling Allen, who was flapping at it with frantic arms. It all looked extremely surreal and if Tess wasn't so horrified, she'd be laughing. She had no idea what to do—she knew nothing about cows. But when she saw Allen being chased by the large chocolate-colored animal, she figured it was time to intervene.

Wishing she'd put on her sturdy boots instead of her heels, Tess awkwardly scaled the fence and tottered across the rough grass. Pulling off her scarf, she approached the brown cow, who now had the

CEO cornered against a rock as she lovingly blew her grassy breath in his ear.

"Hey, cow, go away!" she called, shaking the eggplant wool in the air. The big brown beast didn't even look her way. She went closer, trying to put the scarf in between the cow and the CEO. "Get out of here. Go!" She snapped the scarf at its wet nose, sending silent apologies to the gods of cashmere when she realized she'd actually made contact and there was now cow drool on the beautiful fabric. "Go!" she shouted again.

She glanced at Allen. This was his company, and he'd chosen to site his project on land that he knew had been leased to a cattle ranch. Couldn't he at least help her? But he seemed frozen in fear. A ghostly pale, geeky man-boy who had spent most of his life in front of a computer screen and couldn't figure out what to do in the face of a real-world problem. Well, a cow-town problem. "Go away!" Tess commanded again.

And then she heard the laughter. Whirling around, she saw Slaid leaning on the gate, his truck parked haphazardly on the side of the road behind him. He'd clearly pulled over in a hurry to take in the disaster that was her video project. He was probably thrilled to watch it all fall apart after the way she'd given him such a hard time at the harvest festival.

"If you're not here to help, go away!" she yelled to him. And then realized how bad that sounded.

She looked back at Allen and saw the shocked expression on his face. Here she was, the public relations consultant they'd hired at considerable expense, orchestrating a video shoot overrun by curious cattle and screaming rudely at the locals. In that instant, she could see it all through his eyes and it did not look pretty.

Slaid was still laughing, but to his credit he swung a long denim-clad leg over the gate, then another, and jumped down into the pasture. Despite his football-player build, he moved quite gracefully. In his cowboy hat, shearling jacket and boots, he exuded a manly confidence that made the quivering CEO behind her seem even more like a frightened child.

Apparently the cow had lost interest in Allen because it was now investigating Tess's hair. Slaid came up next to her and gently but firmly pushed the cow's nose away.

"Move along there," he ordered quietly, and the cow obediently walked a few paces from Tess and then glanced back. "Go on, get going now." Slaid gave it a friendly swat on its rump and the cow hustled off. Then he quietly and confidently dispatched its curious buddies before walking back to Tess. He wasn't laughing out loud anymore, but the humor was still there, gleaming in his gray eyes. "Anything else I can do for you?"

Allen pushed himself off the rock. "Thank you, man," he said, reaching up to give Slaid a high five that the mayor good-naturedly returned. "Good thing you came along. I'm afraid my public relations gal here wasn't really prepared for cows."

Gal? He'd really just called her a gal? Ed would rue the day he sent her out here.

Slaid moved past the CEO and came to stand before Tess, tipping his hat. "Ms. Cole. I'm really sorry I was late getting out here today. I know we agreed I'd be here an hour ago."

Tess studied his face, confusion swirling. He was either trying to help her out or dig her deeper into this awkward hole—she wasn't sure which. And then she understood. He was trying to help her out—taking the blame for this fiasco by pretending he was some ranch hand she'd hired.

Gratitude and guilt were an odd mix. She didn't deserve his kindness. She hadn't been kind when she'd mocked his homemade flyer at the fair. "I understand, Mr. Jacobs. Although *you* understand—" she couldn't keep the saucy tone from her voice "—I will have to dock your pay?"

"Of course, ma'am." He was all contrition, except for the muscle in his cheek that twitched from trying not to laugh.

"Could you please stick around during the rest of the shoot to help manage the cattle?"

"Certainly, ma'am," he answered, and delivered a very sexy wink before walking away with an exaggerated, bowlegged swagger. She bit her lip to keep from laughing out loud. Slaid put himself in between the camera crew and the cows, and she hoped the smile she gave him expressed the appreciation she felt.

Allen turned toward her.

"So let's try this again. Are you ready for your close-up?" she said brightly, making sure she kept the upper hand. *Gal*, indeed.

"That was really farsighted of you to hire a wrangler," he told her, maybe hoping to redeem himself after his *gal* comment.

"Thank you. Unfortunately he was running late this morning. I'm just glad he finally made it." She could see Slaid over the CEO's shoulder, and when their eyes met he quickly looked away, but not before his grin melted her knees a little.

Fortunately, the rest of the shoot went smoothly. The cows stayed where Slaid told them to and they got Allen's speech in just two takes. Then the camera crew went off to get more footage of the hills and Tess walked over to where Slaid stood. "Thank you for taking care of the cows."

"Yes, thank you!" Allen appeared by her side. "Hey, would you mind if we took a picture together?" At Slaid's look of surprise he added, "The wife and kids would get a kick out of seeing that I was hanging out with a real cowboy."

"Um, sure?" The look he shot at Tess over Allen's head was full of disbelief and delight at the absurdity of this man. He gamely stood there as

Allen posed next to him and Tess took the photo on the CEO's phone.

"And now I've got to get back to town. If you don't mind, Tess? I've got a meeting scheduled with the mayor."

Tess looked at Slaid, horrified, and he met her glance with his own expression of alarm. Had he not checked his calendar today? He seemed to understand the question in her eyes because he shrugged sheepishly and then turned to the CEO. "How about I give you a ride back to town? There are a few things I think I need to explain. Do you mind waiting by my truck over there while I square things away with Ms. Cole here?"

He spoke with authority, and the CEO went willingly. After he'd left, Slaid grinned at Tess. "I've got us in a real mess now."

"It's my fault, too. I shouldn't have played along. What are we going to do?"

"I'll explain what happened and take the blame. I don't care what he thinks of me."

"Well, maybe if he gets mad, he'll fire me and I can go home," Tess mused. "I'm not sure that would be a bad thing."

"Depends on your perspective, I guess."

She didn't understand that and wasn't sure she wanted to. "Look, no matter what happens, I appreciate the rescue today."

"So when can I pick up my paycheck for my cattle-wrangling services?"

"You weren't working out of the goodness of your heart?" It was impossible not to joke with him a little. It felt good after all the tension that had been between them. Plus, he was giving her his half smile that just made her want to see more of it.

She was rewarded when he flashed her a quick grin. "Are you kidding? I had half a mind to let that cow give Allen a big old hug. After all, that guy's project is messing with my best pastures. But I couldn't let you look bad in front of him."

Tess sobered. "Considering how I teased you about your flyer at the festival, you could have just sat back and watched me fail. But instead you took the high road and helped."

"I guess that's just more my style." He was studying her face as if trying to read something there and Tess looked away, conscious that *her* style wasn't nearly as gracious as his.

Allen had reached Slaid's truck. He had his arms crossed over his chest, waiting. "You'd probably better go," she reminded Slaid. "Thank you again."

"Don't mention it."

"And, Slaid—" if he could be gracious, then she had to try, too "—I'm sorry about the harvest festival. I shouldn't have sprung all that on you."

"Hey, we're professionals, right? No apologies needed. Isn't that what you told me the other night?"

"Well, yes, but…"

"Plus, maybe *I* should be thanking *you*. You schooled me at the festival—showed me how this community-relations work needs to be done. Next meeting I set up, I'll make sure to sneak in some food and music."

Tess smiled at that. "It always helps. Especially food."

"Thanks for the tip."

He stood there a moment, looking at her with a crooked smile. Tess shifted uncomfortably.

"Look, if you really want to thank me for my cattle-control services, you could come riding with me tomorrow."

"I don't ride." Although the thought of seeing Slaid in his element was tempting. "You saw me today. I can't even handle a cow. What would I do on a horse?"

"I'll teach you."

"I'm pretty sure some things just can't be taught, cowboy."

He laughed. "Wait and see. Come on. Consider it my payment for my hard work today."

She should say no. Nothing good could come of them spending time together. They'd probably just fight. Yet despite their differences, she was starting to look forward to their various run-ins. He might be intent on making her wind project fail, but she kind of liked him. After all, he'd just pretended he was her hired hand and was about to take the blame for just about everything that had gone wrong here today.

"Okay. I'll go. On one condition. We can talk, *really* talk, about this wind project."

He was still smiling, and she couldn't look away. "We can talk."

"And be prepared. I wasn't kidding when I said I don't ride."

"Tess, I have no doubt you're successful at anything you put your mind to." Slaid's eyes were dark and intent on hers now, but humor still quirked a dimple along his cheek. "Except maybe wrangling cows. But give you time, and you'd get that, too."

Tess shoved her hand in her pocket to keep from running her finger down the dimple in his cheek. She remembered, suddenly, doing exactly that, at the hotel bar, in Phoenix. She turned away to where she could see the CEO pacing impatiently in front of Slaid's truck.

"Tomorrow," Slaid said quietly. "I've got a lunchtime meeting, but I can pick you up afterward. How about around two?"

Tess tried to remember her plans for tomorrow and failed. Tried to remember all the reasons she should say no and failed. All she could remember was the last time he'd looked at her this way with such a deep, seeking glance. It was when he'd lain over her in the bed two years ago. He'd turned the desk lamp on so he could see her. Her skin shivered with the visceral memory of the way he'd watched her in the lamplight, the way he'd touched her. "Okay," she answered finally. "Tomorrow. And thank you again for today."

They walked in silence back to the road.

She'd spend tonight and tomorrow morning studying up on her facts and figures. And tomorrow during the ride, she'd help Slaid see how easily his cows and these windmills could coexist. And she'd just have to ignore whatever feelings seemed to be between them. That was her specialty, right? Ignoring feelings and doing what needed to be done.

When they got back to Slaid's truck, Allen was leaning on it with his arms crossed, tapping his foot. "Everything okay?"

"Oh, yes," Tess answered. "I was just thanking Slaid one more time."

"Well, be sure to pay him well. Hiring help in a strange place is always tricky," the CEO said wearily as he got into the truck.

Tess looked at Slaid, but he just shook his head slightly and grinned. He swung into the driver's side and Tess heard him say, "Mr. Tate, I think there's been a little misunderstanding," before he turned the ignition and the engine roared to life.

She wondered if Slaid's political skills could save her job once Allen found out that his cowboy was actually the mayor of Benson.

Tess walked over to say goodbye to the camera crew and got into her rental Jeep with relief, grateful to be out of the cold. Grateful to have twenty-four hours to get ready for her ride with Slaid. The image of him shooing the cows away and calling her ma'am afterward flitted into her tired brain, making her smile. She couldn't believe she'd played along with Slaid's ridiculous charade. Maybe she'd let herself be unprofessional because it felt so good, and so rare, to let her guard down and be a little silly. And there was something about Slaid, something about his confident humor and the sparkle in his eye, that gave her the courage to try it.

CHAPTER TEN

IT WAS EARLY afternoon, and Tess was getting ready to meet Slaid for the dreaded ride. All morning she'd had visions of falling off the horse in multiple ways—tipping off the side, sliding right off the back and, worst of all, the horse putting on the brakes suddenly with Tess flying over its ears, cartoon-style. Although she felt a flutter of excitement inside when she thought about spending time with Slaid, she wished she'd insisted they spend their time on solid ground.

Her cell phone rang just as she was trying to decide how much makeup was too much for a horseback ride in the middle of nowhere. On one hand, she wanted to look good. After all, she was going riding with a gorgeous guy. On the other she didn't want it to seem as if she cared too much about what he thought of her. Luckily, the name flashing on the screen of her phone belonged to the only person she knew who loved makeup more than she did. Her and Samantha's other best friend, Jenna Stevens.

In place of hello, Tess said, "How much makeup is too much for a horseback ride?" Jenna would know. She'd fallen in love with a man from Benson and had spent a fair amount of time riding the mountain trails with him on their visits from San Francisco.

Jenna laughed. "You're talking to a ballroom dancer—I don't think there *is* such a thing as too much!"

"Seriously, Jenna, I'm out of my element here. What do you do about makeup when you visit Sandro's family on the ranch?"

"Just the basics. Mix some foundation in with your sunscreen so it's just a light layer. A little eyeliner, mascara and blush. Clear lip gloss."

"Thank you!" Tess wiped off her red lipstick. "So what's up, Jenna? How are you? How's Sandro?" While Jenna chatted away about the flat she and Sandro had just purchased in San Francisco, Tess removed most of her foundation, trying for the casual look Jenna had described.

"Who are you going riding with?" Jenna asked. "Is he cute?"

"Yes. And he's a really long story."

"I've got time," Jenna said. "I'm packing things into boxes."

So Tess told her about Slaid, about the one-night stand and how they were now on opposite sides of a bad situation.

Jenna was delighted. "Tess, it's about time one of your escapades came back to bite you."

"Jenna, that's mean!"

"No it's not. You know last time I read your tarot cards it said you were heading for big change and personal growth. With growth comes growing pains." Jenna loved all things mystical and insisted on trying out all her groovy interests, like tarot cards, on her friends.

"Well, Slaid can definitely be classified as a pain."

"He can't be *that* painful if you're going riding with him," Jenna teased.

"We argue all the time, but I suppose I like him a little," she conceded. "He's nice. He took me shopping *and* he rescued my video shoot from disaster."

"This is so exciting! You *like* someone. Has that ever happened before?"

"Not really," Tess admitted. "Well, honestly, I've never really gotten to know any of the guys I've... er...spent time with."

Jenna laughed. "Nice euphemism. Spent time *in the sack* with, more like!"

Tess giggled. "Yep, that's about right."

"Are you doing okay otherwise? Are you surviving life in Benson?"

"I *am* surviving, but it's not easy. I can't believe you willingly come out here so often!"

"I love it," Jenna told her. "We have so much fun on Sandro's parents' ranch. And I like the town. But we only visit for a few days at a time—living there would be totally different."

"Well, let me tell you, it's quiet. At night it's almost unnerving, it's so silent."

"But don't you love the stars?"

"They make me nervous. There's too many of them. I feel outnumbered."

Jenna laughed. "Oh, Tess! We need to get you back to San Francisco as soon as possible. Maybe I'll hang a big banner on the building across from Ed's office window that says Free Tess from Benson! Or maybe I'll start a petition and send it to him."

"I'm not sure how many people you'd get to sign it," Tess said, fishing lip gloss from her makeup bag. "I think my assistant is having a pretty good time with me gone, and I don't exactly have the busiest social life."

"You do, too. And speaking of that, we need to talk about Samantha's baby shower. I sent a couple emails about it. Have you been avoiding me?" Jenna said it in a teasing way but Tess could hear real concern behind her words—Tess was usually prompt with her email. But she hadn't been looking forward to planning the shower, so she'd put off replying.

"I'm sorry, I guess I've been pretty overwhelmed… and working remotely makes my inbox a little crowded."

"Well, I'd like to have some kind of plan in place before Jack's birthday party tomorrow night."

"You're coming to Benson for Jack's party? I

didn't know! I mean, I should've realized, with Sam throwing such a big bash, but I didn't think. I'm so excited!" It had been months since she and Jenna and Samantha had all been in the same place at the same time. "I can't wait to see you!"

"It will be fun, but we need to be able to tell Samantha *something* about her baby shower. I know you're really busy with work. If you need me to plan most of it, I don't mind, as long as we can have it at your apartment."

Tess was definitely overwhelmed with work right now, but that was nothing new. The real problem was that the baby shower made her think about babies, and that made her sad and uneasy. But she couldn't share that with her friend.

"I'd be so grateful if you could plan it, with work being so crazy. And of course we can use my apartment. Hopefully I'll be back in the city for good before then."

"Great! Can we talk about the menu?"

They chatted for several minutes about the food and decorations, and Tess did her best to sound enthusiastic. But the knot of anxiety inside of her, combined with guilt over not being excited about Samantha's baby, finally won out. "Jenna, I have to leave any minute. It might be easier if you make these decisions on your own. Would it be okay if I do the invitations and you handle the rest?"

"Sure." Jenna kept her voice bright but Tess

knew her well enough to recognize the underlying disappointment.

They said goodbye and Tess put her phone down with a profound feeling of relief. At least they had a plan in place. A plan where Jenna did most of the planning. Invitations, Tess could handle. Donating her apartment to the cause was easy. But deciding which games to play, which food to eat, what baby-themed decorations to buy all made her stomach churn.

Tess walked to the front hallway to start bundling up. She was actually looking forward to the ride now, if only to clear away her unsettling feelings. Later tonight, with a big glass of wine in hand, she'd write up the guest list and order invitations.

It was a beautiful, clear day, but when she opened the front door to check the temperature, she found that the sunshine didn't provide the slightest bit of warmth. Tess picked up her scarf—cow slobber long gone, thanks to a thorough washing in her bathroom. She studied her reflection in the hallway mirror. Slaid had been right about the color bringing out the purple in her eyes.

She reminded herself for the hundredth time that it didn't matter *what* he thought about her or her eyes. She was here on business, and what mattered were the wits in her brain and the arguments she presented that would convince him to support the windmills.

She heard his truck pull up outside the house and

the metallic clank of a tailgate opening. Then she heard the clop of hooves on pavement. He'd brought horses here? Into town? Tess flew to the front window. Sure enough, Benson's mayor was unloading two large horses from a sleek trailer painted with the words *Jacobs Ranch*. She turned away from the window with her heart pounding. She was intimidated by how gigantic horses were, and by how handsome Slaid was—especially right now, with the concentration on his face as he worked. The gentle strength he used to handle his horses was evident in his every move.

One final check in the mirror and Tess pulled on her parka. When she stepped outside, Slaid was brushing down a huge brown horse with a black mane. He smiled at her over the horse's back. Tess racked her brain for the name of the horse's type of coloring. She'd been studying up, figuring she'd better memorize some terminology if she hoped to fit into a community of ranchers. *Bay.* The word came to her from the one tiny portion of her brain that wasn't too busy enjoying Slaid's smile to help her out. *It was a bay horse.*

"Nice bay," she said, walking up to the huge beast and holding her hand out for it to sniff, hoping neither the horse nor Slaid would notice it shaking. The horse's dark nose snuffled her quaking hand, then continued up her arm to her shoulder. It blew gently into her hair, and Tess stepped back in surprise.

"All my animals seem to think your hair is hay," Slaid said, leaning with one arm over the horse's back. There was something about him that gave her confidence and calmed her heart. No. She had to stop thinking things like that—she was perfectly capable of calming her own heart.

"Meet Puck," he said.

"Puck?" It seemed an odd name for a horse. Not that she had any idea what horses were generally named. "You're a hockey fan?"

"*A Midsummer Night's Dream?* Shakespeare?"

Tess looked at him, aware of the play yet unable to make the connection.

"He's playful. And fast. Remember when Puck says, 'I'll put a girdle round about the earth in forty minutes'?"

No she didn't remember, and she was surprised he did. "You're a fan of Shakespeare?"

"I like to read. Occasionally I'm in the mood for a classic."

A Shakespeare-quoting cowboy of a mayor. And she already knew he had fabulous skills in bed. Her resolve to keep this all business was already crumbling, and she'd been in his presence for about ninety seconds. "You're quite the renaissance man," she quipped.

He smiled. "I try to keep life interesting. Now come on over here and meet Wendy."

"Wendy?"

"Well, she came to me with a buddy, and they're

always together. And he's this gangly little guy. We named him Peter Pan. Wendy just seemed like the logical choice for his best friend."

"And do most of your animals get their names from literature?"

"When it suits them. Which is most of the time. There are a lot of good books out there."

Tess walked around Puck's enormous backside, giving him a lot of space, and there, tied to the other side of the trailer, was a beautiful black mare. She was significantly smaller than Puck and daintier, with smaller hindquarters. "She's so pretty. But she's a different kind of horse, right?"

"Puck here is a quarter horse. He's got this big old rear end so he can chase down cattle and turn on a dime. Wendy, however, was born in the wild. She's a mustang."

"You're kidding!" Even city-girl Tess had heard about America's own wild horses.

"When they get overpopulated, the government rounds them up and auctions them off. And though it's not supposed to happen, sometimes they go to slaughterhouses. Other times they're just held at these rundown government facilities because no one knows what to do with them. A guy in town, Todd, made it his business to help change that. He's got a ranch now, kind of a sanctuary. The guy's amazing—really passionate. He convinced Jack to help him train them. After Todd and Jack trained Wendy some, I bought her."

Tess smiled at this further evidence that Samantha had married a good man. "So you're going to put a beginner like me on a half-wild horse?"

Slaid laughed. "Don't panic. Jack's phenomenal at what he does. And my son, Devin, and I have worked with her a lot. She's the sweetest."

His son. It was easy to forget how serious, how settled his life was. She needed to watch herself. Slaid was a family man through and through. Now that they both seemed resolved to be a little more cordial, she had to be careful not to flirt. She didn't want to give him any ideas. She'd already hurt him once.

Slaid must have read her mind. "I know we're not supposed to talk about what happened between us two years ago, but isn't it kind of strange that back when we first met, I knew Jack and you knew Samantha? And out of all the other people your boss could have sent to Benson, he sent you?"

"Coincidences happen all the time," she said dismissively.

"Right," he said, handing her a brush. "Maybe to you. Not so much to me."

Tess figured it was best not to answer. What was the point? It *was* strange that they'd met again, but that didn't mean it signified anything. In her experience, it was best not to analyze things too much. In real life, things didn't mean much. They just happened, and then you somehow figured out what to do next.

Tess carried the large wooden brush over to Wendy. There was no evidence now of the mare's freewheeling past. She had a sweet face, with a white star on her forehead and petite pointed ears that perked up when she snuffed at Tess's hand. "So what do I do with this thing?" she asked Jack, holding up the brush.

"Just run it along her coat, in the direction the hair grows. Make sure there's no dirt on it."

"Um...okay." Tess ran her hand tentatively down the sleek muscle of Wendy's neck, glad that the horse just stood there placidly. She began brushing and had worked her way around to Wendy's other side when Slaid walked over and handed her a small metal tool with a bent end.

"Hoof pick," he said. He demonstrated how to lean gently on Wendy's shoulder until she obligingly picked up her foot.

"You're kidding, right?" Tess looked down at her manicured nails with their pale pink polish.

"Not kidding." He showed her how to use the pick to clean around the bottom of Wendy's hoof.

"You don't know where that hoof has been!" Tess exclaimed in dismay.

"Well, actually, I do. She was in a stall last night, so it's been in straw, maybe a little manure—"

"Exactly my point!"

"If you're gonna learn to ride, Tess, you'll have to get a little less squeamish. And, not to tell you how to do your job, but a little hard work like *this* will go a long way toward earning this town's trust." He nodded his head in the direction of the house across the street, and Tess looked just in time to see the curtain pulled hurriedly shut by an invisible hand inside. "Mrs. Barnes over there will be sure to let people know what she sees today."

He was right. She had to put on a good show for Benson. She pulled her fleece gloves out of her pocket and slid them on.

Slaid grinned as she took the pick from him. "You sure are girlie, Tess Cole."

"If anyone had told me a week ago I'd be cleaning a horse's foot I'd have told them they were crazy." But she slowly leaned into the muscles at the top of Wendy's leg, and the mare's foot came up like magic. It was difficult to hold up the weight of her hind leg, and Slaid leaned in behind her to show her how to place it on her knee. His hands on her back, guiding her, felt huge. She could feel the strength of them, even through her many layers of clothing.

"You're doing great," he assured her, and his breath warmed her cheek and that warmth went on to other parts of her, as well. She struggled to concentrate on dislodging a small rock in Wendy's hoof and Slaid's hand came over hers, guiding the hoof pick, showing her how to get the point under the rock and flip it out. "See?" he said in her ear. "It's not so bad."

She set the hoof down from her wobbly knees—

not sure if they were wobbly from Wendy's weight or Slaid's proximity. They went around Wendy to clean her other two feet and Tess realized that there was a strange part of her that was actually enjoying this, and not just because she was pressed up against the gorgeous mayor. She liked learning to care for this little horse with a big history, whose very presence here was proof that there were people out there who did the right thing, who tried to protect something precious.

She'd always been so worried about keeping herself on track, making sure she had enough and felt safe enough that she'd never given much thought to helping others. But here, today, she was playing a small part of taking care of this rescued horse and it felt good.

"I can't believe how calm she is." Tess gently set the last clean hoof on the ground.

"She's sweet, like I said. She knows you're a beginner and she'll go easy on you."

Or maybe it was because Wendy knew she'd met another creature just like her, raised feral, adopted out, who'd somehow found a way to land on her feet.

CHAPTER ELEVEN

SHE HADN'T FALLEN off yet. Tess was repeating Slaid's equestrian advice like a litany. *Heels down, toes in, ball of the foot in the stirrup. Try to keep your weight in your legs. One hand on the rein, keeping it loose.* The other hand was supposed to be relaxed by her thigh, but it seemed to have a stressed-out mind of its own, grabbing at the saddle horn whenever Wendy went up or down a hill, or stepped over an obstacle.

Wendy's short, quick steps ate up the path that wound through the fields behind Tess's rental house. Although it was strange to call them fields, because that word made her think of meadows and grasses, while here it was sagebrush and something that Slaid called soda straw that had strange, dried, puffy-looking flowers on it. And in between the sparse plants was mainly rocks. "So I take it this isn't grazing land?" she asked Slaid.

"Nope. Most of our good pastures have had a little human intervention to get the grass growing. These are the native plants. Tough as nails."

Tess looked at the shrubs with new respect. They

were tough, and prickly looking, too. She could appreciate any creature that survived under tough conditions. Like she had.

Ugh. Benson must have introspection in the air. She found herself constantly thinking of parts of her life that she had no interest in revisiting. She urged Wendy up closer to Slaid and tried to think of conversation to distract her from herself.

"I haven't been fired so far—do I owe that to you?"

Slaid looked over his shoulder and grinned. "You might owe me a little. That CEO has no sense of humor, but I told him I was completely responsible for any misunderstanding about me being a ranch hand. I embellished a few things to make sure it was clear that I'd done all the lying. And then I played it off as some dumb cowboy practical joke. I figured he was so hell-bent on seeing me that way anyway, I might as well take advantage of it."

"I appreciate it. I shouldn't have played along. I should have cleared it up right away but…" She trailed off, not quite sure how to explain her total lapse of professionalism.

"He called you a gal?" Slaid finished for her.

"Yes, he did. It just bugs me, you know? No matter how hard I work and how successful I am, there will always be things men will feel free to say to me simply because I'm a woman. Things they'd never say to a man. Anyway, I appreciate you helping me out."

"No problem. It was kind of nice to be on the same side for once."

Tess laughed, surprised by his take on it. "You're right. We've been upset with each other since the moment I arrived." She paused and then decided to say what was on her mind. "I'm sorry if I hurt you in any way when I left your hotel room in Phoenix without saying goodbye."

Slaid was quiet for a moment, as if trying to think of how to answer. "Thanks for that," he finally said. "I'm not sure *hurt* is the right word. *Disappointed*, maybe? The whole one-night thing, it's just not something I have much experience with."

Tess thought of and rejected a few different responses. How could she possibly explain to this nice guy, this small-town, wholesome man, that the whole one-night thing was pretty much all she *had* experience with?

The track had merged with a dirt road, and Slaid slowed Puck so they could ride beside each other. Tess cast around in her brain for a new topic. "So where are your parents?"

"They retired to Palm Springs." He shook his head. "I find it hard to believe, but they've actually taken up golf. Guess they'd had enough of the cows and the snow."

"I can understand that sentiment, and I've only been here a couple weeks."

He grinned at her. "And it's not even snowing yet."

"Exactly." That grin would be her undoing. That

and the way his eyes crinkled at the corner and she could see glimmers of humor in their gray depths. She looked out at the mountains, growing closer and looming higher as they rode. Then she made the connection. It was the perfect segue. "They have a lot of windmills out in Palm Springs."

"They sure do. Hundreds."

"And they're not so bad, right?" Tess tried to keep her voice neutral, but the look Slaid gave her told her he saw right through her attempt to win him over.

"Honestly? I think they're ugly. I want clean energy and I want to prevent pollution, but I don't want to look at windmills every day, and I don't want them on the land I lease."

"So you have NIMBY syndrome."

"I have *what*?"

"NIMBY," Tess answered. "It stands for Not In My Back Yard. It's really common. People might believe in the importance of something like windmills, or a homeless shelter, but no one wants them in their neighborhood."

Slaid laughed. "Yeah, well, I guess I've got a *bad* case of NIMBY, then."

"You know the windmills could really help Benson. You could even stipulate that they have to be manufactured here, and that local young people have access to training for those manufacturing jobs."

"We have jobs. Ranching. Tourism."

"Ranching's in trouble," she countered. "I did a little research. There are more than a few ranchers in the area who've already sold a lot of their cows because of the drought."

"We've had droughts before and we've gotten by. We will again."

"But communities will have to make some sacrifices so we can get off fossil fuels."

"Yes, but why *my* community? Especially now that we're trying to install solar panels. And by the way, don't even get me started about the grid crashing. I was up all night reading about it and now I know that's just speculation, mainly fueled by big power companies who don't want to change their ways."

"We could argue about that for a long time," Tess said.

He glared at her, but she saw humor still there. "Let's not, then. So my point was, why shouldn't the community who will use this energy provide it?"

"Maybe they don't have wind?" Tess asked.

"Sure, but again, why does Benson have to be the one to supply it?"

"Because it's windy here." It was a lame answer but it was all she had.

"There are a lot of windy places. And, quite frankly, the folks in this area are tired of our land being sacrificed."

"I'm not sure I understand."

"I would've thought someone like you would have done her homework. You must have seen the trickle that they call the Owens River. The dust flat that used to be Owens Lake."

"Well, yes. But we're in the worst drought in history. Of course it's all dry."

"It's *always* a trickle. Because Los Angeles stole that water years ago and now we have barely any to make our farms and ranches possible out here."

Tess felt a sense of foreboding that she'd walked into a bigger mess than she'd realized. She made a mental note to read up on the history of water in this area when she got back to the cottage tonight. For now, she had to keep her voice neutral. "That's unfortunate. I knew LA got its water from somewhere around here. But it's history, Slaid."

"And it's repeating itself."

"Southern California also provides a lot of those tourists you're so fond of."

Slaid's voice was quiet. "I don't want history repeated on my watch. I'm not willing to sacrifice the beauty out here so that LA can build more houses and turn on more lights." He paused and looked at her, smiling faintly. "We keep having these conversations and we get nowhere. I really liked the few minutes we spent today not arguing—can we agree to keep the peace for the rest of the ride?"

Tess knew she shouldn't agree. She'd prepared for today, made sure she had facts memorized, her responses formulated. But he was right—it would be nice to take a break from all the arguing. "Okay, a truce. As long as we're clear that I've always delivered what my clients want, and I don't plan on disappointing them this time." But when she looked at the wide-open spaces around her and tried to picture windmills there, she felt a lot less confident than she was trying to sound. She might not be comfortable in the wild beauty of the Eastern Sierras, but that didn't mean she wanted it scarred forever by wind farms.

She reminded herself that it didn't matter how she felt. Her job was simply to shed a positive light on the windmill project and be the best spokesperson she could be. If she did that she'd succeed, just like she always had. It was a simple equation, so why the anxiety?

The wide track was leading them up hills that were quickly getting steeper. Out here things went from valley to mountain range all in the space of a mile or two. Stunted pines started to appear on the hillside, their thick trunks betraying their old age.

Slaid and Puck led them onto a side trail at the top of the hill, and Tess nudged Wendy to follow. From here they could look back over where they'd ridden. Benson looked like a collection of dollhouses. She could even pick out her little cottage, and Slaid's trailer—a speck parked in front of it.

Slaid dismounted gracefully on the flat hilltop while Tess awkwardly swung her leg over and groped for the ground with her foot. Relieved to make contact with land, she pulled her other foot out of the stirrup, grateful that Wendy, who was watching her efforts with a quizzical expression on her face, stood solidly.

Slaid led the horses over to an area that had a little more grass than the rest of the hilltop and let them graze. Then he held out his gloved hand. Tess hesitated, then took it, feeling a strange peace when his strong fingers wrapped around hers. They walked to a flat rock that jutted out, surrounded by the breathtaking view.

"Well, it isn't a fancy restaurant or anything you're used to from the city, but want to have a seat?"

With one wistful thought of how much she'd like to be in a fancy restaurant right now, especially a warm one, Tess plunked down on the rock, her various layers and big boots making her feel clumsy. Slaid sat next to her and tipped his felt cowboy hat back a bit, looking out at the view. He had a great profile—a strong nose but not too big, cheekbones just visible and a clear jawline that she had to resist tracing with her fingers. His skin was a natural golden color that many women, herself included, paid lots of money to replicate with bronzer.

"So what do you think?" he asked.

"Of what?" She looked at him, wondering if she'd missed something he'd said while she'd been ogling him.

"All of this." He gestured with his hand, encompassing the view around him.

"Oh, the nature?"

He turned to her, an incredulous smile on his face. "Yes, *the nature*! Have you *ever* been outside of the city before?"

Tess stared at the view, trying to figure out what to say about it. She was starting to like it a little, and she'd just realized that she'd rather it wasn't ruined by windmills, but she couldn't tell him that. "Well, it's large, and impressive." She paused, suddenly aware of her choice of adjectives. She raised an eyebrow at Slaid suggestively. "The nature, I mean."

He flushed a little, but ignored her attempt at humor. "Not so forsaken as you thought?"

Evidently he wanted a serious answer. Tess tried to think of the right words to describe how it made her feel. "It's beautiful, of course, but overwhelming. You have to understand, aside from Samantha's wedding, I've spent zero time in a place like this. I've never camped. I've rarely hiked. I was raised in a city and I've stuck to them ever since. So when I come out here, it's almost like I don't have the brain cells to process it, or the vocabulary to describe it."

"That just means you need to spend more time out here."

Tess smiled. "Perhaps. *Or* maybe it means I need to get back to the city, where I belong."

"Cities are nice places to visit. This is where real life happens."

"We have very different ideas of what counts as real life."

"Opposites attract."

He was looking right into her eyes, and she had a hard time looking away. But somehow she did. "That's what they say."

She studied the view, trying to come up with words to do it justice. Across the valley were hills, dry, stark and tumbling on, one after another. They were so barren that she could see every detail of the land's contours. It was like being able to look through someone's skin and see their bones.

"Those hills are my pastures." Slaid's voice was quiet. "The ones I lease."

Tess pictured more windmills, and felt a little sick.

"Tess, you know in your heart that if it happens, it will be a big loss."

Just her luck to get stuck with an ex-lover who has mind-reading powers as her opponent in this struggle. "My heart can't get involved. Is that why you brought me out here? To convince me that it's too beautiful to spoil?"

"No. That's not why I brought you here," he said.

"Then why?"

"Because I want to be around you. There's something about you…" He looked away as if trying to collect his thoughts. When he looked back, his expression was sheepish. "Well, I just want you to see what I see when I look out at this land. I want you to see the beauty. Not for any real purpose, just to see it."

Tess stared at him. "You want me to like it."

"Yeah." His cheeks were a little flushed, as if he'd just realized how silly that sounded.

"Because *you* like it."

"I guess." He looked out over the hills again.

"Well, okay, then." She looked in the same direction, trying to see the landscape through Slaid's eyes this time. Trying to see the beauty that he did. The skeletal hills were lit golden in the afternoon light, their cracks and crevices in deep contrasting shadows. That was kind of pretty. Rocks jutted through the thin soil like abstract sculptures, and she liked modern art.

"I can see beauty, but it's so vast and aloof—it seems so lonely. I don't know how people ever feel at home here." She shivered. "And it's getting cold!"

He moved over on the rock and put his arm around her.

She shouldn't let him, as much as she wanted to. "I'm fine."

"Let me help," he said. "I keep forgetting you're not used to our weather, probably because you being here, in Benson, feels so right to me."

Tess couldn't hide her surprise. "What part of me being here seems *right*? Because I can tell you, I've never felt more like a fish out of water."

"I know small-town life is all new to you, but seeing you again after two years of wondering about you, that's the part that seems right."

Suddenly it was hard to breathe. She slid out from under his arm. "Trust me, there is nothing *right* happening here. Slaid, you need to forget about that night."

"I can't. And you may have forgotten my name, and not recognized my face, but I think deep down you haven't forgotten that night, either."

Tess stared at him, shocked. He stared right back as if daring her to contradict him. "Just because I haven't totally forgotten doesn't mean it's a good idea for us to get involved." She continued staring—she wouldn't be the one to look away. But as she watched, something in his eyes darkened and his focus shifted from her eyes to her mouth. A faint voice in her head whispered that she should get up and walk away, but the purpose she saw in Slaid's expression had her cemented to the ground. It was hard to breathe, let alone leave. He brought his mouth down closer. Tess felt the attraction between them like the force of two magnets, slamming together over that final tiny distance.

His kiss was just like the ones that had scorched her memories for the past two years—strong and insistent. His confidence—the way his hand felt so large as it settled firmly on her jaw and held her so he could deepen the kiss—sent the last remnants of reason tumbling away. And when he pulled her closer so she was facing him, she realized that those remnants might never come back. There was something about him, his size, his strength, or the way he seemed so calm and capable, that met a need inside her she hadn't known she had.

Her hand went up of its own accord and reached behind his head, pulling him closer. All she could think was how much she wanted his mouth on hers, in a kiss so firm it was almost punishing.

Slaid seemed to sense her urgency. He wrapped strong fingers in her hair, pulling her still closer. She recognized the taste of him as one she'd been seeking since Phoenix.

But it was only a taste, and she wanted so much more. Her hand went to his parka and yanked the zipper down. Then she was running her fingers over his solid chest, over the bulk of his linebacker shoulders, the ridges of muscle in his abdomen, wanting to feel his skin there instead of the layers of fabric. "Slaid…" she gasped.

He pulled her up onto his lap so she was straddling him, his mouth somehow never leaving hers. The demand of his kiss matched that of his hands as he yanked her sweater up and ran his big hands along the bare skin of her back, her sides and then over her bra.

The cry that tore through the air was hers. She felt as though something inside of her was famished, had been waiting for this moment. She squirmed on his lap and he eased her back, slowing their pace, dictating how it would be between them.

The desire that flooded through her blocked out everything else. All she wanted, the only thing that mattered, was to feel his body along hers. She leaned in, trying to force him back onto the ground so she could lie over him. Instead he scooped her up, set her on the ground next to him and, leaning on an elbow, continued the kiss as his free hand roamed down her body, over her jeans, finally wrapping around her thigh. Tess moaned and rolled toward his hand and something prickly stabbed her at the waist.

"Ouch!" she yelped, and he was off her in a flash, helping her sit up and get away from the sharp spines of the little gray-blue innocent-looking plant that had been crushed beneath her. "What was that?"

Slaid's breath was uneven and rough. "Thistle." He grinned at her. "Sorry about that."

"Hazardous around here." She couldn't help smiling back. The desire she felt was exhilarating, and despite the menacing thistle, she couldn't wait to kiss him again.

"Maybe this little guy did us a favor," Slaid said, poking at the plant with his finger. "As much as I was enjoying myself, this probably isn't a great idea."

Reality was such a miser, pulling the golden heat between them right out of her grasping hands. "Remind me why not?" She rubbed her hand over the skin that the thistle had stung. "Besides the fact that plants out here have teeth?"

He laughed softly and tipped her chin up so he could look into her eyes. "Because we already did this."

"We haven't done *this*. Trust me, I'd remember."

"We've already slept together. Two years ago. And it was incredible. And obviously, if we slept together again, it would be even better."

"So why, exactly, are we stopping?"

"We're stopping because I want more."

"That makes no sense. I want more, too. So let's have more." It occurred to her that she was starting to sound a little desperate.

His voice was gentle, his eyes almost hypnotic the way he held her gaze so intently. "I want you, Tess Cole. Like I've never wanted anyone. But not like this... Call me old-fashioned, but I'd really like to get to know you better first. Before we..."

His voice trailed off, and Tess hid her confusion with a practical tone. "Well, I expect you will. I'll be around for a month and we'll be working together. Or against each other."

He looked at her in exasperation. "You know what I mean."

She sighed. Of course she did. "You mean you want a few formalities before we sleep together again."

His deep gray eyes opened a little wider. "You

really don't have a scrap of romance hiding in there, do you?"

That stung, though it was probably true. "I just don't understand why we have to go slow if this is something we both really want. We're consenting adults. It doesn't have to affect our business relationship. We can keep it professional during work hours and..." She couldn't help the suggestive note that crept into her voice. "Keep it very, *very* non-professional in our off-hours."

He smiled at her insinuation. "We could. But that's not really my style. I want to take you out, spend time with you, talk, do things together, have a meal. I want to get to know you so there's more between us than just sex."

She had no idea how to handle this. "But why worry about all that? I'm only here for a couple weeks. If we date, all we'll do is find out we have nothing in common. You like all these outdoor activities and cows and stuff, and I like shopping and being in the city."

"Have you enjoyed this today? Riding Wendy out here?"

"Yes, I have." She hated to admit it.

"So maybe there's a whole lot of other stuff out here you'll like, too."

"Fine, let's say we go on a few dates. We're on opposite sides of a very public controversy. You're the mayor of Benson. What will your constituents say when they see us out together?"

"I dunno…that we're a cute couple?" He picked a pebble off the ground and threw it down the hill. Somehow that boyish gesture, right in the middle of their very adult conversation, went straight to her heart. "I'm not worried about what people will think about us dating. Dating is healthy and natural. I'd be a lot more worried about what people would think about us sleeping together, no strings attached. That's not really the example I want to set for my kid or my town."

"I don't date, Slaid. Ever. Sorry." There, it was out.

His eyebrows shot up. "Ever? You mean you've never been on a date with anyone?"

"Well, maybe once or twice, years ago, but I don't do relationships."

"You mean you haven't before. No reason you can't start now." The side of his mouth quirked up and that gentle teasing light was back in his eyes. "Branch out, try something new."

"I think today was enough new for a while."

"Tess." He reached over and took her hand, wrapping it up in the warmth of both of his. "The fact is, by some crazy coincidence you showed up in my life again. And I won't lie—I've wanted you to. For the past two years, I've wanted you to."

"Us meeting again is a random occurrence. It doesn't mean anything."

He laughed outright at that. "I don't think that's possible. Don't you believe in fate?"

"No! There's no big plan, Slaid. There's just life—it's hard and a lot of bad stuff happens. So you have to grab the fun when you can and not let things get too serious."

"So basically you're saying you like to sleep around."

His words stung. She met the pain in her usual way, with defiance. "Yep."

"Why?"

There were probably a million pieces of psychobabble she could give him. But each of them would reveal a bit of her past that she didn't want to talk about. She looked away from him. Stared at the view, trying to convince herself she didn't care what he thought of her.

"Tess, I'm sorry. I shouldn't have said that."

She glanced over and saw sincerity in his eyes. And hurt, as well. He needed an explanation, but she didn't have a good one. "Don't you ever walk up to a cliff and wish you could step off the edge, just to see what happens?"

Slaid looked startled. "Maybe, but I think I *know* what happens. Even if it's exciting at first, you hit the ground."

"Well, maybe I just like that excitement." She stood up and walked to where Wendy was eating. She'd let this get out of hand. She was supposed to be keeping things professional between them, but obviously the attraction they shared was too big for that. And he wanted more, and he made her want more, and she couldn't have it.

"Tess, I never meant to make you uncomfortable." He'd followed her to Wendy's side.

"Well, you did. You know, not everyone is like you, Slaid, with your small-town values and your concern for your reputation. If you stepped out of Benson once in a while, you'd see that there are all kinds of people who live like I do, and there's nothing wrong with that. Now, I'm ready to go."

"Tess, I…" He didn't finish. Instead he reached up and took the edges of her wool cap between his fingers and delicately pulled it down over her ears, ensuring she'd be warm for the ride back. The tenderness of the gesture softened her outrage and melted something icy inside. Made her wish she could be someone else. Someone who could give him what he wanted.

Slaid turned toward Wendy, ran his hand down her neck and took up her reins. The little horse reluctantly pulled away from the grass she'd been munching. He circled her around and pointed her toward the trail home. Tess managed to get herself in the saddle not *too* awkwardly, and Slaid handed her the reins before going to Puck and swinging into the saddle in a fluid motion that made it look easy.

They rode back in silence. And though she tried not to, Tess couldn't help thinking about their kiss, and the way it had felt to be back in his arms. But the memory was tarnished with regret and something new, a dark sense of despair. She'd been given a glimpse of something gilded and beautiful that she'd never get to have.

Back at the trailer, Slaid helped her dismount, and he put Wendy in a halter and tied her to one of the metal loops on the trailer. Then he turned to Tess. "I'll try not to judge how you live your life. But I know how I want to live mine—and I won't change that."

Tess nodded. "Well, at least we understand each other. Thank you for the ride."

He kissed her cheek, just a gentle brush across her skin. A final reminder of what they might have if she'd just do things his way.

Inside her house, Tess leaned on the closed front door and slid down to sit on the floor. She pulled her knees to her chest, wrapped her arms around them and waited.

The relief she felt when she heard the truck pull away was expected. But the regret and sadness were the kinds of feelings she had worked very hard over the years not to feel. She wanted nothing to do with them.

When a tear slid down her face, Tess brushed it off and stood up abruptly. What was wrong with her? What was all this self-pity and weird longing? She'd learned long ago that she didn't have the emotional skills to be in a relationship, that she did best when she was on her own.

Tess walked into the small study, unwrapping her scarf as she went. A file was on the table and she opened it, forcing herself to read the contents and get her mind back on work. Then she reached into her tote bag and yanked out another pile of files, slamming them onto the desk. *This* was her focus. *This* was her life.

Tearing off her coat, she sat down in the chair and picked up a pen, willing her mind to absorb the flowchart in front of her. By sheer force of will, she shoved all thoughts of Slaid aside and worked.

The afternoon outside her window faded away to dusk, but Tess remained at her desk. She read document after document, hoping they'd have some magical ability to patch the hole Slaid had just made in the armor around her heart.

CHAPTER TWELVE

"WHAT A GREAT PARTY!" Tess hugged Samantha and looked around the crowded restaurant. Her friend had rented out Benson's new Italian bistro in honor of Jack's birthday.

"Thank you!" Samantha exclaimed, giving Tess a kiss on the cheek. "But where have you been? I thought we'd be hanging out every day while you were in Benson. But you've been so hard to reach."

Tess saw the reproach in her friend's eyes and wasn't sure how to answer. The truth was, she'd been trying to avoid talking about babies. It was understandably Samantha's favorite topic these days. And the conflict over the windmills added a whole other layer of awkwardness between them.

"I'm sorry, Sam, it's harder than I thought to work on my own like this, away from the office. I have no assistant, and everything has to be done by phone and email—it all seems like it's taking forever."

She saw the hurt in Samantha's eyes and knew this was the point in the conversation where she should promise to spend more time with her. But she couldn't. So she changed the subject. "Well, Jack seems to be having fun at his party."

"You think so?" Samantha looked over to where her husband was talking with a group of people by the fireplace. He seemed to have a sixth sense where his wife was concerned, because he immediately looked over and smiled.

He really was a handsome guy. Tess could see why Samantha was so fluttery around him, even after over a year of marriage. He came over and enveloped Tess in a hug. "Hey, Blondie," he teased. "Great to see you. How's the windmill business?"

She didn't want to answer too seriously. It was a party after all. "It's a breeze."

He gave an appreciative chuckle at her lame joke. "I'm sure it is." While they chatted, Tess watched Jack wrap his arm around his wife. She noticed the way Samantha leaned into him so comfortably. What that would be like to be so close to someone like that? It was almost as if Samantha and Jack were speaking a foreign language. Tess couldn't imagine that level of ease and contentment with a man. Yet it seemed to envelop Samantha and Jack like a happy cloud.

"Oh, my gosh!" came the shriek from the door. "I can't believe we're all here!"

"Jenna!" Tess and Samantha said their friend's name simultaneously.

The petite redhead flew across the room and threw an arm around each of them, pulling them in for a group hug. "Look at your tummy!" she exclaimed to Samantha.

Her fiancé, Sandro, strolled through the door, watching Jenna with an expression laced with so much masculine pride and tenderness that Tess looked away for a second, feeling as if she was intruding on a private moment. When she glanced back, he spotted her and grinned.

"Hey, Tess." He pulled her in for a quick hug. She saw so much of them in San Francisco nowadays that Sandro felt like family. He even teased her on occasion about the first time they met, when she'd propositioned him at a party, not realizing he was Jenna's date. But who could blame her? Sandro was the epitome of tall, dark and handsome, with enough urban artsy scruffiness thrown in to make most women think dirty thoughts.

"Sandro! You were able to escape from your restaurant for the weekend?"

"Got myself another chef now, and a manager. I can't believe we're doing so well in less than a year. It's incredible—and it frees me up to spend more time with my future wife." He reached for Jenna and pulled her in under his arm. She was so tiny and he was so tall that she fit right under his shoulder. He grinned at Jack. "Plus, my silent partner here seems pretty happy."

"Hey, I know a good investment when I see one. Did we tell you, Tess, that we're thinking of opening *another* restaurant?" Jack asked.

"Ooh, put it downtown, so I can get some decent food after work," she requested.

"We're considering it. Or maybe Hayes Valley."

"No! No one can park there, your customers will all give up in frustration."

"Or they'll come eat there before heading to the opera house…"

"I hate to interrupt all this business talk," Samantha said, "but the birthday boy here needs to mingle."

"Later," Jack said, lifting his beer to Sandro and Tess. "We value your opinion, Tess. No one knows San Francisco dining like you do."

"That's because she never cooks." Samantha and Jenna said it together and collapsed against each other in giggles.

"Well, I spend my time perfecting other talents," Tess defended.

That admission brought another round of laughter. Then Samantha and Jack excused themselves and wandered off through the crowd, arm and arm, to greet their guests.

Sandro looked around the room eagerly. "I need to go check this place out and have a chat with Dan, the owner."

"Is it strange to be here when it was going to be your place at one point?" Tess asked. Not too long ago, Sandro had been in the process of opening a Basque restaurant in this building. Then he'd met Jenna and decided he'd try his luck in San Francisco.

"A little odd. But I have no regrets. All my dreams are coming true." He leaned down and kissed Jenna on the top of her head. "Life is good."

Jenna looked up at him and smiled. "It really is," she said softly.

"And how are things at the ballroom?" Tess asked Jenna. "Is your tango class surviving without its star student? Meaning me?"

"Barely. Seriously, Tess. I think a couple of the guys dropped out when they realized you weren't coming this session." Jenna giggled. "But a few of the ladies seem pretty happy. They have a chance to shine now."

"See? I'm just doing a favor for my sisters in dance. And hopefully I'll be out of here in a few weeks and back to perfecting my moves every Wednesday night. I miss my favorite teacher."

"I miss you, too," Jenna said, reaching out and squeezing her hand briefly.

"Tess, do you want to come with us to meet Dan? I just saw him over by the patio doors."

"You go ahead," Tess said. "I'm heading to the bar for a drink." The last thing she wanted to do was trail after her coupled-up friends like a third wheel.

"Make sure you admire the bar. I built it." Sandro grinned at her and Tess laughed.

"I'll be sure to ooh and aah."

She watched Sandro and Jenna walk away, moving as one unit across the dining room. There was

envy wriggling under her skin—something she'd
never felt before and didn't want to feel now. Hopefully a good Scotch and some light conversation
would distract her from the strange sensation that
life was moving on without her and she was getting left behind.

TYLER SEEMED AS IF he was used to girls jumping in
bed with him. Tess could see why. Tall and lean,
his muscular arms bulged from beneath his vintage
Waylon Jennings concert T-shirt with the word *out-
law* scrawled across it. His blond hair had darker
brown beneath it, making a girl want to run her
fingers into its depths. It was hard to look away
from his eyes. They were big and greenish brown,
and he knew how to use them to flirt outrageously.
Plus, he was funny and could spin a good yarn.

He was leaning his elbow on the bar, a bottle of
Budweiser in hand, telling her a story about being
in boot camp in the army and how a rat had found
its way into his bunk mate's duffel. The image
made her squeamish, but at least the story was more
entertaining than the obvious lines he'd been trying out on her earlier. And she appreciated the entertainment. It almost took her mind off a long list
of topics she wanted to avoid thinking about at this
party, including windmills, babies, baby showers
and happily coupled-up friends. And Slaid. Though
even with her superhuman powers of avoidance

she wasn't sure it was possible to stop thinking about him.

Tyler had to be about five years younger than her, but to his credit, after she'd told him there was no way she'd ever go home with him, he'd stuck around to chat anyway. And he seemed to be the only local who was feeling chatty. Although she'd met many of the guests here tonight at the harvest festival and they'd seemed friendly enough then, tonight they drifted away as soon as they could without seeming rude. Maybe they'd been recruited by Slaid and his solar-panel plan. Whatever the reason, she'd been a social pariah in the bar until Tyler had shown up.

She wondered just how many people Slaid had contacted so far and how many had gotten on board with his idea. Well, in a few days she'd be showing the CEO's video and answering questions at the community center, and she was offering a full three-course catered meal to everyone who attended. The RSVP had been coming back at a brisk pace and most had been marked yes.

At the thought of the mayor, her eyes scanned the room again. And if her heart gave a little jump when she saw that Slaid had arrived and was talking with Jack, well, that was her bad luck. It was one more of life's little ironies that the man she wanted so badly that it was keeping her up at night turned out to be the one guy who didn't want to sleep with her.

And in that moment, he caught her staring. She flushed as he lifted his glass to her in acknowledgment. She looked away trying to focus on Tyler, wondering if it was too early to leave this party. She didn't want to hurt Jack's and Samantha's feelings, or cut short any time she might get with her girlfriends, but she had work to do, and she was pretty sure that her buddy Tyler would be moving on soon to find a more willing partner.

"Tyler." Slaid was standing next to her, and his voice was low and a little less good-humored than usual. Was he still upset about their ride the other day?

"Mayor Jacobs." Tyler's moved just a little closer to Tess as if asserting his prior claim.

"Mind if I have a word with Tess for a moment?"

Tyler looked as though he wanted to say no, but Slaid had age, size and the office of mayor on his side. Tyler reluctantly pushed off the bar and raised his bottle slightly to Tess. "It was great talking to you, Tess. I'll catch up with you later tonight."

She had to give him credit. The mayor might have succeeded in chasing him off, but young Tyler had scored the final blow.

"What the hell did he mean by that?" With Tyler gone, Slaid's voice was low and furious.

Tess was just a little gratified that he was jealous.

After all, he should be made aware that not everyone would pass on what she offered. "Nothing you need to know about," she purred over her drink.

Slaid took a deep breath, glancing around the bar as if reminding himself of where he was. "I think I already know. Tess, you can't go sleeping around in this town."

Anger curdled her tone sour. "First of all, I'm tired of you accusing me of *sleeping around*. It's about a half step up from calling me a slut, and if that's what you think of me, fine, but I don't need to hear it. And second, I didn't realize that being mayor gave you jurisdiction over other people's personal lives."

"I meant no disrespect," he said stiffly. "Look, I'm not the only one in this town who has a more traditional outlook on things. If you want to be successful here, you can't act the way you might at home or on another business trip. People will find out, they'll gossip, and your credibility will be damaged."

Tess took a deep breath and reminded herself that slapping the mayor would damage her credibility. "So let me get the twisted moral code of Benson straight. If I chat with Tyler at a party, I'll be accused of sleeping around. But it was okay for *you* to spend a night with me?" She paused, feigning surprise, sarcasm snapping her words out. "Oh, wait, of course! You're a man, so that makes it okay. Or your morals just exist within the narrow-minded borders of your small town—they don't cross state lines."

The more she thought about his hypocrisy, the angrier she got. She set her drink down on the bar and grabbed her purse. "You know, I think I'm done standing here while you judge me, and tell me how I should behave."

"Tess…"

She started walking, tears stinging her eyes. No way would she let them fall. She rushed into the coat check and found her parka, shoving her arms through the sleeves as she pushed out the door.

"Tess, wait!" Slaid was right behind her, jogging down the front steps. "Hang on."

She stopped abruptly. "Why?"

"Because I'm an ass. I didn't mean to say those things."

"You mean you have some strange affliction where you can't control the words that come out of your mouth? I'm not buying it."

"No. Yes. I mean, only when I'm with you. I want to get it right and instead I say all the wrong things."

"There. That is one thing we can agree on." Tess was cold and she wanted to go back to her cottage. She walked up Main Street. Slaid's long strides made it easy for him to keep up.

"I don't regret that night together. Not at all. And I don't judge you for it."

"Well, that's very reassuring," she said. "Except it's obvious that you *do* judge me."

"Maybe I'm judging myself. I don't do things like that. But I did and it was amazing, so I'm conflicted."

"You need to work out your inner conflicts on your own. It's not fair to blame me for them."

"You're right. It's not." He turned, walking backward so he could see her face. She refused to look at him. "Please accept my apology."

"Slaid—" She was weary now. "Maybe later I can accept it. Right now I just want to be alone." Another tear threatened to escape. Why was she so upset? Why did his criticism hurt? Normally she'd just laugh and write him off as a judgmental prude.

And then she realized. At the party she'd been an outsider with her coupled-up friends *and* with the residents of Benson. Slaid's lecture on her behavior had driven that point home. Driven it right into the sore spot deep down inside.

Growing up in foster homes, transferred from school to school, she'd always felt as if she was on the outside of normal life. Other people had families and friends—she didn't. Other people knew how to behave and what to say—she'd never been taught any of that. Tonight had given her that same feeling and she hated it.

With profound relief she unlatched the gate on her picket fence. "Good night, Slaid." Her hand was shaking as she tried to get her house key into the lock. Suddenly he was behind her, gently taking it out of her hand and opening the door for her.

"Good night," he said softly, handing back her keys. "I am truly sorry."

She pushed through her door and into the warmth of her cottage, sliding the bolt behind her. Dropping her coat and kicking off her shoes, she went straight into the bedroom, where she flopped down on the bed and pulled the blankets over her. Tears made hot trails down her cheeks, but she fought the urge to break down entirely. If she'd learned anything from her rough past it was that crying got you nowhere. It only made you weak in a world where you needed to be so very tough and strong.

CHAPTER THIRTEEN

"I CAN'T BELIEVE you've never done this." Samantha jabbed at the eyeball of her jack-o'-lantern. "How is it that you've never carved a pumpkin?"

Tess cursed herself for letting that information slip out. "I don't know. We had all kinds of other Halloween traditions. Just not this one."

"What kinds of traditions?" Jack asked. His brow was furrowed in concentration. He was determined to make his pumpkin look like a horse, but right now it just looked slightly maniacal.

Years ago, Tess had told Samantha that she'd grown up in New England. She'd invented the perfect family in the perfect location, simply because she hadn't wanted to talk about the childhood she'd really had. Frantically scanning her memory for what kinds of Halloween traditions her fictional New England family might have had, Tess remembered something from a book she'd read once. "Bobbing for apples!" she exclaimed.

Her friends looked at her, probably surprised at the triumphant tone of her voice.

"They were really, really into bobbing for apples," she added lamely. "And decorations. They hung up a lot of stuff. You know, fake spiders, all that."

"Where in New England did you grow up?" Jack asked.

"Connecticut," Tess answered, and quickly changed the subject before she had to come up with more lies. "Okay, so I've got all this gook scraped out. What do you guys think? Happy face or mean face?"

Despite the web of falsehood she'd just been spinning, it was fun sitting out here on her back patio with Samantha and Jack. They'd lit a fire in the fire pit, and the warmth of it compensated somewhat for the chill the setting sun had left behind. The smoke from the pine logs mingled with the scent of the sagebrush around the patio and created a smell in the crisp air that was pure fall. Perfect for Tess's first real Halloween.

She'd celebrated the holiday before, of course. There'd been the school parades, and a few years where the parents at a foster home had taken her and the other kids trick-or-treating. But mostly it had been a stressful holiday. She'd worried that she wouldn't have a costume, or that some kid from school would tease her about whatever battered, hand-me-down outfit a teacher or foster parent could come up with.

But something about being in this tiny town, experiencing real fall weather, had her excited about

Halloween for the first time. Jack had helped her put spiderwebs and orange lights around the front door of the cottage earlier today. She'd bought enough treats for every kid in Benson ten times over and had even made hot apple cider from a recipe off a website. As she went inside to get the candles for their jack-o'-lanterns, Tess realized she was happy and content, moods she wasn't very familiar with. It was nice to let go of her worries and frustrations about work and just focus on a silly holiday.

She rummaged in the paper bag on the kitchen counter and pulled out the candles. A knock at the door surprised her. It wasn't even five o'clock yet—a little early for trick-or-treaters. She grabbed the bowl of candy off the counter anyway.

"Coming!" she called, and ran to answer it, jumping back in surprise when she saw Slaid on her doorstep, smiling tentatively at her from beneath the felt brim of his tan cowboy hat. He had a pumpkin in one hand and a bottle of Scotch in the other.

"Trick or treat."

"Why are you here?"

"Ouch. I guess I deserved that. Well, I've been hoping to talk with you, to make things right, but it seems as though you've been avoiding me."

"I haven't been avoiding you!" Tess protested. What was another lie in an evening of so many?

"Tess, I saw you duck down in the aisle when

you noticed me at the market on Tuesday night. And on Wednesday as you were coming out of the library I called your name from across the street and you ran."

"I was late for something. And I didn't hear you call."

He raised an eyebrow and her face flushed.

"Should I even mention Thursday?"

She'd been out running in the early morning and unfortunately, so had he. In the dim dawn light she hadn't realized the approaching runner was Slaid until he was about five yards away. She'd darted across the street, and when he'd shouted her name, she'd just run faster. "No, you don't need to mention Thursday."

"So when Jack said you were carving pumpkins this evening and invited me to stop by, I figured I'd better take him up on it. It might be my only chance to make up for the way I behaved at the party."

Tess mentally kicked herself for telling Jack to invite any friends he wanted to. It should have occurred to her that he might choose Slaid. She wanted to take Jack's spooky horse pumpkin and plop it right on his head for not warning her.

"I saw you order a Scotch at the party. I hope this is good enough to at least get me in the door." He put the bottle in her hands and what she read on the label had her gasping.

"An eighteen-year-old Talisker?"

"It's good, right?"

"It's way more than good. It's rare, expensive and divine." Just staring at the label and anticipating the smoky, sweet flavor had some of her anger fading. "But you're still only getting in the door if you agree to refrain from all sermons, lectures, barbs and judgments."

"I swear I will do my level best to stop acting like an idiot."

"Well, come on in, then." She sighed. The spookiest thing about this Halloween so far was that she was actually happy to see him, which made absolutely no sense. She stepped back, opening the door wider.

"Hang on," he said. He reached forward and pulled a pumpkin seed with some orange goo on it out of her hair. "One of the many Halloween hazards," he said, giving her a smile that melted another layer of her anger.

She led him through the cottage, conscious of him walking behind her, knowing that if she was walking behind him, she'd be checking out his ass, so she put a little swing in hers, just in case.

"Slaid!" Samantha said in surprise, then looked at Tess with a raised eyebrow.

"Don't look at me," she murmured, and pointed to Jack while he and Slaid were busy shaking hands and smacking each other on the shoulder, manstyle.

Samantha looked at her husband, shaking her head. "No wonder you haven't wanted to hang out with us. I'm pregnant and boring and my husband is turning into a meddling matchmaker." She picked up her finished pumpkin and waddled off with it toward the front yard.

Tess turned back to her own jack-o'-lantern to finish carving it, hoping the project would calm her inexplicable turmoil at seeing Slaid again. Samantha returned, flopping down in one of the Adirondack chairs and putting her feet up on the rim of the fire pit. She stared at the flames dreamily while Jack sat on the flagstones nearby, chipping away at his pumpkin again. Slaid sat down across the patio from them to start working on his own creation.

They all looked so peaceful, and Tess wondered if they were really that content inside. Or was everyone like her…housing a dormant volcano of emotion with only a smile plastered on top to hide the chaos?

Slaid looked up and caught her watching him. "You doing all right with that pissed-off pumpkin?"

Tess giggled. It did look angry. "Hey, it's art!"

Slaid's laugh was low and rich. "Uh-oh. Doesn't art reflect the artist's inner feelings?"

Jack looked over. "Man, if that's true, don't mess with Tess tonight. That thing is scary."

"It's Halloween. I thought that was the idea." She picked up her pumpkin and walked around the side of the house, placing it near the front door, lighting its candle. It glared at her with a contorted expression that really was unsettling.

"If that's how I made you feel the other night, then I should've shown up with a lot more than a bottle of Scotch." Slaid placed his simple smiling pumpkin next to hers and reached into the bag on the porch railing for a candle.

"Let's just say it didn't help much."

"I know it's not a great time to talk, and I'll leave right now if you'd rather I go, but I'd like to stay and show you that I can be a good guy, a nonjudgmental guy. If that's okay."

"It's fine." And it was. She couldn't explain it, but she was looking forward to spending Halloween with him.

A child's high-pitched laughter trilled, and Tess ran to the front gate to peer up the street. A small group was making its way toward her cottage—four small kids in costumes wielding pumpkin baskets, and three sets of parents trailing behind.

"Trick-or-treaters!" Tess squealed. "Come on!" She darted past a surprised Slaid, reaching out to grab his hand and pull him into the house. "Hurry! We have to get the candy bowl!"

He burst out laughing. "Man, you have got to get out of the city more often."

THE STREAM OF witches, princesses, monsters and other assorted ghouls had slowed to a trickle by the time Samantha and Jack took their leave. Slaid pulled on his coat, but he didn't want to go without making sure things were all right with Tess.

He'd been kicking himself all week, wishing he could take back the words he'd said at the party. But they were out there, and they'd caused a huge rift between him and the woman he couldn't stop thinking about.

He watched as Tess closed the door behind her friends. She was so beautiful, with her hair down in messy waves past her shoulders, dressed in jeans and a sweater. He loved this relaxed version of her, the one she didn't willingly show the world.

"What did you think of your first Halloween in Benson?" he asked.

"Pretty different than any I've had," she answered.

"What kind have you had?" He wanted to know all about her. He knew so little.

"Well, I live on the thirtieth floor, so I don't get any trick-or-treaters up there. And I—"

"Trick or treat!" The voices of the kids outside the door sounded older, almost Devin's age, and Slaid had a moment of worry thinking that maybe it *was* Devin. But then he remembered that Devin was at his aunt's for a slumber party, probably having a blast with his cousins—all of them hyper and crazed from way too much sugar. Still, he stepped out of view when Tess opened the door.

Tess handed out candy and lavishly complimented the kids on their costumes. She closed the door and set down the bowl. "That has to be the last of them."

"You might get a few older kids, but you can always leave the bowl of candy by the door if you want to call it a night, or go sit on the back patio with me and build up that fire again."

"You're just trying to get your hands on some of that amazing single malt you brought over."

"You caught me."

She opened the door again to set the bowl on her front stoop. Then she pulled on her parka and hat, and led the way back through her little kitchen, grabbing the bottle and two glasses.

Out on the patio, Slaid threw some wood into the fire pit. Then he accepted the glass Tess offered and took a sip, relishing the smoky flavor. "I can feel all my Scottish genes stand up and cheer," he said.

She laughed and sat on a bench. "It's my absolute favorite drink. I'd take it over a cocktail any day."

"Not the most common drink of choice."

"I'm happy not to have the word *common* associated with me."

He sat down next to her. "Definitely not a word I'd use. Confusing, confounding and commotion causing, yes. Common, no."

She laughed, low and husky, and he listened to the sound fade into the darkness around them. He could sit here all night just listening to her laugh. And then it hit him. He hadn't come here just to apologize. He'd come here tonight to try one more time to convince her to go out with him. It made no sense, they made no sense, but when it came to his feelings for Tess, making sense just didn't seem to matter.

TESS SIPPED HER Scotch and stared at the fire. She could feel Slaid's muscular arm against hers on the bench and she resisted the urge to lean her head on his shoulder. They weren't like that. Couldn't be. It had all been discussed and resolved on their ride and made so painfully obvious at the party. They weren't meant to be involved.

"Tess, I have a real dilemma on my hands," Slaid said quietly. "I know you don't date, but I want very much to take you out."

"That would be a mistake." She felt the strangest sensation—her heart was rising in something like hope while her stomach was sinking in dread.

"We like being together. Let's just give that a chance to grow."

She wanted to. Part of her really wanted to. But another part was terrified, and that was the part that spoke. "What's the point of giving it a chance? We're such different people. When this project is over, I'll go back to San Francisco and then on to wherever my company sends me next. I don't plan on coming back to Benson too often."

"You might change your mind," he said softly.

"You think I might do what Samantha did." Her laugh came out harsh in the dark mountain stillness. "You *really* don't know me."

"So give me a chance to know you better."

A cynical response was on the tip of her tongue, but he sounded so earnest. Instead she looked over at him and, seeing the questions in his eyes—the wanting—she realized that he was torn about all this, as well. For the first time it truly occurred to her that there were two people in this equation— it wasn't only about her and her fears. It was also about Slaid. He was caught in the night they'd shared, in the chemistry that still sizzled between them, and she needed to find a way to help him get free. But how, when it all haunted her, too?

"Look, I know it's hard for someone like you to understand," she told him. "You grew up here, in this one town, surrounded by people who know you and like you and care. I didn't have that kind of life, and maybe I never learned how to live quite like a regular person."

"Will you let me show you how? I mean, I can't speak for all *regular* people, but I can show you how *I* live, how I'd like it to be between us."

"But what if it's not how *I* want it to be?"

"Then you just go back to your life in the city. No harm done."

Tess didn't know what to say, so she sat in silence, sipping their Scotch.

"Look up," Slaid said softly, and she did. Out beyond the patio was the dark night sky. It looked like someone had scattered millions of tiny rhinestones on black velvet. It was a completely different sky from the occasional glimpses of stars she got through the San Francisco fog and constant city glow. And with Slaid by her side and the fire crackling nearby, the vast expanse of sky didn't seem so lonely as she'd feared. In fact, it was beautiful.

"Gorgeous," she breathed. She was starstruck. Held in her seat by the enormity of it all.

"*This* is the kind of thing I want to share with you, Tess."

"I admit, it's nice. But I don't get it. You're a guy. Aren't you supposed to want a no-strings-attached, no-dates-required kind of relationship?"

He smiled at that and the firelight lit his profile with a golden glow. "Guess I'm not like most guys, then."

"Oh, come on, Slaid," Tess chided. "Men want women to be sexy. Sexy first and foremost, and also successful and a domestic goddess in the home. I've seen it over and over with my friends."

"Don't get me wrong, I think you're sexy. Incredibly so. And successful… Well, we both know you're kicking my butt with this windmill project. I don't know about the domestic-goddess part. Although—" he winked at her "—as a single dad, it does sound kind of nice."

"But I'm never going to be the domestic goddess of your fantasies, so why not just enjoy the smart and sexy aspects? Why not just keep it simple?"

"Your offer is pretty damn tempting. But there's so much more to you than that. Somehow, Tess, you've missed out on the fact that you are a smart, funny, warm and fascinating person. And I want to spend time with *all* of those parts of you…"

"Well, that's where we're stuck, then," Tess said regretfully.

"Why not give it a try? I promise I won't do that weird dating ritual where I ask you a hundred personal questions right off the bat."

"Good, because that sounds miserable."

"I'll do my best to talk only about myself if that'll make you more comfortable." He laughed. "Hell, most guys probably do that anyway. Doubt I'll have to try that hard."

Tess laughed, but she knew better. He wasn't the type of guy to go on about himself, and he was the type to want to know all about the woman he was involved with. He'd just told her as much. But she also knew that if he said he would try not to ask personal questions he would keep his word.

She stared into the fire. She remembered the happiness she'd seen between Samantha and Jack earlier. The wistful feeling inside when she'd watched the way that Sandro looked at Jenna. For the first time, she caught herself wanting something like that.

She took a deep breath and nodded. "Okay."

He'd been leaning back, staring into the flames, one long leg crossed over the other. "Yeah?" He glanced over and a grin spread across his face, revealing that dimple she liked.

"I'll try it," she qualified. "One date. Then I'll see."

"How about Thursday night? Dinner. I'll pick you up at seven."

"Okay."

If he kept looking down at her like that, with that big old smile and sexy dimple, she was going to kiss him. "Don't get too cocky, Mayor Jacobs."

"So it's mayor now, is it?"

"I like a man with a little authority."

He raised an eyebrow at her suggestive comment. "Okay, then. My first mayoral edict between us is, let's settle back and enjoy these stars." He put his arm around her, pulling her close so she could lean her head on his shoulder, lean her body into his warmth and strength. "Is this okay?" he asked.

"Mmm…" Tess murmured. "It's good." She wished it wasn't quite so good.

Slaid kissed the top of her head. "See? Good old-fashioned dating. Not so scary. Now take a look up in the sky. I'm going to show you a few of our local constellations."

He was all farm-boy eager, and she couldn't help teasing him. "Ooh, you sure know how to show a girl a good time, Mr. Mayor."

He laughed. "I'm only just getting started, Ms. Cole."

CHAPTER FOURTEEN

TESS KNEW THEIR date was a terrible idea the moment they stepped into the steak house on Thursday night. It was packed, and everyone was thrilled to see the mayor. Slaid backslapped and hand shook his way through the restaurant on the way to their table. He inquired about the Johnsons' sick cattle, and Mr. Elliot's tractor that apparently had been on the fritz. Somehow he knew that seven-year-old Ariel, out dining with her proud parents, had had a book report due yesterday.

She stood next to him, feeling awkward as he introduced her to what felt like half the town of Benson. It hadn't occurred to her that not only was she going on the first date she'd been on in a decade, but that it would be a very public event.

Once they got to the table, Slaid's politician joviality faded. "Sorry about that. In a small town you get to know folks pretty well."

Tess glanced around the room and saw several pairs of eyes dart hastily away. "How do you live in a fishbowl like this? Everyone's watching us."

Slaid turned to the gossiping room and gave a

big grin and a little wave. Several people caught it and started laughing. "You get used to it. You just gotta laugh about it."

"I don't think I could ever get used to it."

"Well, you're here working on what could be a pretty controversial project, so you might need to try."

"I don't mind the work stuff. I can speak in front of any group, talk to the press, it's no problem." It was the personal stuff that had her stomach churning. There was no way to explain to Slaid how during her childhood, her private life had been so public, so completely *without* privacy. Committees of social workers, teachers and foster parents hashing out the details of her care in meetings, asking so many personal questions.

And then the most public event of all—her pregnancy at sixteen.

All that was behind her now. She *knew* that. But it was why she kept her private life so very private now. Tess's heart pounded, and she felt sweat breaking out on her back. A wave of dizziness washed through her, and with it came panic.

"I'm sorry. I can't do this." She stood up, grabbed her purse and coat and rushed for the door, weaving in and out of tables filled with surprised faces. She needed to be gone, to be alone. Needed to breathe.

Luckily, in a small town there was no need to stand around hailing a cab. Tess pulled on her coat and turned toward her cottage, taking in huge gulps of the night air as she walked. She could almost feel the buzz of gossip that must be following her and knew that her hasty public abandonment of the beloved mayor wouldn't help her sell the project she'd been sent here to represent. Going on a date with Slaid had been a mistake.

"Tess!"

She stopped but didn't turn around, and Slaid fell into step beside her. "Are you okay? What's wrong?"

Hot tears spilled from her eyes, much to her horror. She mopped angrily at them with her sleeve and kept walking.

Slaid's voice was gentle. "Tess, I feel terrible. I didn't mean to put you in a situation where you'd be uncomfortable. It never occurred to me. You always seem so poised, so confident."

She whirled to face him. Anger, her old friend, came to her aid. "Well, I'm not, okay? So just stop being so nice. Stop trying to get to know me, because that person you met in Phoenix? That woman you think you want to get to know? She doesn't exist. Not in her off-hours, at least."

"I think that night in Phoenix *was* your off-hours. At least, I hope it was. Otherwise I might be a little confused about your profession."

"Really? You're going to make *another* joke about that night? Only this time I've graduated from *sleeping around* to full-on prostitution? Great, Slaid."

"That is not what I meant. Jeez, Tess, I was trying to make you smile."

"News flash. That is *not* how to make your date smile." She swiped another traitor of a tear off her cheek and picked up the pace.

"Yeah, I got that. I'm sorry. Again." He softened his tone. "I guess I just get really confused. You act so worldly, making these sexy jokes, acting as though you don't care what anyone thinks of you. But you obviously do."

She didn't know what she cared about anymore. It all just felt too complicated. So she said what was easy. "Tonight was a mistake."

"How do you know that? Every time we have a chance to really get to know each other, you storm off. I'm starting to wonder if that's easier for you than facing whatever fears are keeping you from having real relationships!"

He was way too close to the truth. "What do you know about my fears? All you know is who you *think* you know—a woman you slept with one night. A night you're ashamed of, and you're taking that shame out on me with insults and a morally superior attitude instead of dealing with the fact that you aren't the perfect small-town family-values guy you pretend to be!"

"I have values because I have relationships, with my town, my community and most important, my son. I might not be perfect, but I want to be a good example. I don't see anything wrong with that. But apparently you exist in a vacuum, Tess, where you can do whatever you want because you keep everyone who cares about you at such a great distance that no one could possibly be affected by your actions!"

And he'd summed it up. The lonely dead-end dilemma that was her life. Scalding tears streamed down her face as she stared in him in shock. "I can't let people get close," she blurted out. "And I can't explain why I am this way."

It was his turn to look shocked. He reached for her hand, took it gently in his own. "What the hell happened to you, Tess?"

And there it was. The pity in his eyes. She wouldn't have it. "Nothing. It doesn't matter. Look, you have your way of living, Slaid. I have mine. Can't you just accept that?"

"I dunno, Tess. I guess my way is all I know. What my parents had. What I was taught to expect. A traditional relationship. A marriage."

"You *think* you want that," she corrected him. "But you had a taste of something different in Phoenix, and you've been asking for more of it ever since I got to town!"

"Not more of *it*. More of you. I can't explain it, Tess. I'm like a moth drawn toward a damn flame. I know you're likely to incinerate me, but I just keep coming around anyway."

She started laughing. How could she not? His image was just too perfect. The tears still ran down her face and her mascara was probably all the way to her chin and she was standing in the freezing Benson street laughing so hard her stomach ached.

He stared at her for a moment, and then he was laughing, too. He pulled her in and hugged her close. "Damn, Tess, we are a fine pair."

"A complete mess." She felt his chest shaking with laughter, and it made her giggle harder. "I'm crying and laughing. I think I'm hysterical. You might need to slap me."

He looked down at her, serious now. "How about this instead." His fingers were under her chin, tipping her head back. He brushed his thumbs, featherlight, under her eyes, wiping away the tears and makeup. And then he brought his mouth to hers, warm, strong and reassuring and she kissed him back with all the hysteria that had welled up inside.

His lips lingered over hers before he pulled back. "Give me a chance to spend time with you. I promise, nothing public. No restaurants. Just you and me and all this." He waved his hand to encompass the mountains, the stars, the vast space around the town.

"Slaid—" She started to protest again but he interrupted her.

"And if we need to eat, we'll cook something at one of our houses. My place is away from town and very, very private."

She stared at him, in awe of his persistence, wondering what it was he saw in her that made him willing to keep trying. "If I say yes, will you kiss me again?"

"Say it," he challenged, his voice low and rough.

"Yes," she whispered.

And his mouth was on hers again, his hands coiling in her hair to pull her up to him as he leaned down, and she kissed him ravenously, wanting to taste that mixture of goodness and flaws and strength that seemed to make him what he was, make him able to stand up to what she was. And then he was lifting her, kissing her as they walked, kissing her all the way to her doorstep, where he set her down, breathless and laughing.

"See?" he said. "Reputation be damned. Half the town saw that and I don't care."

She laughed. "Well, I might care when I have to get up in front of them and answer all their questions at my next public meeting, but I appreciate the gesture."

"So will you meet me Saturday morning?"

"Far away from town?"

"I've got just the place. And I'll bring a picnic. We can hide behind a rock to eat, somewhere no one can see us."

"A very large rock?" she asked.

"I'll find you the biggest one I can." He paused, and then that smile was back. "Can I see your phone for a minute?"

"You need to make a call?"

"Just hand it over."

So she pulled it out of her purse and gave it to him. He opened it to the notes page and typed something. Then he handed it back.

His phone number was there, and a note that read "Saturday, 10:00 a.m." along with directions for a trailhead south of town on Highway 395. "We're going hiking?"

"Not exactly. But wear your walking shoes." He glanced down at her feet and his eyebrows came up. "Though I do like those."

Tess looked down at her burgundy boots with a four-inch heel. "Me, too." She smiled up at him. "But I won't bring them on Saturday."

He looked genuinely regretful. "Another time, maybe."

Tess felt a twinge of guilt. There probably wouldn't be another time. She'd promised him one date and she'd go, but her panic tonight was proof that she couldn't let this go any further. Just this one mystery date, where she'd eat lunch with him behind a rock. That was all she could give him. Hopefully it would be enough for both of them.

CHAPTER FIFTEEN

TESS TOOK A deep breath of the pine-scented air. After a busy few days, it felt good to be away from town and the controversy over the windmills—and the frustration. Fewer people were attending her informational events. She hoped it was because everyone had the information they needed, and not because they all simply opposed the project. Either way, she'd been running herself ragged trying to improve attendance, and she was tired.

She was early for her rendezvous with Slaid, but even though she was alone by the side of the remote highway, she didn't feel nearly as intimidated as she had when she'd first arrived in Benson. Was it possible she was getting used to the place just a little bit? She occasionally caught herself appreciating the beauty and the quiet.

Though not always quiet. She turned as she heard the roar of a truck engine.

"Hey, stranger, want a ride?" Slaid jumped down from the truck and came around the front to open the cab door for her.

"Sure." He looked amazing in his faded jeans

and straw cowboy hat. She climbed into his truck, trying to contain what she was pretty sure was a smile of pure lust, and he slammed the door behind her. When he got back into the driver's seat he leaned over and gave her a chaste kiss on the cheek.

"Great to see you, Tess. You look beautiful. Thanks for meeting me. Sneaking around is kind of fun."

"Of course it is," she said. "Glad you're finally seeing my point."

He laughed. "We may be sneaking, but we're still dating. See? Compromise. It's all part of a successful relationship."

"We're not having a relationship..." Tess protested. Then cut herself off when she saw that he was laughing. "You're messing with me, aren't you?"

Slaid swung the truck back onto Highway 395 heading south. "I knew you'd get all huffy if I used the *R* word."

She laughed. "That's because it's a bad word. So where are we going, Mr. Mayor?"

"That would be Slaid to you. I'm off duty right now. And we're going to Bodie."

"Where?"

"Did you not read one book, article or website about this area before you came?"

"I read a lot—about wind power."

"But nothing about a perfectly preserved ghost town?" A brown sign for Bodie State Park came into view on their left, and Slaid swung onto the road next to it.

"Nope."

"Well, it's a good thing you ran into me during this exile of yours. You're in for a treat."

The narrow road that wound down through dry hills quickly became dirt. Tess held tightly to the handhold above her window as the truck bumped along the treacherous track. "Are you sure we'll make it to this place in one piece?"

"Yep." Slaid kept his attention on the road. "I checked the weather and there's only sun ahead. That's the main thing. This road gets closed in bad weather, and once the snow comes your only hope of getting to Bodie is by snowmobile or skis."

Finally they were on flat ground, and they pulled to a stop in an empty unpaved parking lot. "The tourist office closed for the season a couple days ago," Slaid told her as she stared at the weathered wooden buildings scattered over the high desert. "I figured this would be the perfect date for someone who doesn't want to be seen."

Tess laughed. "You're right. I don't think I've ever been to a place that feels more empty."

"It was a mining town back in the late 1800s. After gold was discovered nearby it grew from just a few people to a population of over ten thousand in just a few years."

"I can't imagine that many people living out here!"

"They say at one point it was a Wild West boomtown. I guess most of it burned down. This is just the little bit of town that survived."

They crossed the deserted parking lot to the small trail that led to the buildings. Tess thought she'd seen a lot of lonely on this trip, but this had to be one of the loneliest sites she'd come across. Unpainted wooden buildings, many leaning, scattered across the dry soil. It was silent in a way that Tess wasn't used to. They couldn't hear the highway from here, just the desert wind whistling faintly as it blew through the buildings and the crunch of their footsteps on the rocky soil.

Slaid pointed to the closest house. "Take a look in the window." Tess walked gingerly up onto the rickety planks that served as a front porch and peeked inside. She pulled away with a gasp. "It's furnished!" Not just furnished. She looked back in. An ancient wooden table stood in the middle of the room, surrounded by chairs arranged haphazardly, as if people had just stood up after breakfast, pushed them back and left forever. A plate was still on the table and some silverware. Dishes were stacked on a cabinet; a dish towel hung on the knob. Everything was covered under a good inch of dust. "It looks as if they simply got up and left."

Slaid came up next to her and peered in. "I've heard that's true. That it's just as its owners left it. I guess it was too much trouble to carry their stuff out of the valley."

They walked from building to building. There

was an old store with shelves still stocked with ancient goods, and even a rickety church. Each structure was filled with furniture and various items its owners hadn't been able to take with them.

"Why did they all leave?" Tess asked as they stood at the cemetery fence looking at the weathered graves.

"The gold was gone," Slaid answered. "Or not so easily available. People moved on to other gold rush towns or to cities, or they took up farming and ranching. Some folks stayed on. My dad was born and raised in Benson, and he says there were still people living out here when he was a kid. Just a few, though."

Tess looked around in wonder. "I had no idea this was here. It makes me realize how little I know about the area. I mean, of course, in San Francisco they're always talking about the gold rush, that wealth from the gold mines basically built the city way back when. But to be out here where people were working and living in such harsh conditions…"

"It's humbling, isn't it?" Slaid smiled at her. "I mean, you and I, we're both pretty hardworking people, right? But these folks worked night and day, and in such an insanely dangerous world compared to ours."

"Well, except when they were out drinking!" Tess exclaimed, reading one of the informative signs. "How could this town support fifty bars? And almost as many brothels?"

"Not much else to do for entertainment, I guess," Slaid said. "Hard to imagine it, though… People being so open about sex. 'Hey, I'm just going to step on into this brothel for a while. I'll catch you later!'"

Tess laughed. "It *is* hard to imagine. But probably healthier, in a way. We always look back at people in history and assume they were more uptight. But maybe it's modern people like us who are all hung up about sex."

"You're right, and I'm learning in my short acquaintance with you that apparently I'm more hung up than most." He held out his hand, and Tess took it.

They walked back through the ghost town, looking in a few more windows. Tess realized she'd never done anything like this with a man before—gone sightseeing, walked around holding hands and talking history. And despite the emptiness around them, despite the creepy ghost-town feeling, she felt safe next to Slaid. Safe and happy to be out here in the middle of nowhere, with him.

He looked down at her, a mischievous glint in his eye. "We haven't seen a single other person. I don't think we have to hide behind a rock down here, do we?"

"No," she answered, laughing softly. "I think

we're safe from prying eyes. Maybe not ghostly eyes, though."

"So is it rude to eat a picnic with ghostly eyes watching? Because there *are* tables." He pointed to a picnic area near the parking lot. "I mean, if you're really worried, I do see a few boulders out there…" He pointed away from the town, where the desert just kept going.

She had to laugh at his teasing. "The table will be fine," Tess answered.

"Are you ever going to tell me what your reaction at the restaurant was really all about?" Slaid asked, wrapping her hand more closely in his.

"Probably not," Tess answered. Might as well be truthful when she could.

His smile was thoughtful, but Slaid didn't pressure her for more, just led her to a rough, wooden table and offered her the bench with a flourish of his hand, like some maître d' at a posh restaurant. Then he walked to the truck to get the picnic.

Tess sat where she could see the town, so still under the bright midday sun. The dry heat felt good beating all around her, baking her muscles just enough to relax them. The hissing wind, the dull thumping of Slaid opening and closing the truck door all lulled her, making her a little sleepy.

She studied the abandoned buildings, still littered with the remnants of long-ago lives. People had been born and lived and loved and died here, and now there was nothing but the wind whispering through the buildings. This place was a reminder that time passed quickly; lives were lived in the blink of an eye. Tess suddenly felt a sense of urgency—that she needed to be braver, more alive, than she had ever been.

She heard Slaid's footsteps on the rocky soil and looked up as he placed a basket, a real picnic basket, on the bench beside her. He set a cooler next to it, and as she stared in astonishment he opened the basket and pulled out a blue-checked tablecloth. He shook it out, and she helped him spread it over the splintered surface. Next came two wineglasses, real plates, silverware and cloth napkins. Finally she found her voice. "You are pretty serious about your picnics, aren't you?"

"I'm pretty serious about our date. You made it clear I only have one more chance, so I wanted to make it good." He winked and pulled out a bottle of white wine from the cooler.

Tess looked in the basket, finding a corkscrew there. She walked over to Slaid and handed it to him. "Well, I'm flattered that you'd go to so much trouble. You didn't have to."

"I wanted to." His eyes were dark under the brim of his hat. Maybe it was the sun behind him, leaving his face in shadow, but Tess thought it was something else. She couldn't look away, and Slaid didn't, either. He set the unopened wine and the corkscrew down on the table with a thud.

And then his hands were in her hair and his

mouth came down, warm and firm, on hers. So much sensation blasted through her that Tess gasped. How could one kiss be so much...bring so much?

There were a million reasons not to do this, but she wasn't planning on listening to them today. She'd let so much time pass in her life by playing it safe. At least the ghostly people of Bodie had the courage to try for more, to take huge risks for a better life. She'd been such a coward, maybe it was time for her to risk a little.

Slaid pulled her still closer until she could feel the strength of his massive thighs and his broad chest along her body. His arms wrapped around her, holding her up as she kissed him back with a fierce hunger that was all mixed up in the quiet of this place, all the passion and life here that had been lost and stilled by time. She breathed in the scent of him, a combination of minty aftershave, sage and fresh air.

Every part of him, every touch, left her feeling more awake and alive—just the way she wanted to feel after exploring the dusty remnants of other people's lives.

Tess unzipped his jacket, then hers. She didn't want to break from his mouth, from his warm, dark kisses, so she kept one hand behind his head and brought her free hand under his flannel shirt to where his white T-shirt was tucked into his jeans. Slaid made a sound, low and rough, that she felt in her own throat when her hand found the soft skin and the taut muscle at his waist. If there was a way to feel more of him, right here next to the Bodie parking lot, she wanted to figure it out.

And then things got blurry. Slaid must have felt her urgency, because he pushed her back toward the table until she could feel its rough wooden edge pressing at the back of her thighs. There was a *thunk* as the wine bottle rolled off the table and hit the ground, and a clanking as the silverware followed. Somehow he managed to lift her onto the edge and move the wineglasses to the relative safety of the basket while still kissing her. And then he pushed her down onto the tablecloth and leaned over her, barely fitting himself alongside her on the narrow surface, blocking out the sun and sky when he kissed her again.

His hand went under her T-shirt and had the front clasp of her bra open in such a quick twist of his fingers that Tess wondered briefly if he was a bit more experienced with women than he let on. But then his huge palm was cradling her breast, his rough fingers circling the tip in a way that had her back arching, her hips pushing up, inviting his hand to travel down so his fingers trailed under the waistband of her jeans.

"Tess." He pulled back just a few inches, his breath unsteady, flickering across the skin by her ear. "You are so beautiful."

Something in her glowed at his praise. It was a

strange, exhilarating feeling to be with him here under the open blue sky. And then his hand was wrapped at her waist and he was tugging at her lower lip with his teeth and she pulled him down for more.

Slaid put his knee between hers, and she got what she wanted—the feel of him all down the length of her—and she pushed her hips up, feeling the hard length of his erection and the pinch of his metal belt buckle. She reached up, trying to remove his belt. He raised himself up on an elbow to accommodate her and gave a yelp of surprise when he slipped off the edge of the narrow table.

His reflexes were quick. With a curse, he somehow caught himself with a hand on the bench before he completely crushed her. She burst out laughing, despite the frustrated desire. "Are you okay?"

"Just mildly humiliated." He gingerly lifted himself off her, one hip precariously balanced on the edge of the table as she slid out from under him, hopping to the ground so he could scoot over and bring his arm back up from the bench. He sat on the table looking at her with the most sheepish expression, and she laughed even harder. He pulled a large splinter from the palm of his hand and held it up. "This outdoor making-out thing just isn't working."

Tess dabbed at her eyes with her sleeve. "No. First the thistle, and now this table. We're ridiculous."

There was a drop of blood on his hand where

the splinter had been. Tess reached into the picnic basket, pulled out a paper napkin and dabbed at his palm. "See? This is one reason I don't date. It's hazardous. Why not just own up to the fact that we want each other and jump into a nice safe bed?"

He burst out laughing. "I hate to admit it, but you may have a point. Normally I wouldn't consider dating hazardous, but there's something about you…" He paused, pivoted on the table so he was seated on the edge, his feet on the bench. He reached out for her, taking her hands and bringing her between his knees. He pushed back her mussed hair. "I've never wanted anyone like this. So much that I can't stay away. Even when it's dangerous."

She brought her teeth to her lower lip and realized her lips felt bruised, they'd been kissing that fiercely. "I don't know if I can stay away, either," she confessed.

He leaned forward, put his knuckle under her chin and tipped her head up. "Look at me."

She met his eyes, stunned by the tenderness there. He kissed her, so gently this time, just brushing his lips over hers. Offering something, asking a question with his kiss, then backing off to wait for her response.

Tess paused, knowing somehow that if she kissed him back it would be an answer. A yes to whatever it was that kept bringing them back together. Desire, but so much more. This tenderness, this connection threatened to change everything.

She could back off right now and hide from it, or she could lean in and accept it. Being here in Bodie made her want to reach out and try something new—to live. Here was her first chance to put that lesson into action. She leaned in, put her hands behind his head and kissed him with no hesitation.

The taste of him was familiar now, but with Slaid familiar wasn't the bad thing she'd always assumed it would be. There was nothing boring about the way he pulled her roughly between his legs, or the way she knelt upon the bench so she could better reach his mouth. There was nothing boring about the way he kissed her as if he was claiming her, branding her—as if he never planned to stop. And with a sense of shock, Tess realized she didn't want him to.

She'd reached for more, and she felt more alive than she could remember being. Awake in this moment, in this wide-open space of earth and sky and history, with this man, so warm and strong under her mouth. Exhilaration, and a sense that she was exactly where she was supposed to be, prickled cold and warm over her skin. She ended the kiss and wrapped her arms around him, burying her face in the comfort of the spot where his shoulder met his neck.

He pulled her close, cradled her in a security she'd never known she'd needed until now.

"Hey," he whispered. "Just so you know, there's a car coming down the road."

He was so careful to remember the privacy that she'd asked for. But she didn't want to let go of him yet. "Just another minute." She clung to him more tightly, needing more of whatever this feeling was between them.

"I've got you," he murmured.

She took a deep breath and just tried to inhale all of him. All his kindness and warmth and the way he'd made this day so perfect. Only when she heard the crunch of car wheels on the gravel of the parking lot did she pull back.

She stared at Slaid in a daze, trying to connect what had just happened with any experience she'd had before. But she'd never felt this close to anyone. So close it kind of hurt now that they weren't connected physically. "I didn't expect it to be like this," she confessed.

"I did. And I want more of it. More of you." He brought fingers to her cheek and caressed her skin with his knuckles.

Tess stared at him, stunned by his sweetness. He wore a calm smile and there was a quiet happiness about him. He was unlike anyone she'd ever met.

She kissed his fingers as they went by her mouth. Then took his hand and opened it, examining the mark where the splinter had been. "I'm sorry we didn't get to finish what we started here."

He kissed her softly on the mouth, but when he pulled back there was laughter in his eyes. "Who said anything about being finished?"

"And you're thinking that will happen…when?" She glanced over to where the Subaru station wagon had just pulled in. A hassled-looking woman was unloading a little boy and a baby while a man let a dog out of the hatchback.

"On our next date."

"You're pushing your luck there, cowboy." But something inside her lit up at his words.

"I know you enough, Tess Cole, to guess that you like to finish what you start."

She watched as he pushed himself off the table and went around the side of it to rescue the wine bottle from the dirt. "Okay, another date," she conceded. "Though I'm not sure how you'll top this one."

Slaid pulled a paper towel from the picnic basket and wiped the dirt off the bottle, then reached for the corkscrew. "I'm not worried. I know you don't believe me, but there's plenty to do out here around Benson." He uncorked the bottle and poured a glass of wine. He handed it to her and poured his own glass and raised it, arching an eyebrow as he smiled at her over the rim. "To our next date—and all the ones after that."

Tess had the feeling that she was stepping off the edge of something bigger than she'd meant to, bigger than she'd wanted. But looking at Slaid's laughing gray eyes, his full mouth turned up in a smile she wanted to see so much more of, she knew he was right. She wasn't finished. Her answering smile was hesitant. "To our next date," she agreed, and in the clink of their glasses she heard a hopeful sound, a sound of possibilities she'd never allowed herself to consider.

CHAPTER SIXTEEN

SLAID WASN'T KIDDING when he said they'd have privacy on his ranch. Tess was at least a mile outside Benson and Slaid's house wasn't in sight yet. The road was heading up slopes that would soon give way to sheer mountain. The land was mostly covered in brush, but a few pine trees began appearing, and bigger boulders dotted the rocky landscape. It was sunset and the last rays were shining around her. Then she passed into mountain shadows where dusk had already fallen.

The road zigzagged up a low ridge. Partway down the other side she saw the ranch, spread across a high valley, mountains behind it and hills rolling out below. Even to Tess's urban eyes, it was nice. A low modern-looking house sprawled out on the uphill side of the property, surrounded by patios and a garden. Below it was a huge barn, a few smaller outbuildings and several paddocks.

Glancing at Slaid's directions scrawled on a piece of paper on the seat next to her, she drove down the hill and turned into a gravel driveway that ran alongside the barns and paddocks. Looking past them, Tess saw vast fields where cattle grazed.

A familiar truck was parked by the barn. What was Jack doing here? Had Slaid invited him and Samantha for dinner, too? Tess pulled her Jeep up next to the truck. Stepping out she saw more pickups parked alongside the barn, with Full Power Solar emblazoned on their doors. She took a few steps back and looked up. Several men stood on the barn's roof discussing something. Just then Slaid and Jack appeared in the doorway of the barn.

"Tess!" Slaid called, hurrying over. "Sorry about all this." He waved vaguely at the roof. "I thought they'd be gone by now."

"You're really doing it, huh?" she said. "You're installing solar panels?"

"Gotta lead by example." He had the grace to look a little sheepish. "Sorry if this is awkward."

"Tess is tough. She can take it," Jack said, his border collie, Zeke, at his heels. "How's it goin', Tess?"

"I assume if they're here at Slaid's, that you and Sam already have your panels installed?" Tess asked.

"Just yesterday."

"I guess I should say congratulations," Tess said drily. "And can I ask how your other plans are going? Are many people signing on to go solar?"

The two men glanced at each other as if trying to figure out what to reveal.

"Never mind," she said. "I don't plan on sharing my plans, so I won't pry into yours."

"I'd better be getting home," Jack said. He gave Tess a long look. "Samantha would love it if you'd come by for dinner with us sometime, Tess."

She had told Samantha she was way too busy to come over for dinner, yet here she was ready to dine with Slaid. She'd thought the solar panels were the most awkward thing between her and Sam, but maybe this was worse. "Sure," she said, keeping her voice casual. "I'll call her to pick a date."

"Okay," Jack said, but Tess could tell it wasn't.

"Talk to you tomorrow," Slaid said. Jack nodded and walked to his truck, calling Zeke to follow.

Slaid gestured toward his house. "Shall we go on inside?"

Tess hesitated. "Maybe this is just too awkward…"

"We're adults. We both know I'm working on getting panels up and you're working to promote the wind farm."

"Yes, but it's uncomfortable."

"It doesn't have to be. Let's just be straight with each other. I'll start by telling you something I hate to admit. So far, the solar plans are going slowly. We're having more trouble getting state funding than we'd anticipated."

Tess felt a twinge of guilt. She suspected that he was having trouble getting funding because the CEO and the board members of Renewable Reliance were extremely well connected at the state capital. She wouldn't doubt that they'd called in a few favors to ensure that this wind project happened. "That must be frustrating" was all she said.

They started up the drive toward the house, walking side by side. "How was your informational evening last night? Did people like the video?"

She smiled despite her discomfort. "It was nice. A few people came and asked a lot of good questions, mostly about the impact on birds, wildlife and tourism. And somehow they'd heard the story of the video shoot. About the CEO and the cows and a certain cowboy who came to my rescue."

"Hmm…" Slaid winked. "I have no idea how word got out on that one."

"Yeah, right." Tess gave him a friendly jab with her elbow.

He laughed. "Well, I might've mentioned it to one or two people. Can you blame me? It's too funny a story to keep to myself."

"No, I don't blame you. But when I showed the video, I don't think they were paying much attention to what Mr. Tate was saying. They were just looking for glimpses of the wild and crazy cows."

He laughed. "I'd love to see that. But I'm sorry if me telling the story messed up your evening."

"Hey, any interest in the project is good interest as far as I'm concerned. If the CEO had a sense of humor, I'd ask him to let me show an outtake video so people could actually see your cows in action. But I don't think he's the type to appreciate that."

"Well, if you can get your hands on the bloopers, I'll pay top dollar for a copy. I could set up a showing and serve beer and pass out antiwindmill flyers."

Tess laughed. "No chance! I'd be aiding the enemy. Speaking of which…" She reached into her tote bag and pulled out a folder. "I saved you your very own copy of all the literature, including the environmental impact report."

"It's in here?"

"Just got it yesterday, barely in time for the meeting. So I've got another dinner scheduled in a few days to give people a chance to ask questions informally. You're welcome to come."

"You're fearless, aren't you?" Slaid asked. "I wouldn't want you at one of my meetings."

"Really? I promise I'd behave." She gave him a wink that told otherwise.

Slaid just kissed the tip of her nose and took the information packet.

He opened a gate that led onto the flagstone patio. It was surrounded by a low stone wall that had desert plants growing all the way along it. There was a fire pit and a bunch of comfortable-looking chairs. A gas grill was beside the house, and Slaid paused to light it. "We'll just let that warm up for a few minutes. I've got some chicken marinating."

Tess shivered. "You grill at this time of year?"

"I've been known to grill with snow on the ground. It's easy…and less dishes when you're done." Slaid motioned to the furniture as they walked across the big space. "We spend a lot of time out here on summer evenings. Though this time of year, it's a little too cold for most people."

"But obviously you're not most people if you grill in the snow."

He grinned at her, a teasing sparkle in his eye that had the power to melt. "I grew up out here. I don't feel the cold so much as someone like you."

"You mean someone wimpy?"

He laughed outright. "Your words, not mine." He lifted her hands, his warm fingers twining through her freezing ones. "You've proved my point." He kissed her knuckles. "Icicles. Let's get inside."

Tess pulled her focus from his kiss to take in the house more closely. "Hey, wait a minute! What's a mid-century modern doing out here?"

Slaid smiled. "Should have known you'd recognize it."

"Recognize it? I'm a huge fan! I wandered the streets of Palm Springs for a few days once just drooling over these types of houses. How did it get built here in Benson?"

"Well, my dad and mom honeymooned in Palm Springs and he decided then and there that this was the kind of house he wanted."

"But it makes no sense," Tess exclaimed. "These houses are all about the indoor-outdoor living. And those huge floor-to-ceiling windows... Don't they let in all the cold air?"

"A little. But they're double paned." He showed her the extralong eaves to keep the snow off, and once inside, he had her place her palms on the floor. The stone tiles had radiant heat and were warm to the touch.

It was a modern icon but it was definitely a home, complete with comfortable furnishings. The large painting hanging on one of the living room walls depicted the mountains but was just abstract enough to be interesting. Slaid gave her a tour—it was one of the most serene homes Tess had ever been in. And then they passed a room that could only belong to Slaid's son. Posters of football players adorned the walls and a few shelves were full of trophies. Schoolbooks were stacked neatly on the desk. "Where is Devin tonight?" Tess asked.

"At my sister's. She loves having him over, and she has a son about his age. The boys are really close."

It was none of her business, but she was curious. "How long were you with your ex-wife?"

Slaid leaned on the wall by Devin's door. "We met in high school and got married right after graduating from college."

"So you had Devin right away?"

"Devin's adopted," Slaid answered. "He's my cousin's son actually. She got involved with drugs and eventually landed in jail—where she is now. I got a call from social services one day, asking if

I'd take him in. So we did, and we adopted him legally a few years later, when it was clear his mom wouldn't ever be able to take care of him."

Tess was stunned by this new image of Slaid. "You're a good man," she finally said.

"I got a good kid," he answered. "I'm lucky to be his dad. I can't believe he's fourteen already. Kids grow up quickly."

Tess did the math and swallowed hard. Fourteen. She'd had her baby fourteen years ago. Her son. Adam. She rarely let herself say his name—Adam would be the same age as Devin. Did he have similar sports photos on the wall? Did he have a shelf full of trophies, too? She tried to drag her mind away from those thoughts—picking at an old wound did no good. She was glad Devin was at his aunt's tonight. She wasn't prepared to meet him. Not yet. Probably never.

Slaid continued the tour of his house, but Tess was having difficulty paying attention. She shouldn't be here, getting involved with someone who had a son—especially an adopted son. What would Slaid think of her if he knew about Adam?

Focus on the present, she reminded herself. The same four words she'd been using as a mantra ever since Adam's adoptive parents had taken him home from the hospital, leaving her lost and devastated. *Focus on the present.*

Slaid led her through the living room and into

the kitchen. Its clean lines and windows up by the roofline gave it a light and airy feel, even at night. He pulled a bottle of white wine from the refrigerator, opening it while she looked around, taking in the big dining table along the glass walls that lined two sides of the room. In the daytime the views must be spectacular.

He handed her a glass and she sipped it, appreciating the dry, bright flavors on her tongue.

Slaid was watching her as he drank from his own glass. "I'm glad to have you in my house, Tess," he said. "Though I have to admit, after a couple years of fantasizing about you, it's kind of strange to see you standing right here."

Surprised, Tess's laugh burst out. "You didn't really fantasize, did you?"

His laugh matched her own. "Can you blame me?"

"Well, I hope the reality of me can measure up. Two years is a lot of time to build up unrealistic ideas about someone."

"Oh, you've far surpassed anything I could think up. Smacking my cow with a scarf, for example."

"That cow was crazy! What was that about?"

"Well, sometimes we get a cow who needs to be bottle-fed, and it gets kind of attached to people. And Devin likes to baby those ones a little too much. So that cow, Number Fifty-Eight, also known as Rosco, is way too used to the good life."

"Rosco? It suits her—a pushy name for a pushy cow."

Slaid grinned. "Not pushy. Just very, very loving."

She was still giggling when Slaid went out to his chilly patio to put the chicken on the grill. Tess looked around his gorgeous home and sighed. Of all the houses in Benson, this was the one she'd want to live in. She could see herself sitting in the sun on those patios, appreciating ranch life from a safe distance, and cooking up a meal in this perfectly planned kitchen. When Slaid came back in she was so deep in her domestic reverie that she actually jumped. And then felt almost dizzy when she realized where her thoughts had been taking her.

Tess Cole, the queen of dry cleaning, takeout and maid service, had been lost in a fantasy that involved cooking? She had never cooked a meal, nor had a single domestic yearning, in her entire life. It was disconcerting to find herself having them here in Slaid's home. The home he shared with a teenaged son. The home that was in Benson, so far away from her own world.

"I'd give a lot more than a penny to know what you were thinking just then," Slaid said as he picked up his wineglass.

"Oh, highly classified. And you do not have security clearance," she joked to cover her confusion over where her thoughts had just been.

"Does anyone have access to Tess Cole's secrets?"

"Absolutely no one," she said firmly, feeling that familiar panic seeping in. *Change the subject.* "So tell me more about life on a cattle ranch."

For the next little while he entertained her with stories of cows and horses, downed fences and snowstorms, and somehow made life on his ranch sound fun. Not full of the grit and hard work that she knew was the reality. He kept up the conversation all through the cooking and then as they ate dinner. He seemed determined to put her at ease and, although he did ask about her work and her apartment in the city, he didn't ask about her family or her childhood—and for that she was grateful.

Once they cleared the table, Slaid built a fire in the living room fireplace, and as they were curled up on the couch with the last of their wine, Tess felt a part of her unwind—a part she hadn't realized was coiled and tensed. And she wondered if she'd ever felt so at ease with another person in the room.

He must have sensed it somehow because he turned to face her and said, "I really do want to get to know you better, Tess. But if my questions get too personal you can toss this pillow at me. Sound good?" He threw a rust-colored pillow in her lap.

Despite the twinge of anxiety at his request, she burst out laughing. "How about we just have a pillow fight? I think it would be way more fun."

"How about you tell me where you went to college?"

Well, that was easy. "I graduated from UCLA." He didn't need to know about the years at community college and her struggle to pay for the two years of university once she transferred.

"And why did you choose to work in public relations?"

"I'm good at talking people into things." A skill she'd had to learn young. The first time had been when she was probably four years old and she'd talked the local storeowner out of a candy bar. She'd been so damn hungry.

"But not cows."

"Apparently my skills are not very effective with cows, no."

He laughed. "Favorite color?"

"Red."

"Food?"

That was a tough one. Tess loved all food. Maybe it was from growing up without much of it. "If I had to pick one thing, maybe peaches. Right in the middle of summer, when they're completely ripe." Fresh food had been a rarity in her foster homes. And nothing was fresher than a peach in summer.

"Favorite place to travel?"

"Paris, of course!" The ultimate symbol of how far she'd come from her roots.

"Can I have another date?"

She threw the pillow at him and he caught it with one hand. "We'll see," she said.

SLAID CAUGHT THE pillow with a sense of regret. The interview was over and he'd only learned a little about this mystery woman. He wondered about the stories behind her answers. Because there were a bunch, he could tell. Emotion flickered behind her concise words. She was obviously an expert at deflection, just like Jack had warned. Her quick humor was like a defensive weapon, so subtle you barely realized she was using it on you.

He wanted a firmer answer to his question about a date. But he knew if he asked her for one, she'd throw up a barrier between them. He glanced around the room, looking for inspiration, for something to distract her from her instinct to hide and flee. His eyes lit on the chessboard he and Devin kept set up near the fireplace. Devin was learning and Slaid had always loved to play. "Chess?" he asked.

Tess started, then threw back her head and laughed, long and low. "Oh, my," she purred. "You do know how to show a girl a good time, don't you?"

Damn, she was sexy when she teased him like that. When she laughed, her throat was a long, elegant column, and he remembered the silk of the skin from their kiss in Bodie. He remembered the satin of her when he'd been inside her back in Phoenix. In an instant he was hard and grateful for the pillow in his lap. "Hey, don't knock it till you've tried it. It's a good game. I'll teach you."

"Teach me?" She cocked an eyebrow in worldly disbelief. "I'm pretty sure I've got a few moves I could teach *you*."

He reached for the coffee table that held the game, and slid it closer to the couch. "Why am I not surprised?"

Tess turned out to be a formidable opponent. Lower lip caught in her teeth, a glass of Scotch swirling gently in her hand, he could have watched her concentrate all night. A faint line appeared between her fair brows when she drew them together in thought. And a satisfied smile molded her lips when she made yet another killer move on the board. Slaid whistled low when she slipped her queen behind her rook and murmured, "Checkmate."

"You're a shark, Tess. Where did you learn to play like that?"

"Boys and Girls Club after-school program. They had to keep us housing-project kids out of trouble somehow." She froze. Her skin went pale and she kept her eyes glued to the board, as if by not moving she could somehow pretend the information wasn't out there.

It wasn't the answer he'd expected. Tess was so refined, cultured and polished, he'd assumed she'd come from a privileged background. And he realized in a rush of understanding, that that was exactly what she wanted him to believe—what she worked so hard to make *everyone* believe. Which was why this revelation had her almost glassy-eyed in shock.

He shoved down the curiosity that fizzed and popped in his mind. It wouldn't serve him now. She was in distress and needed his help. "Well, whoever it was, they taught you well. Or maybe I've gotten rusty, playing against a fourteen-year-old."

She still wouldn't look at him. She took a long sip of her Scotch and stared into the fire. When she looked back at him, all signs of distress had vanished. Her shoulders were straight and that feline smile was back on her lips. "Or maybe I *can* teach you a thing or two, Mr. Mayor."

He knew now that the smooth, sexy banter was an act. But he played along.

"I think you already have." He saw the heat in her eyes and knew exactly what she needed right now. He needed it, too. He took the drink from her hand and set it on the coffee table. He leaned in and brought his hand to her hair, pushing the thick blond mass behind her shoulder. Her usual I-dare-you look flashed from deep in her eyes, and he took her up on the challenge, bringing his mouth to hers and kissing her sassy half smile until it melted into a heated response.

He'd promised himself he'd take things slow, that he'd show Tess what it was like to get to know someone, but when he was near her, slow just didn't seem to work out. He lived his life with a lot of discipline, but he had almost none when it came to Tess. His entire focus centered on kissing her, on exploring her dark depths. His hand left her hair and found her full breast, and instead of caution, all he felt was frustration that there was a wool sweater between them. He must have let his feelings show, because her lips curved in a slight smile under his. Then she pulled back and tore off her sweater, all confidence now.

"Is this what you were looking for?" she murmured, meeting his eyes with pure seduction in hers.

Her bra was the color of deep red wine, and he reached for the lace without thought, only need. She laughed, low and satisfied, until he stopped the sound with another kiss, rough this time. He wanted to break through that facade and find the real Tess. The one he'd glimpsed in Bodie, the one he'd seen without makeup on Halloween, the one he saw every time she forgot herself and just laughed.

He eased her down onto the leather sofa and assaulted her mouth with kisses that wouldn't let her hide or pretend they didn't matter. Grabbing a wrist, he held it over her head while his mouth raged over hers, taking her lips, nipping at her jaw, sliding down to her delicate shell of an ear before capturing her mouth again, inhaling her surprised gasp with his ragged breathing. His other hand roamed, taking in a collage of sensation—her warmth, the muscles of her abdomen and the outrageous curve of her hip.

Tess moaned and moved under his hand, pressing her body into his erection, driving him crazy. Her free hand slid under his T-shirt and over his back, trailing along the waistband of his jeans. He opened his eyes and saw that hers were closed, her cheeks flushed. The composed woman had turned inward, wild and wanton and like nothing he'd ever seen in her or anyone else.

"You're incredible," he murmured, sweeping his cheek across hers, running his tongue along the rim of her ear, gratified by the way she whimpered at his touch and pushed against him. "I don't care where the hell you came from, or what all those secrets are that you're so damn careful to hide. I love being with you." He kissed her again, but pulled back when he felt her hands on his chest, pushing him away.

He sat up. Knowing instantly he shouldn't have let his thoughts come to the surface like that.

Tess reached for her sweater. He was closer, so he handed it to her, watching with regret as she pulled it over her head.

"What's going on, Tess?"

"Just seems as if maybe we're getting in over our heads. Wasn't it you who talked about taking things slow?"

"Dating doesn't mean celibacy. It means we do things together besides just having sex."

"I told you I don't date—I shouldn't have let you talk me into it."

She was so good at putting up walls, he could almost see them rising, brick by brick.

"Tess, what's this really about? Are you scared because I said that I love to be with you? Or because you mentioned something about your past? I don't care about your past. Why would I care that you grew up in a housing project? Or hung out at the Boys and Girls Club?"

"I don't want to talk about it," she said softly, straightening her sweater.

"Then we won't. But just so you know, I think you're feeling ashamed by things that aren't under our control. We don't pick where we're born or who our parents are." His voice was raised now but he didn't care. He'd do whatever it took to crack that stubborn shell she wore around her like a shield.

"It's easy for you to say. You haven't lived like I did. You need to understand, Slaid—you're in over your head," she said flatly. "I can't give you what you want."

That bugged him. "How do you even know what I want?"

"You've told me you're a traditional relationship kind of guy. That will never happen with me. I'm over here pretending that it could, but I'm like a kid playing house. It's just a game. It's wrong to let you get involved."

That pissed him off, too. "*Let* me get involved? I'm a grown-up, Tess. *I'll* decide who I get involved with and how much."

She stood up, looking pale and pissed. She walked to the entryway and picked up her coat and bag. "I'm going to head home now."

He didn't know what to say, so he just grabbed his coat and walked her to her Jeep. They stood at the vehicle's door, and the silence seemed to breathe between them. When she reached for the door, he put a gentle hand on her arm, determined to try once more to reach her. "I had a great time earlier tonight. Let's not end it on a bad note."

"Oh, it's not bad," she said with a brightness he now recognized as fake—and was thoroughly sick of. "It's just like you said—we had a nice time."

"Stop pretending everything is fine for once. If it was, you wouldn't be running out the door."

"Look, it's obvious that we really like each other—but want different things."

"What *do* you want? Because a few minutes ago I was pretty sure you wanted me."

"I want things simple, Slaid. I've been telling you since I got here. I don't have heart-to-heart talks. And I don't do relationships."

"Seems as if we already have a relationship."

"We have a crazy chemistry. That's different than a relationship."

He'd had it. His mind was reeling with his desire for her and the knowledge he felt so deep down that they *could* be great together. "So that's it. We have one accidental mention of your past and you run out of here and go hide in that little house of yours? Ignore what's between us? I thought you were braver than this."

She stiffened. "I'm brave enough to face the truth, Slaid. That you see what you want to see in me. You think you can get me to conform to the life you think everyone should have, to live up to your ideals of how you think a relationship should work. But I can't. So let's stop this now, before someone gets hurt."

"You're walking away because you're scared."

"I'm walking away because I'm smart." She leaned in and kissed him, her mouth bold on his, her touch sending nerves rippling. "Good night, Slaid."

He didn't answer. The only words in his head were *don't go*, and no way would he be that pathetic. His fists clenched, coiled in frustration, as she climbed into the Jeep and drove off.

Slaid walked back to his house, slamming his fist on the door as he opened it. He looked around the room, at the dishes stacked in the kitchen, at the couch in disarray, at the clock on the wall. It was only nine o'clock—not too late. He refused to sit here and think about what he'd just lost. Devin was gone and he was free to do what he pleased.

He grabbed his keys and drove to town, parking in front of The High Country Sports Bar on Main Street. From the sidewalk he heard a band playing inside. He pushed his way through the front door, into the chaos, in search of a beer, a game of pool, a conversation—anything to get his thoughts off Tess Cole.

CHAPTER SEVENTEEN

TESS SAT ON the bench in the small front garden of her cottage. She was wrapped in her teal parka, her computer on her lap, hot tea in a travel mug next to her. The air was crisp, but the thin layer of afternoon sunshine hitting the front of the house had enticed her outside. She couldn't stay cooped up a minute longer. The sunshine here might be twenty degrees cooler than at home, but it still felt good on her skin.

She glanced at the document she had open, trying to concentrate. But for the past week, concentration had been almost impossible. *Thank you, Slaid Jacobs,* she thought bitterly. But he wasn't really the problem. Her idiot brain was the problem. Why did it have to get obsessed with the one guy she'd ever slept with who wanted more than just sex?

Everything had been going so well between them, and then he'd made those comments about her past. And there'd been something close to pity in his tone. She'd spent her childhood being everyone's charity project—she didn't want anyone's charity, or pity, ever again.

She should have known better than to agree to date him. There was something about Slaid that lowered her guard. That made her forget that it was always best to keep her personal business to herself.

And now everything was complicated. Though things had ended badly between them the other night, she'd still looked for him all week. While lunching with the Benson Women's Club to talk to them about the wind project, she'd found herself wondering if she'd run into him at the restaurant. The Sierra Club met in the library across from city hall, and when she'd gone to their meeting to seek an endorsement for the windmills, her gaze kept straying out the window, hoping to see him walk out of the old granite building. Her video screenings and information sessions each evening had been fairly well attended, but he hadn't been in the audience, no matter how many times she'd wished he might walk through the door.

The odd thing was, she had no idea what she'd do if she saw him. They were at a dead end. But she missed him, and it was unsettling. Tess had always cherished being alone. But for the past several nights she'd tossed and turned, wanting Slaid with her. She ate her solitary meals in the cottage kitchen wishing he was on the other side of the table. If he was here right now, they'd sit on this bench together, and she'd be tucked under his arm, braving this cool afternoon with his warmth surrounding her.

But she'd pushed him away so hard this time that he was most likely gone for good. It was for the best, she reminded herself as she sipped her tea. He wanted to know her better, but if he knew the truth about her, he'd run away fast. She'd done the right thing, saved them both a lot of useless trouble, and now she'd just have to learn to live with it.

Out of her peripheral vision an object came flying and hit the picket fence a few feet away with a *thunk*. A piece of the old fence broke off and landed with a clatter on the flagstones under Tess's feet. She jumped, her heart in her mouth. "What the…?" She stopped when she saw the boy. A young teenager staring at her in shock, his backpack split open at a seam, its contents scattered on the sidewalk in front of her fence.

"Are you okay?" Tess asked, opening the gate and stepping onto the sidewalk.

"I'm sorry." The boy's fair skin was flushed, his light brown eyebrows drawn into a heavy scowl. "Sorry about your fence. I just…" He gestured helplessly at the backpack and bent down to collect the scattered books. Tess knelt down and picked up the ones nearest her, putting the pieces of the puzzle together. He'd obviously been upset and chucked his backpack.

"Seems as if you're having a bad day," Tess told the boy, and he looked at her startled, as if he couldn't believe she wasn't going to yell.

"Yeah."

It was none of her business. She should send the boy on his way and figure out how to fix the fence. But she'd been that teenager who couldn't control her temper. She'd thrown her share of backpacks.

"Anything I can do?" she asked, keeping her voice casual.

"Nah," he answered. Then he paused, staring at the hole where the picket had been. Maybe he felt as though he owed her an explanation, because he started talking, not shifting his gaze from the fence. "I lost my temper. At football practice. Another kid was bugging me, kept saying stuff, and it just got to me. I went after him. Hit him. Coach kicked me out of practice for the rest of the week."

"That makes sense."

He looked disappointed. "Of course you'd say that. You're a grown-up."

It took her a moment to realize where they'd missed each other. "No, I meant *your reaction* makes sense."

He looked at her in surprise. "Really?"

"Well, you can't hit people, but if the other kid was goading you I can understand why you wanted to." She'd succumbed to the taunting too many times to count. "But can I give you some advice?"

"You can give it. Don't know if I'll take it."

"Fair enough." She couldn't help but smile at the sassiness. That sounded like her, too. "Look, you've got to realize that when you have a temper, other kids notice it, too. And some kids will try to provoke you, because they know you'll do something wild and get yourself in trouble. It's entertaining for them. So they set you up. And when you have some big reaction, you're doing exactly what those kids want you to do."

"How do you know?"

She hesitated, then decided to be honest, realizing as she said the words that she was revealing more about herself to this boy who she'd probably never see again than she had to her best friends. "Because I threw my backpack, too. And I got in fights at school, and worse." She'd been kicked out of three high schools—once for wrecking a locker, once for fighting and the last time for throwing a chair at the window. It took all of that for her to realize she had to control her reactions.

"No way. You don't look as if you were a kid who got in trouble."

"Well, I don't get mad like that anymore. I mean, people make me mad, of course, but I don't throw stuff or hit them or anything like that."

"What do you do?"

"Leave, if I can. Go someplace else. Or try to talk to them. Or ignore them. And sometimes I'm just really polite to them, even if I want to be the opposite. Like I said, you have to remember that those kids are *trying* to set you off, so don't give them the satisfaction."

The boy sat down on the curb and tried to fit all his books back into his busted backpack. Tess handed him the ones she'd picked up. There was no way the ripped fabric could hold all his stuff. The poor kid must have a ton of homework.

"Are you a teacher?" He eyed her suspiciously.

"Nope. I'm doing some work here in town right now. But I remember being your age really clearly. I got in a lot of trouble, made some mistakes. I guess I know a little about how it is."

"So you're not mad about the fence post?"

"Well, do I wish you hadn't broken it? Yes. And I'm glad it didn't actually hit me. But it's also just a picket. Not a huge deal in the grand scheme of things. I'm sure it can be replaced."

"I'll help if you want."

Tess smiled at his effort to take responsibility. "Thanks. I'd like that. How about if I get a hammer and some nails and a new picket and I'll leave them on the patio? Sometime over the next week, after school or something, you can come by and fix it for me?"

"Yeah, that would be good. Thanks."

They sat on the curb in companionable silence for a minute. Then the boy said, "What's your name?"

"Tess," she answered.

The sound of a truck engine had them both looking up. Tess recognized Slaid's pickup and stood up. The boy did the same.

Slaid pulled up to the curb by the house and jumped out of the cab. "Devin? Are you okay?"

Tess looked at the boy. "You're Devin?" She'd been sitting on the sidewalk having a heart-to-heart with Slaid's son? She felt sick.

"I'm fine, Dad." The sullen look was back on his face, as if he was bracing himself for a lecture.

"Coach Ellis called me, son. Said you got into a fight during practice. Do you want to tell me about it?"

"Nope." Devin looked at the ground and scuffed his feet and Tess had to mask a smile. He was 100 percent classic teenager at the moment.

"We'll talk at home, then." Slaid turned to Tess, and his expression warmed a little. "Hey, Tess."

"Hey," she answered, trying to sound casual, as if she hadn't been missing him every minute for days.

"Can I ask how you got involved in all this?"

Somehow she couldn't mention the fence. Devin had offered to fix it, to make things right. She wanted to honor that. "I was sitting out front, trying to get some sun. Devin was walking by and dropped his backpack. It ripped. His books went everywhere." She gestured to the shredded backpack lying on the ground at Devin's feet.

"Thanks for helping him," Slaid said quietly.

"It was my pleasure." She gave Devin a quick wink. "He's a cool kid."

"Wait, you two know each other?" The horror in Devin's voice was audible.

"We're professional acquaintances," Slaid told

him. The word stung for a moment until Tess realized that of course he couldn't tell his son they'd dated. Especially since they weren't going to date again.

"Do you work in the mayor's office?" Devin asked Tess.

"Not exactly…"

"Tess is working for the company I was telling you about, that wants to put windmills in Benson."

Devin turned to Tess in dismay. "You're the windmill lady?"

Tess smiled. "I guess you could call me that."

"Huh." Devin studied her for a moment, then shrugged. "I don't want windmills, but I liked that band you got for the harvest festival."

"Thanks."

"Devin, we'd better get you home. I'm sure you have homework, and we need to talk about what happened at practice today."

"I already talked with Tess."

Slaid looked startled. "Really?"

Tess nodded, trying not to laugh at Devin's assumption that a chat with a stranger could fend off the inevitable conversation with his actual parent. As if one adult was replaceable with another. She remembered being his age, and how generic grown-ups had seemed.

"Good. She's smart. But you still have to talk to me, son. Let's go."

Devin gave Tess a shy smile. "Thanks, Tess."

"Take care, Devin."

Slaid gave her a long look, obviously curious about what she'd said to his son. But she took a cue from Devin and gave him a shrug. "See you later, Slaid."

He opened the door and waited for Devin to climb up and fasten his seat belt before closing it. Then he turned back to Tess, a troubled look on his face. "A lot's happened between us lately."

"Yes." She knew that was her cue to apologize for the other night, but she didn't want to bring it up. If she did, she'd probably lose her willpower, beg him to spend time with her again. What he said next surprised her.

"We're still agreed to disagree about the windmills, right?"

"Sure," she answered, studying his face, looking for some clue as to why he'd brought this up now.

"Well, all right, then." He looked relieved.

"But I'll give you fair warning, Slaid. Attendance at my meetings is up. They've been going really well, too. At least, no one has seemed too upset."

Slaid glanced to the side. He seemed to be considering something. "Mine are going well, too. Really well."

"I'll just have to work a little harder."

His smile broke slowly over his face. "You are something else."

"I'll take that as a compliment."

"It is a compliment." He walked around the back of the truck and climbed into the driver's seat. "I'll see you soon." The engine came to life, and he and Devin both waved before they drove off.

Tess watched them go, still trying to figure out what that last exchange was really about. Maybe he'd finally accepted that they had no romantic future and he was trying to remind her that it was strictly about work now. The thought made her heart hurt. Even though it was what she'd told him she wanted.

She bent down to collect the pieces of the broken picket. There was a hardware store on the edge of town. She'd bring them the pieces and hope they could find her a replacement. And then she stopped in her tracks, picket in hand. She'd met Devin. *Devin*, Slaid's adopted son, who was the same age as her son. And the world hadn't fallen apart. She hadn't run away screaming, or cried, or felt overwhelming guilt and remorse. In fact, the only thing that was different was that she liked the kid. She was glad they met—glad she'd been able to help a bit, and hopeful that she might get to see him again sometime.

She leaned the broken picket carefully against the wall of the cottage and sank back down on the bench in relief. It was heartening to realize that something that had seemed so scary and life altering could happen in such a quiet way. There'd been no drama, no angst. Just a kid who needed someone who could understand him. She was glad that someone had been her.

CHAPTER EIGHTEEN

"I THOUGHT YOU weren't much of a stargazer."

Tess barely caught the glass of Scotch that went airborne as she jumped out of her skin. "Samantha! Oh, my gosh, you scared me!"

Her friend plunked herself down in one of the Adirondack chairs that surrounded the small fire Tess had made in her fire pit. "Jack had a meeting in town and I came with him. I called you but you didn't answer."

"My phone's inside."

"So you could sit out here and drink alone? Tess, you always have your phone. What's going on?"

"I don't know... Maybe the stars are growing on me."

"Are you okay?"

"I'm always okay, Sam. Don't you worry about me." She'd been sitting out here thinking about all the lies and stories she'd told for years, to her friends, colleagues, everyone. The weight of them was oppressive. Here was her best friend, who had no idea that Tess had been abused by her parents, raised in foster homes and had a baby at sixteen.

And then there was the fictional backstory she'd created. Not purposely… It had just happened over time, as a result of those casual questions friends and colleagues ask each other all the time. Questions that Tess never wanted to answer truthfully because the truth was so depressing.

So when people asked where her parents lived, she'd started saying "New England" instead of "I don't know." When someone asked what her childhood was like she answered "great" and "fun." And from that false foundation, a rickety house of other, lies were built up. Fictional schools, family vacations, pets and, just the other night, Halloween traditions.

She'd never meant to lie, but what choice did she have when most people really didn't want to hear the sordid truth? And she didn't want to see the look in their eyes when they did.

"Seriously, ever since you got here, you've been distant. Different."

Tess sighed. "I guess there's something about this part of the world that makes you think, you know?"

"What have you been thinking about?"

Tess took another sip of her Scotch and for one, brief moment, contemplated telling Samantha everything. But their friendship was already on shaky ground—if she revealed her lies it might totally fall apart. "Do you ever wish you were different than you are? I mean, if I could change myself right now, I might."

"You're perfect!" Samantha protested. "You're Tess. I wouldn't want you to be anyone else. What would you want to change?"

"I'd want to be braver. More willing to take a risk." She stared at the blue center of the flames. "I feel like everyone is evolving, but I'm still exactly the same. First you moved away, and now Jenna is busy with Sandro and her ballroom. I think I'm stuck."

"You could get unstuck."

Tess sighed again. "It's not that simple."

"Maybe the right person will get you unstuck."

Tess immediately thought of Slaid and doubted Samantha's theory. He was the one making her feel the most stuck. "I don't know. I think I'm just incapable of relationships. I've kept people at a distance for so long that now, when I might want to let them get closer, I don't even know how to do it."

Samantha watched her for a moment. "Do you want some advice?"

"Sure."

"Stop running away."

"I don't run!" Tess protested. "I'm always up for a challenge."

"You are professionally, sure. But in your personal life? When you get uncomfortable, you disappear."

And then Tess understood. "You're talking about us. Because we haven't seen each other as much as we thought we would when I first got here."

"Partly, yeah," Samantha answered softly.

"It's hard. You're my best friend, but we're disagreeing over the windmills."

"It's more than the windmills," Samantha said. "It feels as though you might be uncomfortable with me because I'm having a baby."

Tess realized maybe she wasn't quite as good of an actress as she liked to think. "No, of course not!" she said. "It's just that you and Jack, well, you're such a couple. And in the city I spend a lot of time with Jenna and Sandro, and they're so happy and in love. I think I'm spending too much time with couples. Maybe I'm jealous."

"But we don't care if you're a part of a couple or not. We just want to spend time with you."

"I'll make more of an effort," Tess promised. "I'm sorry if I've hurt your feelings."

"You're really not upset about the baby?"

How could she possible answer with complete honesty? No way would she spoil Samantha's joy with her past mistakes. "Well, sometimes I worry that things will change even more. But logically I know it will be fine."

"I can understand," Samantha said. "But please let me know what I can do to help. I miss my friend, Tess."

The hurt behind Samantha's words made Tess's heart ache. Samantha was an incredible friend—kind, funny, loyal and so good to her. They'd started off their careers together, helped each other, coached each other.

And now that friendship was in trouble. Samantha would never come here to talk like this if she wasn't really upset.

Tess stared at the flames, watching sparks pop off the dry wood. She was worse than stuck. She was so mired in the pain of her past that it was threatening the few friendships she'd managed to develop. All the independence she'd needed to survive, all the fear and shame made her push people away. Suddenly, getting unstuck didn't seem like something Tess might do, but rather something she *had* to do. She wanted her friends. She wanted to be able to be a good godmother. She wanted Slaid.

She took a sip of Scotch for courage. "You're right, I do run away. And I don't want to anymore."

"I'd love that," Samantha said, and even in the dim light Tess saw her wide smile. "I'm happy to help in any way I can."

"I think it's something I have to work out." She'd find a way. She'd been through a lot in her past, but she didn't want to let it dictate what she could or couldn't do now. She didn't want to be on the run from it anymore.

Samantha yawned.

"Oh, no, we've finally had a heart-to-heart and you're bored!" Tess was only half joking.

Samantha giggled. "No. I'm so glad we can talk, and I'm not bored at all. Quite the opposite! But I am sleepy. I guess things really are changing. The night is young and all I want to do is go to bed."

Tess walked Samantha through the house and gave her a hug at the door. "Thanks for coming over here and talking to me. I'll try to do better."

"Let's just trust that no windmill, or baby, is going to ruin our friendship."

Samantha started up the walk and unlatched the gate, and then she turned. "And it's none of my business, but if you really do want to let people get closer to you, I know one very handsome mayor who'd really like to do just that."

Tess blushed like a teenager and was glad her friend couldn't see it in the dark. "Just because I'm gonna try to be a better friend doesn't mean you get to matchmake," she teased.

"Can't blame me for trying," Samantha called as she opened the door of her SUV. "You two would be awfully cute together!"

Tess shut her front door and went back outside to put water on the coals. She felt relieved that she and Samantha had talked, but nervous, as well. It was one thing to announce that you were *going* to change, but it was another thing to actually do so. And she knew that as long as she kept her past hidden away and relied on lies, there would always be walls between her and the people she loved.

She wished she could just put herself out there, tell the world her story and damn the consequences.

But she wasn't like that. She had no idea how to be like that.

She turned off the hose and stepped away from the fire pit's billowing smoke. At the edge of the patio, far from the glow of the kitchen window, the stars looked even brighter in the black sky. They unnerved her with their infinite numbers, with their reminder that she was on this spinning planet sailing through space, and pretty much nothing was under her control. But tonight that knowledge was exhilarating, as well. She'd been trying to keep her life under such tight control for so long. Maybe it was time to accept the futility of that, to loosen her grip and just see what happened.

SLAID LOOKED AROUND the crowded bar. Most people at The High Country were intent on the football game, and usually Slaid would be, as well. But tonight he'd come here to meet Jack because they'd hit a dead end. Every finance company they talked to, every politician they got a meeting with had the same answer for them. *No.* Either they were in the pockets of the big energy companies who were reluctant to support residential solar panels or they were allied with Renewable Reliance. Slaid had a dream last night that the hills around town were bristling with windmills. He was glad to wake up from it, and just hoped he hadn't suddenly started having premonitions.

Jack had been fiddling with a bottle cap on the

bar. Flipping it over and over with his index finger, deep in thought. Then he spoke. "I'll pay."

"You'll pay?" Slaid echoed. "Jack, we're talking about tens of thousands of dollars. Possibly hundreds of thousands, depending on the number of folks who can't afford to cover their costs."

"It's worth it," Jack said quietly. "This area is home and it's precious. There's nothing like it. I talked with Samantha last night and she agrees."

"But what if Tess finds out that you and Samantha are providing the money?"

Jack sighed. "Well, if she does—which she probably will—friendship should go beyond this stuff. She must know deep down that we're doing the right thing. She's just focused on winning right now."

"I don't know what to say. This is a totally personal question, but how the hell did you make so much money? It can't be from horse training."

"I wasn't always a horse trainer. I worked in finance. And I've had a lot of luck with stocks and some other investments."

"Well, it's an incredible offer, but I'd hate to drain your bank account. Let's keep looking for funding but if you're serious about doing this, we could use your money to get some of the panels ordered and installed sooner rather than later. The public hearing is coming up. We don't have much time to get this done." He paused, studying his friend. "If you're sure."

"Completely sure. I'll call my accountant in the morning." Jack glanced at the clock and drained his beer. "I'd better get going if I want to spend any time with my wife before she falls asleep. If I didn't know she was pregnant, I'd think she was hibernating."

"Let me get the tab," Slaid told him. "It's the least I can do." After Jack left, Slaid ordered another beer. He wasn't ready to head home yet. Devin was with his cousin for the night. After a few days of his son being grumpy and grounded due to the fight at football practice, Slaid was grateful for the night off.

He had to remind himself how far Devin had come from the scared and angry kid he'd adopted. He still had a temper, but it no longer showed itself at random times. There was some relief in knowing that his fight at school a few days ago had at least been provoked. But he had to find a way to help Devin get control over his reactions—he knew things would only get harder over the next few years as more teenage hormones came into play.

He wished he could talk to Tess about it. He had no idea what she'd said to his son. Devin had been closemouthed about it and Slaid hadn't wanted to pry. But Devin had eventually confessed, a couple days later, that he needed a reprieve from being grounded so he could fix the fence he'd apparently broken. Slaid had been a little miffed that Tess had lied to cover what Devin had done, but he could see why she had. She was letting Devin make it right on his own.

He'd looked for Tess all week but hadn't seen her. It made him crazy because people around him certainly had. Betty Watkins had provided morning muffins for one of Tess's video screenings at the library. Slaid deemed it a brilliant move on Tess's part, as Betty's baking was famous in the area. Betty had told him that while she didn't support the windmills, Tess sure was a lovely girl to hang around with.

His sister, Mara, had chatted with Tess at the bank for a while, and Devin's science teacher had mentioned that he'd invited her to visit his classes to discuss alternative energy. Todd, who ran a machine shop in town and a mustang sanctuary on the side, had had a long talk with Tess after one of her video presentations and was flattered that she'd praised how well he'd trained Slaid's horse Wendy. Jed Watkins had filled him in on Tess's presentation to the local Cattlemen's Association—a meeting Slaid hadn't been able to attend because he'd been home with his grounded son. Seems she'd persuaded them to draft some kind of resolution supporting the compatibility of grazing and wind power, even if they weren't quite ready to come out and say they actually supported the project. She must have worked some serious magic to make that happen.

It seemed as if everyone in town had spent time

with Tess this week. Everyone but him. But ever since he'd seen her with Devin a few days ago, he'd had this flicker of hope. There'd been something between them in that brief moment, an easy intimacy that had him wondering if maybe they had a chance after all.

"Here you go, Slaid."

He looked up, surprised to see Selma Logan, owner of the bar, setting the pint on the counter in front of him. "Where's your hired help tonight, Sel?"

"I gave them the night off to make banners for the parade."

"The holiday parade? Isn't it a little early?"

"No, this is for the parade the day of the big public hearing. Over the windmills. Hasn't anyone mentioned it? We were going to put it on the agenda for the council meeting next week. The publicity subcommittee's been putting it together."

"I knew they were thinking about a small rally, but a parade?"

"Isn't it a great idea? And it's really taking off. We've connected with a bunch of hiking and camping groups out in San Francisco and Oakland, and they got in touch with local activists out there. Now they've chartered buses to bring people out here to protest the windmills. It'll be quite a sight!"

"Well, make sure you apply for all the permits. And you'll need to find somewhere for all these folks to stay. The fairgrounds, maybe? You could set up a campground. Get some portable toilets. Work with the sheriff, too, okay?"

"Yeah, we'll talk more about it at the meeting. I'd better serve these folks over at the other end." Selma walked off and Slaid took a big gulp of his beer. A town full of activists would definitely bring in the media. It would be chaos, but what a great idea. The more people, the more publicity. The more publicity, the less chance of the windmills getting built.

Tess would be upset, and he knew he should tell her—give her a warning so she could prepare. Then he remembered the harvest festival. She hadn't given him any warning when she'd turned it into a pro–wind farm event. Maybe he wasn't obligated to say anything, but he wanted to. Despite all her insistence that she didn't need anyone's help, he felt protective of her. He was caught between wanting to keep her safe from unpleasant surprises and wanting her windmills to fail.

Slaid took another drink and tried to focus on the football game on the TV. Since when did he have to *try* to focus on football? Truth was, tonight he didn't want beer and he didn't want football. He wanted Tess.

He threw his money on the counter and left his beer half-drunk. It took less than ten minutes to walk across town to her house. He thought the night air might clear his head and remind him that she'd sent him packing the last time they'd been together.

But it didn't. If anything, the sharp autumn air, the stars rippling in the black sky made his desire for her more clear, brought all the reasons and ways that he wanted her into sharp focus.

He saw a light on somewhere in her house, but it was ten o'clock. She might be asleep. Fortunately Slaid was past good manners, past trying to be the nice guy, the polite guy. He was just a guy who wanted Tess, more than he'd ever wanted anything else. He knocked softly on her door.

THE KNOCK ON her front door was low, but it jolted Tess out of her thoughts. As she pushed herself up from her chair, she realized how stiff she was. She glanced at the clock over the stove, shocked to see that it was almost ten. She'd been staring out the kitchen window for an hour.

The soft knock came again and she walked to the front of the cottage. Glancing through the window she saw Slaid, shoulders hunched under his shearling jacket, collar drawn up against the wind. She opened the door. "Slaid, are you okay? You—"

He didn't let her finish. Just stepped inside, put his hands on her shoulders and held her while he kissed her. Tangled his fingers in her hair and kissed her harder. Walked forward, forcing her backward, until she hit the wall opposite the front door. He tasted of beer and smelled like fresh air. He didn't stop kissing her, not to breathe or explain.

She'd stopped them before, but she couldn't stop

this now. Not when she'd been sitting here with her loneliness and regret. She reached her hands up behind his head, fingers slipping easily through his short, silky hair. He was tall and massive and dwarfed her with his big hands that had slid down and were spanning her waist, moving downward to cover her ass and pull her toward him.

She moaned against his mouth and brought her own hands down to yank his shirt from the waist of his jeans, to feel the warmth of his skin. She slid her hands up his sides and over his back, feeling him shudder under her touch.

He broke their kiss and looked down at her, thumbs sliding across her cheekbones, his gray eyes intent on hers. "I know I spend a lot of time apologizing and here I go again. I'm sorry you were so upset about our date last weekend."

She could only nod. Her vocabulary was limited to adjectives. *Gray* eyes, *full, serious* mouth, *steel* muscles where her hands cradled his biceps.

"I can't promise that I won't mess it all up again tomorrow, Tess. But tonight I'll play it your way. No questions, no expectations, no past or future. I want you. That's what matters."

His words were aphrodisiac, freeing her from her worry about what he might think of her past, and what he might want in the future. She reached up on tiptoes. "Thank you for coming," she whispered in his ear, and then kissed him where the words had fallen.

The ragged intake of his breath was gratifying. She'd felt at such a disadvantage with Slaid on their dates. He was a pro at small talk, at getting to know someone effortlessly. Now they were in her territory, and she felt all her confidence returning.

She slid her lips to his mouth, still balanced on her toes, using his broad shoulders as support to keep her mouth even with his. It was her turn to kiss him, to push his lips open with hers, to taste and torment him. She bit softly on his lower lip, and he made a harsh sound and pushed her down and into the wall so it was completely supporting her weight. His mouth ravaged hers as his hands came down to her breasts, and she felt his mouth tip up under his in a gratified smile when he discovered that she was braless. His hands dipped to the hem of her shirt and lifted it up, his fingers trailing along the bare skin of her back, his thumbs on her abdomen, and then he slid his hands under her breasts, filling his palms with them.

She wanted his hands there, but she wanted them everywhere else, too. Tess ground her hips against his, feeling him hard through his jeans. His huge hands were under her armpits in an instant, lifting her effortlessly so her legs wrapped around his waist. "Bed," she gasped, and he carried her there, kissing her the entire way, only slamming her ankle into one door frame in the process. He sat her down on the bed and went to his knees, rubbing the offended ankle gently.

"You okay?" he asked, and she knew he meant about all of it, not just the ankle.

"I'm good," she assured him. "Stand up. Please?" She scooted closer to the edge of the bed and grabbed his belt loops as he stood, bringing him closer. She unbuckled his silver buckle and found the button at the top of his fly. When she unzipped, his erection sprang out under the black cotton of his underwear, and she pulled the waistband to free it, taking him in her mouth.

"Tess," he gasped, fisting his hands in her hair. She quickly found the rhythm he needed and lost herself in the feel of him, mouth and hands sliding along his length until he cried out and she tasted him, so sharply salty.

"Hell," he whispered, tipping her face up to look at him. "You in some kind of hurry to get finished tonight?"

"Who said anything about being finished?" she teased, throwing his words from Bodie back at him.

He pulled his jeans all the way off and pushed back the covers on her bed. "Get in here with me."

She glanced down at her fleece ensemble. Not exactly sexy.

"And take those off."

"I like a man who takes charge," she purred, removing the fleece top and watching him admire her breasts when she tossed it aside. She slipped her yoga pants off and slid into bed next to him. "Any other orders you want to give me, Mr. Mayor?"

He studied her face for a moment, a slow smile building. "Sure." He pulled her on top of him so she was on all fours. He immediately filled his hands with her breasts, teasing her nipples with his thumbs. "I want you like this." His words came out ragged, barely audible.

Tess arched her back, reveling in the feeling of being caressed by his enormous hands, letting the intense sensations ripple through her nervous system. She brought her mouth down to kiss him, freezing when his hands moved over her back and down her thighs.

"I need you," she whispered, barely choking the words out, she wanted him so badly.

"Wait," he said, and gently set her down next to him on the bed."

"I like these." He traced the lace border of her emerald green satin panties. And then he slid them off with agonizing slowness, stopping to kiss every bit of skin revealed. And when he reached her toes, and tossed the panties over the edge of the bed, he pulled the quilts over and around her, making sure she was warm.

"Such a Boy Scout," she breathed.

"Well, let me earn my merit badge, then." And he slid under the covers, pushing her knees so she opened her thighs to him.

She closed her eyes, letting the room disappear so it was just his mouth on her, and all her senses focused on only that, his fingers inside her, his hand on her belly, the alternating teasing and pressure, until the feeling raging through her collected and shattered and she shook against his mouth as he held her firmly to the bed.

HE EMERGED FROM the covers, damp with sweat and her, and used the edge of the sheet to wipe his mouth before he kissed her.

"Boy Scout," she teased again, but her voice was languid now, her muscles marshmallow soft in her afterglow.

His mouth came over hers, nibbled gently on her lower lip. "Did I earn my badge?"

"Most definitely." She giggled. "One of them, at least."

"Remember when I told you I was an Eagle Scout?" His hand was between her legs now, circling her most sensitive spots, bringing electric desire back into her sleepy body and brain. She pushed herself against him and he increased the pressure.

"I… Yes…" Her voice was breathless now. It was hard to speak with his hand circling relentlessly, building up that wanting need she'd only just sated.

"So I've got *a lot* of badges…"

"Really…"

"And I know how to be prepared."

It took a moment for his words to penetrate the haze of longing that was cocooning her. When the caresses stopped and he leaned over the bed to pull something out of the pocket of his jeans, the meaning became clear. Tess giggled. "I'm so glad."

He ripped open the condom packet and quickly rolled it on, then resumed touching her. "I know how to build a fire, too."

She was burning under his hand; she didn't think she could take much more of his amazing badge-earning skills.

"Prove it." She wrapped her arms around his neck, bringing him down to kiss her, to lay across her. He held himself up slightly so as not to crush her while he pushed her thighs apart with his knee, and she almost cried with the anticipation of him inside her. She'd had two years to savor the memory of what it felt like. Yet this was better than the memories, better than anything she'd had before or since. Her entire being was focused on his hard length pushing deep inside and over and over until she cried out, clinging to him. His rough gasp escaped on breath that warmed her neck, and she felt him move in her depths, the muscles of his back trembling a little as he rode out his climax.

And when they'd both stopped shaking, he lay next to her, propped on an elbow, with a smile that was all happiness, pride and admiration. "It's better than Phoenix," he whispered.

Tess looked up at him in surprise.

"I know you better than I did that first time. And that makes it *way* better."

"So there are some benefits from this getting-to-know-you business," she whispered languidly, and he laughed out loud.

He pulled her to him. She had just enough energy left to roll over so her back was to his broad chest, her bottom nestled into his groin. She was completely sated and perfectly cradled in his warmth. He wrapped one arm protectively around her, drawing the quilts up against the chill autumn night. "You're right," she murmured sleepily. "This *was* better than Phoenix. And it's my house, so I don't have to tiptoe out of here in the morning."

She could feel his chest move against her back with soft laughter. He kissed her hair and snuggled against her, and his quiet breathing lulled her to sleep.

CHAPTER NINETEEN

"Good morning, beautiful."

Tess opened her eyes and gasped. Slaid was looking down at her, the warm smile on his face quickly fading when he saw the horror on hers.

"It's okay," he said. "It's just me."

Tess sat bolt upright with the covers pulled up to her chin. She was naked under them, in bed with Slaid, and it was morning. Light outside. Which meant smeared makeup, morning breath, and she'd have to come up with some kind of small talk to entertain him, which she was pretty sure she was incapable of precoffee. Irrational thoughts raced across her mind. What did you say to a guy at— she glanced at the clock—seven in the morning?

"Um, excuse me" was all she could think of. She grabbed the small throw draped at the foot of the bed and wrapped it around herself. Her scramble out of bed and her race to the bathroom were probably not very graceful, but she had to get away.

Once inside the relative safety of the tiny bathroom, she took a deep breath and considered her choices. Her running clothes were hanging from a hook on the door, she could pull them on and get out through the window, but it looked cold outside. Plus, Slaid wouldn't appreciate it if she disappeared on him again. Better to try to repair whatever damage she could from last night and face him looking as good as possible.

She splashed cold water on her face, dried her skin with a towel and regarded her reflection, pleasantly surprised. She did look good, actually. Glowing. She remembered how Slaid had made her feel last night, the things they'd done. Yeah, no wonder she was glowing. She smiled, despite the anxiety of waking up with a guy in her bed, and grabbed her toothbrush. At least she could do away with the morning breath.

She heard Slaid moving around in the bedroom. Maybe he was getting ready to leave. By the time she'd finished brushing her teeth and pulling her hair into a ponytail, there were no more sounds in the bedroom. Yay. Hopefully he'd gone home and she wouldn't have to figure out what do next.

She wrapped herself in a bath towel and padded into the bedroom, noting with satisfaction that the bed was made and there was no sign of Slaid. She rummaged through her drawers, pulling out a bra, underwear, jeans and a T-shirt. She had no formal appointments today. Just some work here at the cottage and, of course, the dreaded baby shower invitations—she had to tally up the RSVPs.

"Coffee?"

Tess started and dropped her underwear. The lacy panties wafted down and landed at the ground by Slaid's bare feet. His laughter came out as rich as the scent emanating from the cup he offered.

"I didn't mean to scare you."

"I thought you'd left!"

"I wouldn't leave without saying goodbye." There was outrage on his face at the thought, and then the realization seemed to hit him that she'd done exactly that in Arizona two years ago.

"Oh." It was all she could say, unless she voiced what was in both their thoughts. *I would.*

She sipped the coffee and looked up to where he was leaning on the door frame, smiling at her, his own cup in his hand. In his faded jeans and untucked flannel he looked younger than usual, not the mayor or the busy rancher or the dad, just a guy hanging out after a really great night of sex. She flushed as the recollection of just how great it was heated her skin.

"You've never done this before, have you?"

"Done what?" She feigned ignorance, hoping there was still a way to avoid this chat.

"Woken up with a guy. You completely panicked earlier, didn't you?"

"Well, there's a lot to panic about. Messed up hair, morning breath, wondering if it was fun for you, too…"

He chuckled. "Trust me. No need to panic. Your

hair is incredibly sexy when it's mussed, you don't have morning breath and it was way more than fun."

She just stared at him, wondering at this knack he had for making everything seem so simple.

"And I'd like to wake up with you again, very soon, but right now, I want to take you to breakfast."

"You can't take me to breakfast!"

"Why not? People do eat breakfast, Tess. Though after looking in your cupboards, I'm not sure *you* do."

"Everyone will know that we…"

"It's just breakfast. I'm not planning to have sex with you *in* the diner, though the idea does pose some interesting possibilities…"

"Ew!" She didn't share his humor. "There is nothing sexy about bacon and eggs."

"I disagree. Right now they sound very sexy. Warm…salty…"

"Greasy…"

He laughed. "Come on, let's go eat. Who cares what anyone thinks? Some might think we're together, some might think we were just hungry. Who cares?"

"I've never had breakfast with a guy like this."

"Don't you think it's about time you started?"

Tess didn't have any more arguments. Last night she'd promised herself she wouldn't let her fears hold her hostage. Plus, she was really hungry, way hungrier than the low-fat granola in her cupboard had the power to sate. She grabbed her underwear out of his hand and got dressed. Then she went to the bench by the door and pulled on her knee-high boots.

"That's more like it." He sat down next to her and put on his socks and boots, glanced over and caught her watching him. "Let me guess, you've never sat next to a guy and put on boots, either?"

"Nope." Tess giggled. It was pretty ridiculous, now that she thought about it—how incredibly solitary her life was.

They grabbed their coats and walked side by side to the diner on Main Street. Tess was relieved that Slaid didn't try to hold her hand—she wasn't ready to announce to the town of Benson that they'd just rolled out of bed together. But when she saw his truck parked in front of the bar, she knew that at least some people would put the pieces together and figure out where he'd spent the night.

"You left your truck in the middle of town all night?" she said.

"Well, it seemed better than leaving it in front of your house," he said mildly.

"You couldn't have hidden it in a bush somewhere? Put branches on it so no one could see it?"

He looked at her uncertainly.

"Kidding," she said. "I'm not quite *that* crazy."

They were still laughing when they stepped inside the diner. It seemed as though half the town of Benson was here, and all heads turned toward her and the mayor. Tess paused, the weight of all the attention suddenly stifling.

Slaid put a comforting hand on her arm.

"If this is too much, we can leave."

She was uncomfortable, but she wasn't running anymore. "Hey, it's a morning of firsts anyway, why not add my first successful public date with a small-town mayor to my list of accomplishments?"

"Lucky mayor," he said softly with a smile that was both sweet and sexy.

Slaid managed to get them the booth in the far corner by the window. Tess sat with her back to the restaurant—at least if people were looking at them and speculating, she couldn't see it. And it didn't seem to bother Slaid at all. Every once in a while he'd catch someone's eye and give them a little wave or nod of acknowledgment, but she never turned to see who it might be.

The waitress took their order and filled their cups with coffee. Slaid took a gulp of his before asking "So how's your first morning after so far?"

"Surprisingly pleasant, after the initial shock," she answered.

"It was pretty cute when you took off for the bathroom."

"Don't tease!" She kicked him gently under the table and he caught her leg, bringing it up to rest on the seat next to him, his big hand wrapped around her ankle. Even through the leather of her boot she felt his warm strength.

"Hey, I'm honored. And I meant it when I said that I hope it's not a one-time thing. You wear bed head well."

"No promises," Tess said automatically, sipping her coffee. But strangely enough, she wanted other mornings, too.

Their food arrived, and after one bite Tess decided that bacon and eggs *were* sexy, or at least the perfect breakfast after a long night of incredible sex. And sitting here with Slaid was so much easier than she'd imagined. She'd always feared that the morning after would be full of awkward pauses and unspoken feelings. Instead they chatted about the people who walked by on the sidewalk outside the window, and they argued the merits of the country songs playing over the speakers. It was relaxing.

The waitress took their plates, and they sat sipping their coffee.

"So Devin is back on the football team, raring to go."

"Really?" Tess asked. "I'm glad he's able to play again. I hope he does okay. He seems like a good kid."

"He is. But he was sure having a rough day when you met him. Last week was his birthday. My ex, Jeannette, didn't call, and his birth mother didn't, either. That might've been part of what set him off."

The information scraped over her like sandpaper. Devin wanted to hear from his mom on his birthday. And his birth mother. Did Adam wish for a phone call on his birthday? Was he disappointed every year when it didn't come? "I'm sorry," she answered woodenly. "I can imagine that was hard for him."

"I haven't really thanked you," Slaid said. "I don't know what you said to him the other day, but it helped."

"I'm glad." There was a sort of buzzing of emotion in her ears. She'd had many chances to be in Adam's life and she'd refused. Had she caused her son the type of anger and pain that Devin felt?

Slaid didn't seem to notice her distraction. "I was bracing myself the whole drive to town for Devin to be angry, upset and acting out. Instead he was calm. And he even talked about how he needed to learn to ignore people who might provoke him."

"You must have been so proud of him." She had to focus on the present. This wasn't about her son; it was about Devin and Slaid, who were in her life, who mattered *now*.

"I was," Slaid assured her. "And grateful to you, too. You made a great impression on him. I was almost jealous. I've been trying to teach him those lessons for years. Ever since he came to live with us."

"How old was he?"

"About three. With a head full of anger and a heart full of hurt. We worked hard and he made a lot of progress—until Jeannette left a couple years ago.

She was the only mom he'd really known. Since then, it's been a little touch and go with Devin."

Tess felt sick. What would Slaid think if he knew Tess had so much in common with the women who'd let Devin down? That she'd walked away from her own son and never looked back? Suddenly her throat felt dry and thick and she reached for her water. "Can I ask why she left?"

Slaid stared into his coffee cup. "She never told me, but I think I know. We'd tried to get pregnant for a while. We finally went to the doctor and found out Jeannette couldn't have children. I think she kind of gave up on having a family after that. Once Devin came into our lives, I thought things would get better for us, but she never really bonded with him. It was hard, adopting a kid with a lot of issues. It takes its toll, I guess."

"That must be hard...for you and for Devin."

"Harder for him, I think." Slaid looked out the window for a moment and then back again. "I don't talk about this much," he said. "Never, really. I think we fell out of love, you know? And it was hard for me because I wanted to believe in what I'd been taught, that you get married and it lasts forever and you're happy that way. But we weren't. We met so young that we barely knew ourselves at that point. Over the years we became more and more different—different people, each with separate dreams. By the end, she didn't even want to live around here anymore. She works as a waitress on cruise ships out of Florida now. I hear she's pretty happy."

"And are *you* happy?" Tess asked.

"I'm not gonna lie. I was pretty broken up. I did a few crazy things, had a wild night down in Phoenix…" He winked at her, and Tess flushed. "But then I became mayor, figured I'd better set a good example for my son. And once I realized I was more upset about the marriage ending than I was about losing Jeannette, and once I got used to being a single dad, I realized that it was all gonna work out."

"And has it?"

"Well, there's this woman who came to town, trying to talk everyone into supporting this wind project. It was all good until *she* showed up!"

Humor was familiar territory and helped settle her nerves. "Ha-ha," she murmured, sipping her coffee. "I think, if you just look on the bright side, you might discover some benefits to having her in town."

He raised his cup, and she was glad she was sitting down when he flashed her a knee-melting smile. "Absolutely. And maybe, if I'm lucky, she'll agree to go to Devin's game with me on Friday."

"You want me to go to a football game?" She hadn't meant for her voice to come out at such a high pitch. "Isn't that us getting pretty serious, pretty fast?"

"Maybe. I don't feel serious, though, I just feel

happy. I like you, Tess. And I'm a dad. This is how I spend a lot of my time. So if I want to spend time with you, I have to figure out how to talk you into things like this. Plus, Devin wants you to go, too. He mentioned it."

"Really? Or is that just you talking me into it?"

Slaid laughed. "No! He honestly mentioned it. But...did it work? Did I talk you into it? Will you come?"

The idea of a small-town football game didn't hold much appeal, and about a hundred warning bells were going off in her head.

"It will give us more time together," Slaid coaxed her. "And folks around here will appreciate that you're out supporting our team. It could help with the windmills..."

"Okay, I'll go." She instantly regretted it. On top of all her other charades was the fib she'd told Slaid a few weeks ago about being a football fan. It wouldn't take long for him to realize she didn't know the first thing about the game. She'd just have to hope that she didn't accidentally bust out in a cheer for the wrong team.

"I'll pick you up at three?"

"Sure," she answered. "I'll be ready. Pom-poms and everything."

He smiled at her feeble joke. "I'd like to see that."

"Cheerleading fantasies, huh?"

"Well, I'm a pretty big football fan, so..."

The waitress came by with the check, which

Tess insisted on paying. "I can expense it," she said when Slaid tried to take care of it. "Don't you think Renewable Reliance owes you a breakfast?"

"Well, if I'd known they were paying I'd have ordered everything on the menu."

Tess laughed and stood up. "Come on, Mr. Mayor. This town won't run itself, and I have work to do."

The walked out of the diner and over to Slaid's truck. "I had a great night," he said.

"Me, too," Tess answered.

"So…see you Friday? I really appreciate you giving it a try. Devin will be happy when he hears you're coming."

Devin. The weight of what she'd learned today came back. How his birth mom couldn't take care of him, and his adoptive mom had abandoned him. She knew what it was like, to go through so much upheaval as a child. Maybe it was possible to be there for Devin even just a little, in the way she'd never been able to support her own son.

"I'll see you Friday." Tess gave Slaid a kiss on the cheek. His eyebrows went up at her chaste goodbye. "Oh, what the hell," she murmured, and went up on tiptoe to reach his mouth with hers. He wrapped his arms around her and deepened the kiss, right there on the sidewalk in front of all of Benson. And Tess didn't care because the kiss felt incredible— like the most real and honest thing she'd done, ever.

CHAPTER TWENTY

"WHY DO PEOPLE play football in winter anyway?" Tess asked. "It makes no sense."

"Dunno," Slaid answered, wrapping her scarf around her neck for her and kissing her lightly on the mouth. "But are you all ready to cheer for the Benson Mustangs?"

"Bring it on." Tess pulled on her parka.

"And by the way," Slaid added as she shut the door behind them and locked it, "Devin asked to sleep at a friend's tonight. Just so you know."

"Oh, just for informational purposes?" Tess teased.

Slaid actually blushed at being caught in the act of dropping hints. "Just in case you wanted to invite me over later. Or go on a date with me and *then* invite me over."

"Why, thank you for looking out for me. I'll keep that in mind."

He grinned and took her hand as they walked the short blocks to the high school.

The street in front of the football field was packed with cars and trucks. Tess looked up at

Slaid in shock. "So many people are coming to the game!"

Slaid looked at her in surprise. "Of course. It's a big deal. It's football!"

"But are you sure we should be out together like this? The final public hearing for the windmills is coming up—won't people get the wrong idea?"

He shot an amused glance at her. "I'm pretty sure they'll get the right idea. If people can't deal with the fact that we like each other, too bad. They can recall me. It will give me more time to relax."

She laughed, loving his confidence, wishing she could borrow a little right now. Her knees were almost knocking at the idea of taking their relationship, or whatever it was between them, so public. But she'd promised herself that no matter what, she wouldn't run. She wasn't going to be a coward anymore. And if Slaid knew these people and didn't care what they thought, well, she'd learn not to care, too.

When they turned into the field entrance, she almost changed her mind about that. It looked as if the entire town was filing through the gates. Across the field, Tess saw the bleachers for the visiting team almost as full. Entire families cuddling under blankets, eating, laughing, excited for play to start.

"Hot chocolate?"

"Will they spike it for us?"

He grinned. "Nope."

"Oh, well." She sighed in mock disappointment. "Yes, please. At least it's warm." With the sun behind the mountains, the air had cooled quickly. She could see her breath. Slaid purchased two cups of the steaming cocoa from the food booth and she followed him into the bleachers. It took forever to climb up to their spots because everyone wanted to say hello to the mayor and spend some time looking back and forth between them, trying to figure out their connection.

They ran into Betty Watkins, and a wide, warm smile creased her cheeks when she saw them together. She stood and surprised Tess by pulling her in for a hug. "You are a sight for sore eyes, Tess. Only you could make a down parka and wool hat look as if you just strolled off the runway in Paris."

Tess blushed at the effusive compliment, and Slaid grinned ear to ear. "Isn't my date gorgeous? I'm a lucky guy, Betty."

"Stop," Tess protested, embarrassed.

"Now, you just enjoy it," Betty admonished. "It's clear our mayor is head over heels for you, and most of the single ladies in this town are green with envy. Slaid's a good man, Tess. You couldn't do better."

Betty was apparently trying to make Tess feel less embarrassed, but her efforts were backfiring. Tess wondered if she could ever get used to living her life under the scrutiny of her neighbors. Slaid didn't seem to mind, just came to her rescue, saying, "Betty, I think you got it wrong. Tess is doing *me* a favor, coming out with me today." He winked at her and Tess felt something in her stomach flutter—he was that handsome.

Betty laughed and waved them off. "Go enjoy the game, you two. And, Slaid, I know Devin will do just great tonight. I can feel it."

Betty's husband, Jed, had been grinning through this entire exchange, his broad arms crossed over his big belly. He reached out and wrapped Tess's hand in his own, shaking it. "Pleased to meet you finally, Tess. I've heard so much about you from Samantha and Betty, I feel like we're already acquainted."

She smiled, feeling more at ease already due to his relaxed manner. She'd imagined that people would be upset that she was here, seeing her as an outsider, someone here to change their community for the worse. Maybe it was because she was with Slaid, but tonight, at least, people seemed welcoming.

She sat in her seat in the bleachers, nestled against Slaid's big shoulder, sipping her hot cocoa. People glanced back to get a look at them, but with Slaid's arm around her, bolstered by the good humor with which he acknowledged the town's curiosity, she slowly stopped worrying about the scrutiny.

And then the game started and she was busy watching Devin, excited to see the boy's talent. When she noticed the pride on Slaid's face, she felt as though she was seeing a little piece of the deep love he had for his son—his adopted son. She hoped with all her heart that Adam's parents looked at him with that same pride and joy.

Devin did well, throwing the pass that made the final touchdown, and when his coach put a hand on his shoulder and said something that even from this distance she could tell was a compliment, Tess looked over to see Slaid's eyes glitter with what she suspected might be tears. She squeezed his hand, happy for him and for his son.

"Does it take you back to when you played?"

He cleared his throat. "It sure does. I spent a lot of time out on this field. There's nothing like it, hearing people cheer, seeing your friends and family get so excited."

"You played in college."

He gave her a sheepish grin. "I did. I was good, but other kids were better. I clocked a fair amount of the time on the bench. But they gave me some scholarship money."

They followed the crowd as it meandered off the field and eventually found Devin, who shouted, "Tess!" He seemed genuinely happy she was here, even introducing her to his coach as "the lady who'd helped him calm down." Then he turned to his dad and said, "Pizza!" and Slaid answered him with a high five.

Tess smiled at this display of masculine affection, wondering at the way the word *pizza* seemed to speak volumes about the love between these two. Well, pizza and two of the biggest smiles she'd ever seen.

"You're coming with us, right, Tess?" Devin asked.

She opened her mouth to decline. She didn't want to intrude, plus a bunch of teenagers and their parents at a pizza party wasn't really her thing, but Slaid didn't give her the chance to say no.

"Tess is all about new experiences tonight, aren't you, Tess? You've experienced your first football game, now it's time for your first after-game pizza."

"You *never* went to a game before?" Devin asked in horror.

She turned to Slaid. "You knew it was my first game?"

"You called almost every player the quarterback."

Devin cracked up and Tess flushed. "Oh...I thought... Well, never mind."

"And there was that comment the other week, about the Santa Clara Forty-Niners, that gave you away."

"I was trying to find common ground! It's what we do in community relations. The truth is, sports weren't exactly my thing in high school."

"I can't picture you in high school," Slaid said.

"It's best not to," Tess countered, casting about in her mind for a new subject.

"Aw, come on!" Slaid put his arm around her

and pulled her into his side. "Do you have a high school yearbook picture? How about a graduation photo? I'll show you mine if you show me yours."

Tess froze. She'd never had enough money to buy a yearbook. Plus, she'd eventually been kicked out of school for her poor behavior and finished out high school in a continuation class. They didn't take graduation photos there.

By sheer will she calmed her heart and sent the regret and shame scuttling back to the dank parts of her brain where they constantly lurked. "Oh, no, Slaid Jacobs, you're not conning me. You were the big football star and I'm sure you were handsome, as well. No frizzy-haired photos of me with my braces are ever going to fall into your hands."

"I can just picture it! But how come no football games? You grew up in New England, right? I know they like football there."

"Oh, you know, my parents were pretty strict. I stayed in and did a lot of homework." More lies. She was so sick of them. It was time for a new subject.

"You've talked me into it," she said. "Pizza, I mean, not bad yearbook photos. All this watching Devin exercise has made me hungry."

Devin gave a yelp of laughter at her lame joke. "C'mon, then. We gotta go now or we'll never get a table."

They piled into Slaid's truck and drove the few blocks to the restaurant. It was simple and homey with red-checked tablecloths and candles in mason jars. As they stood in line for a table, Devin begged for quarters to go play some video games in the adjacent arcade room where many of his friends were. It seemed that most of the football team came here after the game.

Slaid kept his arm around Tess, holding her tight against his side. He leaned his head down to kiss the top of her head, and when she looked up he kissed her once, softly, on the mouth. "I know this is all new for you...being out with someone like me. Meeting my kid. Standing in restaurants, and me kissing you. I know it's not your usual way. I just want you to know how much I appreciate you trying it out, trying all this new stuff, for me."

His simple words had tears prickling at her eyes. She loved the way he could be so totally sexy and cocky in one moment and say words like that the next. But she didn't have his heartfelt vocabulary. So she teased. "Well, don't get a big head. Maybe it's not all about you, cowboy. Maybe I've just decided it's time to be more adventurous, check out the wild ways of you small-town folks." She looked pointedly around the pizza parlor, at all the happy families. "And, boy, does it get wild around here!"

His laughter boomed out over the line of waiting diners, and several of them turned to see what their mayor thought was so funny. He pulled Tess in again and kissed her soundly on the mouth for all to see. Tess flushed, feeling all eyes on her. But despite her discomfort, she wouldn't have traded her spot under Slaid's arm in this funky local pizza parlor for a table at the finest Parisian restaurant. This strange small-town adventure, with this sexy small-town mayor as her guide, was exactly the journey she wanted to be on right now.

CHAPTER TWENTY-ONE

DEVIN WENT HOME from the pizza parlor with his friend Cal. Before he left he made Tess promise to visit the ranch the next afternoon so he could show her around. He wanted her to meet all the horses and even offered to give her a horseback-riding lesson. He was a persuasive kid, funny and smart, and she liked him a lot, so she agreed.

But the sweetest thing was when Devin said goodbye. They were standing on the sidewalk near the restaurant entrance. Cal's family was busy loading their three children into their enormous SUV. Slaid had just finished reminding Devin to be on his best behavior, and Devin had just finished giving Slaid a hug. Then he turned to Tess and there was an awkward moment when they just looked at each other. But then he stepped up and wrapped his arms around her, giving her a hug, too. "Thanks for coming to my game, Tess," he said when he stepped back. "I'll see you tomorrow."

Tears threatened. Slaid and his son, this tiny, two-person family, were getting under her skin. She couldn't even speak. She just smiled and waved as the SUV headed off to Cal's house. When she looked back at Slaid she was surprised to see him watching her intently, an expression on his face she didn't recognize.

He cleared his throat, and she realized he was as emotional as she was. "Want to go for a drive?" he asked. "There are some amazing stars out tonight."

"Is that what you all do for fun out here?" she teased, trying to lighten the mood.

"One of the things. Come on, let me show you a real Benson date."

"As long as we avoid picnic benches and spiky plants, I'm good," she quipped.

He rewarded her with that wide smile she was coming to crave and tipped his hat in a "yes ma'am" move. "I'll keep that in mind."

He opened the door of his truck for her and she climbed inside. When they drove out of town, he kept one hand on the wheel, the other wrapped around hers. At the freeway he turned north, then headed east on a small road, just a narrow strip of darkness lit by his headlights. It eventually started climbing upward and became switchbacks for a few minutes. Finally they came upon an open area that seemed like the end of the road, and Slaid parked.

"You are *not* taking me to the local make-out spot, are you?" Tess asked, looking out at the rich darkness around the truck. "And, just to clarify, you're not some kind of serial killer, correct?"

Slaid's husky laughter filled the cab. He leaned

over, put his arm around her and kissed her hair. "Negative to both questions. Well, actually, I haven't been to the local make-out spot lately, so I dunno, maybe this is the new place. Though the kids would probably be here by now if it was."

She tipped her face up. She could barely see him in the blackness, but she felt him, his warm breath on her skin and the brush of his lips across her mouth.

"I wanted to show you a place I love," he murmured.

"Let me guess," she murmured back. "This place you love is outside in the freezing cold."

"It is. But I've got blankets, Scotch and dark chocolate."

"Scotch and dark chocolate is one of my favorite combinations. Have you been talking to Samantha?"

"I may have run into her the other day and mentioned I was thinking of taking you on a late-night picnic."

Warmth filled her at the idea of him seeking out her friend to find out what she liked. "Okay, fine. I'll go out there and freeze with you. As long as we can come back in here and crank the heat when I cry mercy."

"You got it. But I promise I'll keep you warm."

His low voice was already doing the job.

They opened the doors of the cab and Tess gave a little gasp when she took a breath. It felt as if she was inhaling ice crystals. But she met Slaid at the back of the truck where he opened the tailgate and with no warning, put his hands under her arms and effortlessly lifted her onto the truck bed. Then he jumped up and walked to the back, where there were a few duffel bags and a thick foam pad rolled up.

Tess sat on the edge of the truck and watched as he unrolled the foam, covered it in a blanket and pulled more blankets and even a down comforter out of the duffels. Pillows went against the back of the cab.

"Okay, this is kind of cool and kind of creepy," Tess said. "Who brings bedding on a date?"

"Hang on! I'm not finished yet!" Slaid pulled out a small, low folding table and placed a bottle of Glenlivet, two glasses, a candle and an assortment of chocolate bars on it. He lit the candle and, in a final flourish, pulled out a single red rose and handed it to her. Its petals had been crushed a bit, but it only served to release its heavy perfume. Tess inhaled the sweet smell of the rose, completely out of place and exotic in the dark desert night.

"There," Slaid said, with a satisfied tone. "Hopefully more romantic then creepy."

Her laugh was sharp in the intense quiet around them. "And definitely warmer than sitting out here." She got up from her perch and knelt down on the foam, pulled off her boots and climbed under the blankets. He did the same, poured them both a shot of Scotch and they leaned back on the pillows. Slaid clinked his glass to hers, saying, "To new adventures."

The burn of the alcohol and the smoky taste of the whiskey warmed Tess inside, and snuggling next to Slaid under the blankets quickly warmed the rest of her.

"This is very cozy," she said, "but why, exactly, are we here, and not at one of our houses, which are both empty tonight?"

"Look up."

There were more stars above them than she'd known existed in the universe. Without the lights of the town competing with them, with the small moon setting, their glory was astounding. Layers and layers of crystal specks, extending into a space that her imagination couldn't begin to comprehend. Slaid pulled her close, so she was leaning against his strong shoulder.

"I wanted you to see this," he murmured.

Suddenly a light streaked across the sky. "Yipes!" Tess sat bolt upright.

"Amazing." Slaid's voice held a reverence she'd never heard.

"What was that?" Her heart was pounding.

"The Southern Taurids." Slaid pulled her gently back onto his shoulder. "Meteor showers."

"Really? We just saw a meteor?"

"Yep. A bright one. You must be my good-luck charm. I rarely see anything like that."

Tess studied the sky, hoping something else would happen. She took another sip of her Scotch.

"Chocolate?" Slaid offered, passing her a bar.

"Hang on. I want to see if there's any more."

He started laughing. "A girl refusing chocolate? Hmm, I think it's actually happened."

"What's happened?" She thought she saw a faint light traveling across the sky and pointed. "Wait— is that a meteor?"

Slaid craned his neck to see where she pointed. "A satellite."

"Oh." Disappointed, she looked up at him. "What's actually happened?" she asked, going back to his previous comment.

"You like it here."

It took a moment for the words to sink in. But when they did, she realized he was right. The past couple of days in Benson she'd felt more relaxed, more accepting and more balanced than she could ever remember feeling. But she didn't want to get Slaid's hopes up. She'd be leaving soon.

"Maybe," she said. "Or maybe I've just never seen a meteor before."

"Well, I'm glad I got to be here for your first."

Tess set the chocolate bar aside unopened and took another sip of her Scotch before setting it on the small table. "You know how else you could be my first?"

"How?"

"Like this." She turned toward him, pulled herself up to his eye level and kissed him. He tasted like Scotch and warmth and everything she really wanted for dessert.

He pulled back to look at her. "You mean you never had a good old-fashioned make-out session in the back of a truck?"

"I'm a city girl, remember? Most of our illicit activity takes place indoors."

He set down his drink and pulled her up onto his lap, facing him. Then he unzipped her parka. "I can help with this deficit in your upbringing."

"Really?" she murmured against his mouth, kissing him again. "I'd appreciate that."

He hauled the blankets up around her shoulders, cocooning them both against the back of the truck. And then he kissed her, such a slow, intimate gesture that she felt his touch not only in her mouth but along her nerves and over her skin.

When he finally ended the kiss, she wasn't sure she was still breathing, she'd been so completely lost in it. She opened her eyes in shock and saw the same in his, as if he couldn't believe what was happening between them. Then the haze cleared and a triumphant smile tilted his mouth. "That was pretty good, huh?" he said quietly.

"It was great." That was all she could manage before becoming completely distracted by the way her fingers felt sliding through his hair and down to caress the strong line of his jaw. She set her mouth over his, parting his lips, taking the same journey he'd taken, wanting to taste every part of him.

His hands were under her parka, and she felt the touch of air on her skin when he slid her sweater up and unhooked her bra. His palms molded the curve of her ribs, surrounded her breasts, overwhelmingly gentle and insistent at once. She gasped deep in her throat, his mouth catching the sound.

"Tess," he whispered, and it seemed to give her name new meaning. He rolled her off him, laid her down carefully on the makeshift mattress pulling the quilts firmly around her again. His caring gesture only made her want him more. She fumbled with his silver belt buckle, unable to wrest it open with her shaking fingers until his big hand came over hers and they released the clasp together.

He unzipped his jeans and pulled them off, then turned over to meet her gaze with eyes almost as black as the surrounding darkness. The intensity she saw there matched the feelings tangled up inside her, and she sat up and slid her own jeans off, pulling him down under the covers with her. He supported himself on one forearm, and his huge frame radiated heat all along her body; she forgot the intense cold of the almost-winter night, conscious only of its beauty. Every time she opened her eyes he was over her, a dark shadow framed in a million flying stars. His free hand left a trail of warmth in the path it traced over her stomach and hips, a warmth that turned to burning when he touched and teased between her legs.

"Slaid." She gasped his name, wanting him inside her, feeling like if it didn't happen soon she might go up in flames, just like the meteor they'd seen earlier.

He reached for his jeans and rummaged in the pockets, brought the condom to his mouth and ripped it open with his teeth. He growled as he did it, making her laugh as he slid the condom on and rolled to lie fully over her.

His hands were braced on either side of her head, holding him up. With his weight over her, his warmth around her and inside her, she was immobilized, and she loved it. A groan of sheer pleasure vibrated through her but he didn't move, just studied her face. "I want you, Tess. Like I've never wanted anyone. I dreamed of you for two long years, and now that you're here, I don't see how I'll ever get enough of you."

He kissed her then, not letting her answer, maybe tired of hearing her protests and rationalizations about why they could never work out. She was tired of her rationalizing, too—sick of keeping sex in a sterile compartment. Under this blazing, fiery sky, she welcomed the emotions that flooded her, sensation radiating not just through her body but along the pathways of her mind, singing through her synapses until tears poured down her cheeks and she wasn't sure if she was laughing or crying.

And only then did he begin to move inside her, so slowly, making sure she felt every moment. Desire combined with all her wild emotion, and she gripped his shoulders tightly to ground herself. But it was impossible to stay grounded when he pushed himself so fiercely inside her, when her body responded with such blazing joy. When they were finished, and he buried his face in her hair, murmuring her name like a prayer, she watched the sky. There was a shower of sparks above them, and she gasped. Slaid rolled over, looking up to try to see what she had.

"I think you missed it," she said. "I think they were small, far-away meteors. It looked like sparks from fireworks."

He laughed softly. "It's the perfect opening."

"To what?" She was too languid, post sex to actually look at him.

"To say something like, 'Baby, I don't need to see fireworks when we just made plenty of our own.'"

"No!" she protested, cringing at his terrible pillow talk. And he took her hand and held it as they lay giggling, watching the sky for more glimpses of the meteors.

TESS DIDN'T KNOW when she'd been so completely content. She'd enjoyed all her favorite things tonight: Slaid, sex, chocolate and Scotch. Not to mention her new favorite thing: hot sex in a truck bed under a sky full of shooting stars. And then more sex back at her cottage in the comfortable bed. Sex with a wildness that had her gripping the iron bars of the headboard—and hoping her neighbors were heavy sleepers. She closed her eyes, and the memories of the night heated her skin in a way that had nothing to do with the hot bathwater she was immersed in.

"You okay down there?" Slaid was the world's best backrest, though it had been tricky to fit his huge body into the claw-foot tub. She was snuggled down between his thighs, the water up to her chin, letting the hot water take away the soreness of her muscles after all the insane things they'd just done.

"Mmm…" She sighed. "I'm good. Very, very good. You?"

"Never been better." His fingers massaged her scalp. "I could get used to this."

Tess yawned and refused to listen to the voices in her head that conspired to pull her out of this moment by warning her not to get used to it, that all this was temporary. She didn't want to think about that right now.

"You're sleepy."

"No, I'm fine."

"Come on. Let's get you to bed." He lifted her easily to her feet and stood up behind her, holding her steady when she swayed slightly. He stepped out of the tub and insisted on lifting her up and over the edge, wrapping her in a soft bath towel and helping her dry her hair. They brushed their teeth side by side—another first for Tess.

Slaid tucked her carefully into bed before lying down next to her and spooning her. "You want to tell me what's going on?" he said, his breath stirring her hair.

"Just so tired," she breathed, feeling sleep approaching like a peaceful, cool fog. Her voice seemed so far way, as if it was coming from someone else when she whispered, "So tired of being alone. Never felt so safe before. Ever." And then the warm darkness covered her.

CHAPTER TWENTY-TWO

SLAID WATCHED TESS ride Wendy around the corral. Devin was perched on the top rail fence giving her instructions. It was unbelievable, the way his son had taken to Tess. Despite acting tough, Devin missed having a mom. And there was something about Tess that he clicked with, some sort of understanding that they had. Maybe it stemmed from the day they'd met, when Devin had broken her fence. Slaid wasn't happy about Devin's behavior that day, but maybe it was good that his son had met Tess on his own terms, forging a bond with her before even knowing who she was. However it happened, he was grateful that his son liked the woman he'd fallen in love with.

It would take some time to get used to those words. He'd said "I love you" to one other woman—Jeannette. But they'd been together since high school. Sure, he'd had a crush on her back then, been thrilled that she'd let him put his hand on her bra, but had he really been in love? He didn't think so anymore. Not like this, at least—not like last night when he'd lain awake watching Tess sleep, making sure she was okay. Her last words haunted him... What had happened to her that she'd never felt safe before? She'd slept deeply, with a small smile on her face, until he'd kissed her goodbye in the early dawn, determined to get home before Cal's family dropped off Devin.

But he hadn't fooled his twenty-first-century son. Devin had hopped out of Cal's parents' SUV, and come straight over to where Slaid had been loading the truck with hay. "Where's Tess?" he'd asked. And when Slaid had explained with all the false innocence that he could muster that Tess was likely at home where he'd left her last night, Devin had just laughed. "Jeez, Dad," he'd said. "You don't have to pretend with me." And he'd given his dad a wink and headed toward the house, whistling merrily.

From the mouths of babes. How did his son manage to be worldlier than him most of the time?

Tess had arrived at the ranch for lunch. Slaid had grilled burgers and they'd all sat out on the patio, absorbing the meager sunshine while they ate. Devin had picked up where he'd left off last night, teasing Tess about her lack of football knowledge, which prompted them to get a football and teach Tess to throw and catch. And if Slaid had thrown in the occasional tackle, well, he was a guy, crazy about a beautiful woman—who could blame him for wanting to throw his arms around her and bring her, squealing and laughing, down to the ground once in a while?

Once they'd shown Tess where to place her fingers along the laces, how to hold her elbow up to leverage the ball, she'd lobbed it right over their heads—which had impressed Devin. But best of all was the surprised look on her face as she watched it sail away, and the hilarious jumping dance she'd done afterward.

He'd just stared at her, amazed. The icy cool Tess who'd glided into his office in her sexy power suit a few weeks ago was nowhere to be seen. And he was completely in love with this woman, her thick blond hair tossed in the wind, almost no trace of makeup on her beautiful face and her smile unguarded and ear to ear.

Finally finished cleaning the paddock, Slaid picked up the manure-laden wheelbarrow and pushed it to the gate. Not his favorite job, but he figured he'd give Devin a break from his chores since he was having such a good time with Tess.

Orlando came over and nuzzled him, hoping for a treat before Slaid left. "Later, big guy," Slaid told him, patting his neck. Orlando blew out an alfalfa-sweet horsey sigh and wandered off, clearly disgruntled.

"Slaid!" Tess was calling to him, so he latched the gate and left the wheelbarrow where it was, walking down the hillside toward her. "Look at what Devin taught me!" She gently turned Wendy and gave her a little nudge, and the mustang broke into a slow jog around the paddock.

"Push your weight into your legs," Devin called, and Slaid remembered how, not too long ago, he'd been sitting right where Devin was, calling out the same advice to his son. Pride swelled. His boy had come a long way.

Tess slowed Wendy back to a walk and looked over at Slaid, her eyes shining with a tentative pride. "What do you think?"

He smiled, trying to figure out how to put into coherent words the way he felt right now. He couldn't, so he stuck with, "It looks as if you belong up there."

He opened the gate and she rode Wendy out, dismounting stiffly while Slaid held the reins. Devin approached. "That was awesome, Tess!"

She smiled at him, and Slaid saw true affection there. "Well, I had a great teacher," she told him, and Devin beamed.

"Want to go for a ride around the ranch?" Slaid asked. "Dev, we can show her the higher pastures and a bit of the mountains."

"Sure!" Devin had a huge grin on his face.

"Why don't you saddle up Orlando and Puck and I'll grab us some food from the house?"

"I'll go with you," Tess offered.

He took her hand as they strolled up the driveway and kept it when they went inside. It wasn't until he'd decided what sandwich makings to pull out of his fridge that he was willing to let go.

MAYBE IT WAS being with Devin and Slaid and listening to their good-natured, teasing rapport. Maybe it was the bright autumn sunshine, or that the world looked different from the back of a beautiful mustang like Wendy. Whatever it was, Tess saw the mountains differently today. Everything looked brighter, more cheerful, that it had before. The peaks still looked majestic, but not as forbidding as they once had. The creeks they crossed as they went higher up were more of a trickle now at the end of the dry season, but Tess easily imagined the way they'd roll and tumble with snowmelt in the spring. Then Slaid paused in the woods and they watched in silence as the aspen leaves fell around them, drifting like golden confetti through the forest.

The aspen eventually gave way to pines that grew with impressive tenacity through the granite slabs of the mountainside, and it was up there, with a view of the valley below, that they stopped and ate their sandwiches while the horses snacked in a small meadow of sparse grass on the other side of the trail.

Slaid and Devin pointed out various landmarks to her while they ate, and when it was time to head back to the ranch, Tess was filled with genuine regret. She wanted more time up in the mountains.

She wanted to follow the trail they'd been on as it wound higher. Devin told her the path eventually led to a lake with a great camping spot that he and his dad visited often in the summer. Tess tried to imagine camping, actually cooking, sleeping, *living* outside, but it boggled her imagination. Perhaps a quick picnic on a boulder was as rustic as she got, but still, the idea intrigued her *new* more adventurous self.

Back at the ranch, Slaid and Devin got started on chores, leaving Tess to try her hand at cooking dinner. She walked around, opening and closing cupboards with increasing despair. And then she remembered her new goal—to no longer pretend she was okay on her own, but instead reach out to her friends when she needed help. And fortunately, one of those friends was married to a fabulous chef.

She called Jenna and enjoyed a few minutes of small talk, and then Sandro got on the phone. "You mean, you've never cooked anything before?" he asked, sounding slightly horrified.

"Well, I've made toast. Does that count?"

"No. Okay, I'm going to walk you through a basic pasta with vegetables. Ready?"

She told him what ingredients she had and he told her what to do with them, and by the time Slaid and Devin got back she was a regular Julia Child, with the table set and a large bowl of steaming pasta in the middle.

"You *are* a domestic goddess!" Slaid exclaimed.

"Don't get your hopes up. I was merely the hands. Sandro, via the telephone, was the brains behind this meal."

"Well, then, you have the right kind of friends, which is just as important as domestic skills, if not more so," Slaid said. "Come on, Devin, let's get changed and washed so we can eat this Sandro-Tess creation."

She was playing housewife for a night, and it was kind of fun.

Apparently Slaid had similar feelings. They'd finished their meal and cleared the table, Devin had gone off to wrestle with his essay. They'd loaded the dishwasher and had started on the pots and pans, with Slaid washing and Tess drying, when he leaned over and kissed her. "I could get used to this. It feels like family."

"It's nice," Tess answered, walking away to set the bowl she'd dried on the sideboard in the dining room. She didn't want to talk about this. Didn't want to think about how obviously Slaid wanted a family—how he deserved a family—and how she couldn't give it to him. But she loved him, and she didn't want to think of him having a family with someone else, either—

She froze in the doorway. She *loved* him.

"Tess..." Slaid glanced over. He must have seen something in her expression, shock, maybe? Because he walked to the doorway and took the dish towel from her hands and kissed her gently on the mouth. She felt it all over her skin. She was afraid he might voice what she was feeling—she wasn't ready for that.

"Tess, I…"

"Can't we just enjoy this… What we have now?"

"I just…"

She kissed him back then. Threw her arms around his neck and went on tiptoe to reach his mouth and bring him down to her, to show him all the unwanted emotion that was welling up inside her. And to keep him from saying anything that might break them apart when they'd only just come together.

When the kiss ended slowly, lingeringly, she whispered, "*That's* what I want. Can't we just *be*? Like that?"

He hesitated, pulled her in close, and she felt him take a deep breath. "Yeah. We can. For now."

AFTER DEVIN WAS in bed, Tess and Slaid curled up on the couch, watching the fire. It was cozy and perfect as Tess lay against his broad chest, listening to his heart thumping, so steady and reassuring. She yawned and sat up. "I should leave, Slaid, or I'll be too sleepy to go home."

"Stay," he murmured, pulling her back down to him.

She turned to look at him and he grinned at her, slow and lazy and suggesting all kinds of possibilities.

"Is that okay? For Devin?"

"I don't know. At least stay for a while."

He picked her up as if she weighed nothing and carried her to his bedroom. She buried her face in his neck, inhaling his spicy, masculine scent, and with that her last speck of hesitation vanished. She kissed him and he set her on the bed, locked the bedroom door and turned on a small lamp on his dresser. The room became a soothing mosaic of light and shadow.

He pulled off his T-shirt, and Tess drank in the sight of him. The sculpted muscles, the bulk of his chest, his shoulders, arms, and then she couldn't wait. She got up, walked over and ran her hands across his skin. He shivered slightly, but smiled at her, letting her explore his upper body with her hands, and then her mouth.

When he pulled her sweater over her head, it was his turn to look, and he did, surveying her deep blue lace bra, trailing his hands down her arms, along her waist. He ran his fingers under her breasts, around their full curve, and then his mouth came down on hers. She reached her arms around his neck, pulling herself as close as she could.

"You're incredible," she said, so intent on holding him that she barely noticed when he walked her gently backward to his bed. Her entire focus was on her own need to be close to him, to better learn the shape and feel of him.

When he lay her back on the bed, she pulled

away so she could touch him, giving herself room to trace the bulk of his muscles and the lines that defined them, down his chest, over his arms. For once she wasn't racing to fulfill all the desire inside. She wanted to know him, to memorize the way his biceps angled down to his elbow, the way the dusting of hair on his chest tickled.

She loved him. Combined with all her physical cravings was a deep, emotional desire to be as close to this kind and generous man as possible. She was different and everything felt different—newborn and fresh.

She met his eyes. He'd been watching her touch him with a slightly feral curl to his lip, and now he reached out to take her hand and bring her up for a kiss. "I need you, Tess," he whispered against her mouth, and the words went straight down her spine. He slid her jeans off and came over her on the bed. And she realized that *there* was the danger in all this—that desire would turn to need and it wouldn't be possible to face the goodbye that was waiting for them right around the corner.

And then he was touching her and the worry was buried in the avalanche of feelings he sent tumbling through her, and all she could do was cling to him, trusting that there'd be a way to pick up the pieces and glue her back together when she shattered.

They dozed off, and when Tess woke up the lamp was still on. She dressed quietly, not wanting to wake Slaid, and wanting to be gone before Devin awoke. Closing the house door as silently as possible behind her, she walked through freezing air and pitch-black darkness to her Jeep.

The first snowflakes hit the windshield as she turned around in the driveway, and she opened her window for a moment to let them in. When she'd arrived in Benson she'd hoped to get back home before the first snowfall. But now she was looking forward to seeing the mountains powdered white.

WHEN SLAID WOKE up and found Tess gone his first thought was *Not again*. The early-morning light was streaming dim and gray through the window, and when he looked outside the world was white with a few inches of snow—and then he was worried. He called her cell phone, relieved to hear her very sleepy voice say, "Hi," and, "I'm fine, thank you very much." He was pretty sure she'd nearly fallen back asleep by the time she'd hung up, and he took some masculine pride in that. He'd worn her out—not an easy feat with someone as driven as Tess.

He went out into the snow, loving the look of the newly white world, and did the chores. He checked the horses over as he fed them, drove hay out to the cattle, glad he'd brought them in close over the past few days. Then he loaded the truck with more hay to bring to the pastures he leased across the valley before going back inside.

Devin stumbled out for toast and eggs.

"How come Tess didn't stay the night?" he asked.

Slaid almost dropped the orange juice he was pouring. "Because it's important to make sure you really know someone well before you have them stay the night."

Devin took the glass Slaid offered. "Thanks."

Slaid had a blissful moment where he thought his lame explanation had worked, and then Devin said, "Dad, just let her stay here. You guys are a total couple. And it's a lot safer than making her drive home in the middle of a snowy night."

Slaid kept himself busy scrambling eggs as he absorbed Devin's words. He'd never thought he'd be taking advice from his barely teenage son.

"Well, I don't ever want to make you uncomfortable, Dev."

"I like her, Dad." Devin rolled his eyes, exasperated with having to state the obvious. "She's totally cool and it's more fun when she's around."

He didn't know whether to be happy or sad at those words. He worked hard to make things fun for his son. "Well, thanks for telling me. But if you ever feel uncomfortable, you just let me know."

"Dad. I'm not a little kid anymore! It's fine."

Slaid figured that was the equivalent of having a fourteen-year-old's blessing. "Well, then, would it be okay if I brought her back here today?"

"Yeah. She said she'd help me with my essay anyway."

His kid had plans with Tess that he didn't even

know about? And it occurred to him that this all felt right, that he and Devin and Tess were quickly becoming a family. But right on the heels of that thought came the understanding that he had an impossible task in front of him. He needed to find a way for Tess to see that, too.

CHAPTER TWENTY-THREE

"I LOVE YOU." Slaid figured he'd tell Tess right away, before she could protest. "I'm in love with you and I want to be with you."

She'd just stepped out of her Jeep, and he reached behind her to shut the door, hoping that would prevent her from driving off in a panic. He leaned down and kissed her startled lips. She was still for moment, but then kissed him back, her soft lips making him want so much more. But he couldn't have more. It was the middle of the afternoon and Devin was probably somewhere nearby. A snowball hit Slaid in the back, confirming his suspicions.

"Hi, Tess!" his son called as another snowball sailed over, landing a couple feet away.

"So that's how it's gonna be?" Slaid asked, setting Tess aside and reaching for the snowball. He packed it bigger and sent it back, dodging the one Devin sent winging by his ear.

"Snowball fight!" his son hollered, and Tess laughed. Out of the corner of his eye he saw her making a ball of her own to toss at his son.

He had a brief moment of satisfaction that she'd

sided with him before she landed one on his collar, sending snow down his shirt.

He came at her laughing, tossing snow as fast as he could. And then Devin was at her side, and they were a team, showering him with snowballs and driving him back until he had to take shelter behind Tess's Jeep, lobbing his frosty ammo over the hood and then ducking down as a rain of snowballs pelted him.

Finally he admitted defeat and made a dash for the house with them on his heels.

"Truce!" he called at the door. "No snowballs in the house!"

"Hot chocolate?" Devin asked hopefully.

"If you make it," Slaid told him.

"I'm on it." Devin kicked off his boots and went eagerly into the kitchen. Tess and Slaid removed their coats and boots more slowly.

"So you're just gonna spring that on me, huh?" she finally asked.

"You mean that I'm in love with you?"

"Yeah, that."

"Yep. I guess I am."

She was silent and he waited a few beats more for the words *I love you, too.* It didn't happen. Sitting next to her on the bench in the mudroom to take off his boots, he watched her out of the corner of his eye as she studied his profile. When he caught her smiling quietly to herself, he knew. She might not be ready to say it, but she felt it. He knew she did.

DEVIN WAS SHOWING Tess how to feed the cows. The problem was, she was scared of cows, so she kept jumping whenever they moved suddenly. But Devin was a great teacher. He had her leading a cow by a halter, throwing the hay into their mangers, and with his encouragement, she even got up the nerve to pet a couple of them.

"I'm amazed."

She hadn't heard Slaid come into the barn, but he was right behind them, laughing at her. "Almost speechless."

"Almost?" she teased him.

"Well, yeah, it's a rare occasion that I have no words, but this might be one of them. I can safely say that when you showed up in Benson, I never thought I'd see you in my barn, looking after my cattle. And it looks like you haven't smacked any of them with your scarf."

Tess laughed, glancing down at where the eggplant wool wrapped around her neck, cow-slobber free. "It's all Devin. He's a good teacher." She glanced at the boy and saw the grin on his face as he coiled up the rope they'd been using. "Speaking of teaching," she continued, "as soon as we're done here, we're going inside. It's homework time."

Devin looked at his dad as if he couldn't believe his luck. "Tess is helping me with my essay."

Slaid shot her a look of admiration and astonishment. "Normally Devin has to be dragged kicking and screaming to his homework. Tess, you truly are the queen of persuasion."

"Which is why I'm helping him. He has to write a persuasive essay," she explained. "I told him he was looking at one of the greatest persuasive writers in history. It *is* my job after all."

"Yes, and your ability to do it scares me." He was smiling, but she heard the serious note in his voice.

They hadn't talked about the windmills in days, but the conflict hung in the air between them. Tess had been working hard to get ready for the final public hearing and she suspected Slaid was, too. She'd noticed the solar panels on his barn were finished and she'd seen several others going up on homes and businesses. She was planning on taking a drive outside of town later today to get a sense of how much success he was having. She wanted to know where he was getting the funding, but now that they were dating, everything felt more complicated. She wasn't sure what she could ask without prying.

"And we're having hot chocolate while we write it," Devin added.

Slaid nodded, and winked at Tess. "Ah, now I understand the enthusiasm. You two get started. I'll come in a minute and make it for you. I could use a cup of coffee."

Tess smiled. She well knew why he was tired today. Memories of last night came back… She shivered and glanced over, seeing the heat in Slaid's gaze.

"Come on, Devin," she said. "Time to kiss your cows good-night."

"Ew!" Devin retorted. "That's gross!"

SLAID LISTENED TO their good-natured banter as they walked off toward the house together, his heart lighter, his spirit happier than he could remember. It made him realize just how much he wanted Tess in his life, forever. And it wasn't just that he loved her. Tess already felt like more of a partner than Jeannette ever had. And every piece of time and effort she gave to Devin went straight to his heart. How had he lived with his ex-wife for so many years and not even realized she'd had a foot out the door the entire time?

He walked outside and grabbed the wheelbarrow he'd loaded earlier and started down the drive to his compost area. Glancing over his shoulder, he saw Tess and Devin almost at the patio, tossing the football between them now as they walked.

He looked up at the solar panels he'd had installed on his barn roof last week. She hadn't mentioned them since the installation…but *he* needed to. They were becoming a team, and he couldn't let her walk into the public hearing later this week to present all the benefits of wind power without a heads-up that it was probably going to be pretty chaotic.

In the past couple days, the protest movement had grown so fast that he'd been unable to keep up with it. With the way information spread so quickly on social media, it was impossible to know how many people were planning on attending, but Tess deserved a forewarning that a lot of extra people would be rolling into town. And he was pretty sure the news cameras would follow.

He could at least try to make sure she wasn't totally blindsided.

And maybe if he did, she could see that he was truly on her side, and she'd trust what was growing between them. And if he did things well enough, he'd get her to stay in Benson, with him, where he was certain that she truly belonged.

TESS WAS PRETTY sure she was having the best day of her life. It was fun to spend time outdoors on his ranch laughing and joking with Slaid and Devin. And there was snow. Which she thought she'd hate, but it actually made the world very pretty, and somehow warmer. Even though it was cold.

And then there was Devin. What a cool kid. She had no idea kids could be like him. He didn't even seem to mind a bit that she was dating his dad.

He was funny and sweet, with a little teenage-boy swagger to boot.

And Slaid. His calm, humorous way of being, and the way he just got things done. The way he organized sweet dates for her and the way his hands felt on her skin when…

Glancing at Devin, who was tapping his pencil and biting his lip as he tried to think of a topic sentence for his essay, she decided not to think about sex with his dad right now.

"I've got my topic," Devin announced. Tess had told him he had to come up with something he thought should happen in the world, a point he wanted to prove to someone else.

"Okay, good," Tess said, jolting back to reality. "Now try to say it in one sentence."

He thought for a moment. "Okay… One sentence… Here goes. I think kids who are adopted shouldn't have to wait until they're eighteen to find their birthparents."

Tess wondered what would happen if she vomited on the table. Would she scar Devin for life?

"I'll be right back," she told him. "Hold that thought." She went into the kitchen, filled a glass with water, took a few gulps and tried to reason with herself. Devin was adopted; it made perfect sense that he'd feel this way. It wasn't personal; it wasn't about her.

She went back to the table with her water, hopefully hiding her discomfort a little better. She sat next to him. "Great topic! Now think of three main reasons why you think this should happen. Good, strong reasons."

She stared out the big windows while Devin

tapped his pencil for what felt like forever. It seemed as though he might be stuck.

"How about you say them out loud first," Tess suggested. "It helps you figure out if they sound forceful enough." She didn't want to hear them, but she'd promised Devin she'd help him. And from the incredulous look she'd seen on Slaid's face, it seemed as though his son didn't ask for help that often.

"Number one. Don't laugh..." Devin looked at her uncertainly.

"I won't." Cry maybe, run out of the room screaming, but she could definitely promise no laughter.

"Kids would feel happier and more confident knowing *all* their parents." He looked at Tess as if he expected her to argue, but she just said, "Okay, go on."

"Number two. Kids can understand more complicated stuff than their parents think they can. Like they can understand that someone has problems and can't be their parent, or that someone who adopts them is their *real* parent."

"And number three?" Tess asked softly.

"If kids know their birth parents and can understand them, they'd be less likely to wonder why their parents gave them up, like if they did something wrong that made their parents not want to be their parents anymore."

Tess took deep breaths and sipped her water. *This*

isn't about you, she reminded herself. But it was hard not to imagine Adam having the same questions about her.

She looked up, and Devin was watching her cautiously, waiting to hear what she thought of his essay idea. "I hope you know that *you* didn't do anything wrong. With your mom *or* your birth mother," she finally offered quietly.

He flushed. "My dad tells me that all the time. And it's as if I know it in my brain but I don't *totally* know it. And then when my mom left, well, I guess I just felt like it had to be me, if it was happening a second time."

Tess was quiet for a minute. Feeling honored that he'd chosen to talk to her about something so personal, and feeling heartbroken, as well. Did her son secretly wonder if he'd been placed for adoption because he was flawed? He'd been such a perfect baby. It was Tess, sixteen, alone and terrified, who'd been flawed.

"Those are strong reasons. Great work. Now write down each reason on your paper and put a few lines underneath it. On those blank lines, list facts to support your arguments. For example, in what ways, exactly, would knowing their birth parents make kids more confident?"

"That's easy," said Devin. "If they don't know them, it makes them sad, and then they worry about it instead of thinking about normal kid stuff."

"Write that down and try to think of a couple

more," Tess instructed, digging her nails into her clenched hands under the table. A panicky feeling was forming in her chest, fluttering there. Had Adam had a hard time thinking about "normal kid stuff" because of her?

TESS LOOKED AT Devin, his pencil scratching across the page, his tongue caught in the corner of his mouth as he concentrated. And it occurred to her that she'd made a terrible mistake coming here today. She was selfish. That was what it came down to. She'd enjoyed bonding Devin, feeling as if they had this special relationship. She'd liked playing in the snow and pretending to be a family. But that was all she was doing: pretending. She'd go back to her life in San Francisco. And Devin would still be here, wondering why she'd left. And then she'd just be one more woman he'd cared about who'd let him down.

It was hard to breathe. Hard to move, but she had to get away.

"Devin, I think you've got this. Will you be okay? I think I need to get home."

"Yeah, I think I'm okay. Are you sure you can't stay?"

"I need to get ready for the work tomorrow, and you have to finish this and get ready for school. But thanks for a great weekend. I loved it."

"See you later, Tess."

"Yeah." A lump grew in the back of her throat

and she tried to swallow it down as she went for her coat.

Slaid caught up with her just as she got to her car. "Tess, hang on, what happened?"

"Oh, there you are." She tried to sound casual. "I couldn't find you and I need to get home."

"I thought you were staying for dinner. Maybe even longer?"

"Well, Devin's all set and I know it's a school night…"

"Did something happen between you and Devin? Did he lose his temper?"

Tears sprang up and welled over before she could stop them. "No! Devin is amazing… He's wonderful." She couldn't stop the flood now that it had started. She buried her face in her hands as sobs racked her body. And she knew it wasn't just Devin she was crying for.

"Tess." Slaid was by her side in an instant, wrapping his arms around her, holding her while she sobbed. "Tell me what's wrong so I can help," he pleaded.

She couldn't believe she was crying. Anger at herself for losing control helped to stop the sobs, but her words still came out shakily. "I had a baby, Slaid. I gave him up for adoption. I was sixteen. So he's…he's about Devin's age."

"Oh, Tess…" Slaid cradled her tenderly. "I am so sorry."

"I know I did the right thing for him. But…I

never kept in touch. His adoptive parents even asked me to. I said no. And now I wonder if..." Another sob interrupted her words.

"If he's having questions like Devin?"

"I figured I was doing everyone a favor by just moving on."

He stepped back so there was distance between them. She was cold where his arms had been. "And there's more, Slaid. I lied to everyone. You, Samantha, Jenna, everyone. I'm not from New England. I never bobbed for apples. I grew up in the projects of Detroit. My parents did drugs. They hit me, locked me up... Left me... I went into foster care when I was seven. No one adopted me, so I never got out of the system."

"Tess..."

But now that she'd started, she had to finish. "I had a crazy temper. I got kicked out of high schools." Slaid just stared at her, so she went on. "My name was Theresa Cooper."

"Wait, Tess isn't your name?"

"I changed my name legally to Tess Cole when I was eighteen. I wanted a new start, to get an education, to make something of myself."

"I don't get it. You've been lying about all this stuff, all this time? To your friends? To me?"

She sighed heavily. "Yes."

"Do I even know you?" His brows were drawn together in a scowl. He looked like a stranger.

"More than anyone else ever has." It sounded lame, but it was all she could offer.

Slaid looked away, out over the ranch. He was slipping away from her. She could see it. "I've never lied to hurt anyone else, Slaid. Just to protect myself."

He didn't answer, and she knew there was nothing more she could say. He knew it all now. Tess looked around at his ranch, too. Suddenly the warmth and beauty she'd seen in the snowy day was gone. It all just looked bleak.

Finally Slaid spoke. "Tess, I admire you, do you understand? I truly do. I said I love you and I meant it. But the way that you've lied, and stayed away from your son... Well, I just have to think..."

And there it was. The exact thing she'd always known would happen if she told anyone the truth. Rejection. "I'd better get going. We both have a busy week."

"I'm sorry. I have to think of Devin, too. It might be hard for him to learn about your son. We live with the aftermath of choices like yours every day."

"I get it." She couldn't hear any more. No matter how kindly he phrased it, it was judgment.

"I'll call you?"

"Sure." He wouldn't. She could tell. She leaned in and gave him one last hug, took a shuddering breath to inhale the scent of him she'd come to need like oxygen and quickly got inside the Jeep. She put the key in the ignition with shaking hands, fighting hard not to cry again. She turned the car around and headed down the snow-covered driveway.

She followed her own tracks from when she'd arrived, when she'd been feeling so happy and hopeful, only hours before. She glanced in the rear-view mirror and saw Slaid standing where she'd left him, watching her go. Everything hurt: her heart, her head, her raw emotions. This was why she'd avoided love. Because she didn't have the strength to endure losing the person she loved the most—again.

CHAPTER TWENTY-FOUR

IT WAS STRANGE how, even when you were sad and disappointed and angry at the world, you still had to go buy groceries. Tess cruised the street in front of the Blue Water Mercantile, looking for parking. For some reason the lot was full and there were even cars parked down the street. She'd chosen this shop instead of her usual Main Street Market because the Blue Water was generally pretty empty. It was on the edge of town, out by the fairgrounds, and the perfect spot for not running into anyone—especially Slaid. But oddly, it was packed today.

Tess finally maneuvered the Jeep into a parking spot on a side street and walked around the corner to the store. Inside she grabbed one of the last baskets and wandered the aisles, dodging fellow shoppers to grab milk, bread and a few other staples.

She had to wait in a long line to pay. When it was her turn, she asked the man behind the counter, "So who are all these people?"

"I think they're all here for the protest tomorrow," the cashier said. "It's crazy how many people turned up. The city even converted the fairgrounds into campsites since we've got so many folks visiting town right now."

"Wait," Tess said, dread pooling in her stomach. "What protest?"

"Well, they're having that big public hearing on the windmills tomorrow afternoon. And most folks around here don't want them. So there's a march and a rally. A bunch of environmental groups got involved and brought all these people out here. It should be quite an event. And good for my business, too."

"I'll bet," Tess said weakly. She paid her money and practically ran to her Jeep. Once inside, she grabbed her phone and dialed, grateful that Ed answered on the second ring. "It's Tess," she told him. "Tomorrow's the public hearing and I have a big problem."

SLAID HAD HIS feet up on his desk when she got to his office, and for a moment Tess felt a touch of déjà vu. Just a few weeks ago, she'd walked in and seen him sitting just like this. She remembered how handsome she'd thought he was, and how strangely familiar. It felt like years, not weeks, had passed since that day.

He looked up as she stepped through the door. Taking his feet off his desk, he set down the file he was reading and stood up, looking ill at ease for the first time she could remember. "Tess." His voice was low and quiet. "Hello."

"Why didn't you tell me?" she asked.

"Tell you what?"

"About the march and the protest and the fact that this town is flooded with environmental activists and news cameras."

"I meant to, Tess. The other day. But then you told me all that stuff about your past and…I guess I forgot."

"And you didn't remember to tell me afterward?"

He ran a hand wearily over his jaw and Tess noticed the shadows under his eyes. The stubble on his normally clean-shaven chin. She wasn't the only one having a hard time right now. "There's been a lot going on. Here and at home."

"Is Devin okay?"

"He's fine."

The two-word answer said it all—she was no longer privy to the details of their everyday lives. Her chest felt heavy. She tilted her chin up higher and met his eyes.

"I would have appreciated a heads-up. I spotted at least three different television news trucks parked near the hotel."

"Yeah, well, the more I think about it, the more I realize that I would have appreciated you telling me a few things, too. I know you think I'm old fashioned, but honesty isn't just a small-town value."

"Now you're mixing the personal with the professional. We said we wouldn't."

"Seems to me as if you've a lot to learn about the personal, Tess."

That was it. She could take the blame for some things, but not this. "And I warned you about that from the very beginning. I told you I didn't want to get involved, that I didn't do relationships, but you pushed and pushed at me to date. To do what *you* wanted, to be who *you* wanted me to be. And I finally did. And you know what I learned? That I was right all along. When you let people really know you, they can really hurt you. So you can sit there at your mayor's desk and judge me all you want, but I would recommend you take a look at yourself, too. Because from where I'm standing, your way isn't so great after all!"

She spun on her heel and marched out, willing herself not to cry, not to waste one more tear on Slaid Jacobs, the mayor of Self-Righteousville.

"Tess, wait."

She stopped and whirled to face him. "Don't try to talk me into coming back."

He looked even more uncomfortable, if that was possible. "I wasn't going to."

She could feel her cheeks get hot. "Well, what is it, then?" she said sharply.

"We're at ninety-five percent solar."

She hadn't thought she could feel any worse. She'd been wrong. "You're kidding. How did you do that?"

"We got funding."

"But you told me you were having trouble finding investors. That you couldn't find a company to give you a discount."

"We were. But we eventually got a company to work with us, once we got our money together."

And then she knew what he was trying to say. "Let me guess. It's privately funded?"

He nodded.

"Jack and Samantha?"

"Yes. I'm sorry you found out about the protesters by chance. I wouldn't want you to find out about the funding the same way."

"Thanks," she said bitterly. She turned to go, despair pitting her stomach, making her legs feel heavy as she dragged her defeated self down the hall. Not only had Slaid forgotten to mention the huge public protest, but her best friend had neglected to tell her that she and her husband were personally funding the opposition's plan.

How ironic that the two people who'd pushed her to change, who had convinced her to open her heart to let love in, had stomped on it within days. Tess realized she didn't care about windmills anymore. She didn't care about winning. All she wanted to do was get out of Benson as fast as possible.

CHAPTER TWENTY-FIVE

TESS SAT IN her car outside her cottage, willing herself to turn the ignition and get started. Her Jeep was packed and the cottage was closed up.

She huddled in her teal parka, staring straight ahead down the street toward the football field where she'd had such an incredible date with Slaid. Where she'd felt welcomed so warmly by the people of Benson. Now she knew they'd given her such a warm welcome because they didn't perceive her as a threat. By that time they'd had their secret meetings, they'd all signed up for solar panels and called in the environmental activists. By then, everyone had known she was here representing a project that was doomed. Everyone had known but her.

Had they felt sorry for her? Laughed at her? Had Slaid?

Her new understanding of what Slaid and his city council had planned shed a light on so many puzzling events here in Benson. Why people had been so well behaved and asked so few questions at her informational meetings, for one. She'd egotistically thought that it was due to her thorough presentation and persuasive public-speaking skills. Really, they'd just shown up out of idle curiosity. To check out the woman who was dating the mayor while he worked behind her back to make sure she failed spectacularly. They didn't have any questions because they already knew the most important answer—there was no way a wind farm would be sited anywhere near Benson.

Slaid should be thanking her. The wind farm had made him famous. He'd been on every California news channel last night. They'd dubbed him the sunshine mayor, the mayor of Solar City. Not that Benson was a city, but it sounded better than Solar Backwater. Solar Cow Town. Solar microscopic speck on the map that she would never visit again.

So why wasn't she leaving? She reached to turn on the ignition, but her hand dropped back in her lap. She was still too shaken up to drive.

Ed should have airlifted her out of here before that town meeting last night. She'd asked him to, but with his customary lack of imagination he'd told her that the meeting couldn't possibly go that badly.

Ha.

It really hadn't been much of a meeting. Just chaos. A parade of activists had marched from the proposed wind farm site to the town hall, complete with enormous mangled-bird puppets reminding everyone of the danger that windmills posed to the animals. They had signs saying No Way LA, and

You Got Our Water, Hands Off Our Wind. Even Slaid had gotten in the spirit. The literature-loving mayor was mounted on Puck and dressed as Don Quixote, the character from Cervantes's novel who famously attacked windmills. Puck pranced around while Slaid waved a wooden spear, chasing after a large cardboard windmill built on the back of Betty and Jed's truck. A teenager, not Devin, thankfully, followed him on a smaller horse—the perfect Sancho Panza.

It was a joke to all of them. An outrageous victory parade because they knew they'd won… They had the media, every major environmental group and logic on their side. How could the BLM and Renewable Reliance put windmills around a town that generated its own power?

Ed had called her about five minutes after the meeting was supposed to start, while she was standing in the city council chambers looking helplessly out over the sea of people, all waving signs and singing "We Shall Overcome." He told her Renewable Reliance had canceled the contract with their PR firm. And they were canceling their lease with the BLM. They were giving up on the wind project in Benson.

Tess had left the city council chambers by a back door and returned to her cottage to pack. A couple hours later, Slaid had called—she'd hung up on him.

All evening she'd been inundated with calls from

the media, requests for interviews from the many reporters who'd shown up in Benson to cover the rally. She'd turned off her phone; she had nothing to say. The image of her pale face up in front of the crowd in the council chambers, trying futilely to call everyone to order, played over and over on the news, so she'd turned off the TV, as well.

She'd never felt like such a failure. She'd come to this town so confident, her biggest worry how to endure the minutes until she could push the project through and head back home to San Francisco. Instead she'd lost control of the project and failed at love.

The sky was getting lighter. She took a deep breath and started the engine. Thankfully, Benson was such a small town that it took only a few moments of driving before it disappeared from her rearview mirror.

SHE'D EXPECTED ED to be mad, but she'd never thought he'd fire her. Except he didn't call it that. He'd suggested they "part ways, professionally" and promised a good recommendation, and to never let on that he'd asked her to leave.

Tess stared around her quiet apartment, remembering his words yesterday—a jumble of mixed metaphors. He said she'd gotten distracted, missed the clues, fumbled the pass, taken her eye off the ball.

Somehow he'd heard about her relationship with

Slaid. Now that he was the famous sunshine mayor, video footage had appeared on the internet of them kissing at Devin's game. Their relationship had become news fodder. The sunshine mayor had not only scored a victory for his town, he'd scored with his opponent, as well.

As words like *unprofessional* and *incompetent* rolled off his tongue, Ed had toyed with the paperwork on his desk—already prepared. Her firing was a done deal before she'd even set foot back in the office.

Maybe it was time for a change. She'd look for a job with a public relations firm that dealt only with clients in nice cities with good hotels. No small-town energy projects ever again. They were far too dangerous for her career and her heart.

The truth was, she might be furious at Slaid, but she missed him. She missed Devin, and she even missed that funny little shabby-chic cottage. She missed Wendy the mustang and Slaid's ranch and— she couldn't believe she was admitting this—the silent and majestic beauty of the mountains.

She looked around her apartment, clutching a cup of tea that she'd considered dosing with a dollop of Scotch. But even she had rules against drinking first thing in the morning.

Everything about her apartment looked the same as always, but it felt different. As if something homey and alive was missing. Tess studied the sleek, modern furnishings she'd always loved.

Shiny surfaces, no clutter, everything efficient and sculptural. An image of Slaid's living room pieced itself together in her tired mind. The rustic, faded pillows. The bulletin board in his dining room covered in photos and football schedules. His house was modern, too, but it looked as if people actually lived there.

Suppressing the tears that came way too quickly these days, Tess stood abruptly and pulled her purse and coat out of the closet. She might not be able to fix her heart, but she *could* redecorate.

EIGHT HOURS OF shopping in Union Square hadn't taken the hurt feelings away—it should have. Tess held firm beliefs in the powers of retail therapy. But her shopping bags lay empty on her apartment floor, her newly purchased throw pillows, vases, and knickknacks were distributed and her home still felt empty. She flopped on her sofa and picked up one of her new pillows, hugging it to her stomach, trying to relieve the turmoil inside.

Outside her huge windows was the view that made the elevator ride to her thirtieth-floor apartment worthwhile. An enormous cargo ship was going under the Bay Bridge, making its slow and steady way through the bay toward the ocean, with Treasure Island rising just behind it. It was gorgeous, and yet she didn't feel her usual mix of pride and excitement at the view she was able to afford.

She wished her thoughts would just behave, but

ever since she'd left Benson, she realized just how
closed-off and shallow her life was. She'd built up
a material fortress around herself. This expensive
apartment, her chic furniture, her perfect ward-
robe, had provided her with comfort before. But
now, sitting here alone, without Slaid and Devin,
they didn't mean much.

And it occurred to her that she'd been hiding in
this apartment, staring at this view, for years now.
Hiding while other people made new friends, fell
in love, got married, had kids. Hiding while her
own child grew up somewhere else, possibly wondering why she had never made contact.

Tess stood up, went to her bedroom and reached
under the bed. She had to stretch as far as she
could, but she managed to reach the box she was
looking for. She stayed where she was on the floor
and opened it up.

Inside was a photo, faded and battered, of her
sixteen-year-old self in a hospital gown, holding
her newborn baby with panic in her eyes. The social worker had snapped it all those years ago. Tess
stared at the photo, tears thickening. With blurry
vision she groped in the box until she found the key.

She walked back into her hallway and pulled on
her coat again, putting the key in the pocket. She
grabbed the huge tote bag she used for groceries
and left before she could think too much about
where she was going. But she knew in her heart that
this was the real errand she needed to run today.

The real place she needed to go, that just might have the power to fix what shopping could not.

THE POST OFFICE was dark at this time of day. It was past business hours. But the lobby was open and Tess walked the endless rows of mailboxes, looking for hers.

The nice couple who'd adopted her son had handed her the key to the mailbox here fourteen years ago, promising they'd keep the box open for her until Adam turned eighteen. She'd kept the key hidden, never checked the PO Box once in all these years. She just didn't have the courage to know the boy she'd given birth to, or the family who'd made him their own.

Her first thought, when she found her mailbox, was that it was big. It was on the bottom row and was about the size of a file cabinet drawer. She knelt down and somehow got the key in with her shaking fingers. The moment the door opened, letters tumbled out, spilling onto the floor in a giant pile of unopened opportunities.

She sat there, loading them slowly into her tote bag, tears pouring down her face—fourteen years' worth of tears, soaking her cheeks. As she fumbled through her purse for a tissue, a big hand came down and offered her one. She glanced up into the kindly face of the security guard and mumbled a snuffly thank-you as she took it from him.

"Is there anyone you can call, ma'am?" he asked.

Tess blindly nodded and groped for her phone. She opened it and brought her contacts up to the screen, scrolling through without thinking, searching frantically for Jenna's number.

CHAPTER TWENTY-SIX

"So all these years, you've never told us any of this." Jenna sat down next to Tess on the couch and put an arm around her shoulders.

It was a statement, more than a question, but Tess answered, "Yes." She leaned her head on Jenna's shoulder, feeling completely wrung out and relieved. "Thank you for taking care of me all night."

"I'm just glad you let me. I can't believe you've kept this stuff inside all these years. I wish I'd known what you were dealing with."

"Well, I think that's just it. I haven't been dealing with it." Tess stared out at the view, the midday sun lighting up the bay.

Samantha took her hand and squeezed it. She'd arrived about half an hour ago, early enough in the day to prepare for her baby shower tomorrow. They'd planned to spend today shopping and decorating, but so far all they'd done was sit on Tess's couch while an anxious Jenna tried to explain why Tess was such a wreck.

"Tess, I'm so sorry if I have anything to do with all of this."

"You mean me falling apart?"

"Jack and I funded a lot of the solar panels."

"I know," Tess said. "Slaid told me."

"We didn't know what else to do. It seemed as if Renewable Reliance was using their connections to block us at every step. And I was afraid to tell you."

"It's okay." Tess could hear the distress in Samantha's voice. "I mean, I was hurt when I found out, but now I get it. It's your town. And now I'm glad you did what you had to do to preserve it. I was just working for a company that ended up firing me anyway."

"They're idiots. They should be giving you a medal for how hard you worked for them." Samantha paused, then reached out and took hold of Tess's hand. "Okay, so I'm trying to catch up on everything else," she said gently. "Jenna told me over the phone that you went to the post office last night to get letters that had been piling up for the past fourteen years? From the adoptive parents of a baby you had when you were sixteen?"

"Yup." Tess sighed, strangely grateful that the information was finally out there.

"And then you called Jenna," Samantha continued. "And she brought you home and you cried all night."

"And slept late," Jenna added.

"And ate donuts," Tess said, feeling guilty about the calories already.

"I've never ever seen you this upset," Samantha said. "Do you want to tell us more about what's going on?"

"I told Slaid, and now he hates me."

"Well, then, he's an idiot, too, and I'm sorry I encouraged you to date him." Samantha said. "I could never hate you, Tess."

"Me, neither," Jenna said. "Unless… You're not a murderer or anything, right?"

Tess giggled, just like Jenna had intended. And then she told them. Haltingly at first, then with relief and shaky emotion, she finally told her two best friends her story. From her life with her parents, to her life in foster care, to her troubles in school and her pregnancy. She described her years of working full time to finish college. And her friends just listened, asking a question here and there, but mostly just watching her, wide-eyed.

And finally she got to the end. Graduate school. "And that's when I met you two. Jenna, remember, we met in an exercise class at the USF gym? You were teaching it and…"

"You were my most dedicated student. I remember." Jenna smiled.

"And, Samantha, we met in that economics class."

"But I can't believe you never told us anything about yourself." Samantha paused. "Wait…you told me your parents lived on a farm in New England! You even told Jack that story on Halloween!"

"And you told me that your mom was afraid of flying and that's why they never visited," Jenna added.

"I lied," Tess admitted. "I lied about so much. I'm sorry. I just didn't want anyone to know the truth. I thought you'd see me differently. That you'd feel sorry for me or think I was damaged or something. Slaid did."

"We won't. We don't." Jenna leaned forward to look at Samantha. "Do we, Sam?"

"We love you," Samantha answered simply. "We'd love you the same way no matter what your story is."

"Even if you knew that up until my eighteenth birthday my name was Theresa Cooper?"

"Really?" They both leaned forward then to look at her, fascinated. Tess looked back and forth from one to the other, relieved to see only curiosity and acceptance in their expressions. No pity. No judgment.

"How cool!" Jenna said. "No offense to Theresa, but I like Tess Cole better. Way more glamorous."

"I wonder what name I'd choose if I was going to name myself," Samantha said.

Tess couldn't believe it. All these years she'd thought they'd look down on her for her past, and here they were so...*normal* about it.

"Something that sounds good with Baron..." Samantha mused.

"Jacqueline?" Jenna offered. "Then you could be Jack and Jacqueline Baron."

"Perfect!" Samantha and Jenna both burst out laughing, and even Tess had to smile at their goofiness.

"So is this why I barely saw you in Benson?" Samantha was serious now. "Because me having a baby is hard for you?"

Trust Samantha to get right to the very uncomfortable point. "It sounds so selfish when you say it out loud. I am truly happy for you, Sam, but when I'm around all this baby stuff it reminds me of when I was pregnant, and all the guilt I have for walking away from my baby comes flooding back."

"You were a kid when you had him," Jenna said gently.

"But I've been a grown-up for years now. I should have at least read some of these." She pointed to the tote bag, overflowing with letters.

"What do you want to do about them now?" Jenna asked.

Anxiety pitted Tess's stomach and suddenly the donuts she'd eaten seemed like an even worse idea. "I don't know. Read them?"

"Would it help if Jenna and I at least put them in order for you?" Samantha offered. "We could look at the postmarks and organize them from the first ones to the most recent."

Tess looked at Jenna and they smiled. Samantha loved to organize. "Why not?" Tess answered. "It might help."

So she curled up under a blanket on the couch while her best friends stacked the letters into neat piles by year, and when there were fourteen piles on her coffee table, they each gave her a kiss and announced they were going off to buy favors for the baby shower and would return in a few hours with good things to eat and a jumbo-size box of tissues, just in case.

When her apartment door shut behind them, the silence was deafening.

Tess stared at the letters for a long time. Each one had the potential to put one more crack into the armor she'd so carefully constructed around herself over the years. That many cracks would surely cause her to break. But the alternative, of pretending Adam had never happened, or that giving him up didn't hurt, was no longer an option. She'd just have to trust that if she completely fell apart, Jenna and Samantha would figure out a way to put her back together.

She decided to start with the most recent letters. If she saw pictures of baby Adam it might just bring up all that old pain and she wouldn't have the courage to go on. She reached over and took the first envelope off the "most recent" pile, flopped back onto the couch and opened it with shaking hands. A letter came out and with it a school portrait of a handsome teenager with slightly shaggy, sandy blonde hair. He had a huge smile that was slightly self-conscious. His dark blue eyes were her own. Tears threatened to spill, but Tess swiped them away and forced herself to set the photo aside and read the letter. It was written on a plain piece of notebook paper, and it took Tess a moment to realize that it was Adam himself who'd written it, not his parents.

Dear Theresa,
Here is my sophomore-year school picture. I hope you like it. I made the swim team this year and I did well in the first couple meets. My grades are good so far, though geometry is kind of hard to get the hang of. My whole family is doing well, Mom and Dad say to send their love, and my little brother, Cameron, who is a total pain right now, says hi.
Hope all is well with you,
Adam

His signature scrawled across the bottom of the page.

And that was it. Maybe he'd learned just to keep it short and sweet after years of writing to her and getting no answer.

And then the tears came. Again. Tess had no idea that the human body was capable of pumping out such vast quantities of salt water. She cried for all the years she'd missed, all the times he might have felt disappointed or sad that she hadn't reached out, and she cried for the other possibility, that maybe he didn't really care that she hadn't. That she'd made herself that insignificant in his life.

WHEN JENNA AND Samantha got back, Tess was puffy eyed and she'd used up all her tissues, but she'd also made it through most of the letters. Her friends quietly joined her on the couch for hugs and cracked the label on the excellent Scotch they'd brought with them. Tess sipped the potent drink in silence, not trusting herself to say anything. Samantha and Jenna just chatted idly about their shopping trip, respecting her need to pull herself together.

Tess hated how quivery her voice was when she finally spoke. "Thanks for the Scotch, guys, and the letter organizing and, well, everything."

"I'm so glad you finally told us," Jenna said softly. "I wish you'd said something years ago."

"You're our friend, Tess. We love you. Please don't ever feel like you have to lie about who you are."

They sat in silence, and Tess pondered her friends' words, feeling guilty that she'd so casually invented stories about her past for so long.

"You know." Jenna gave her a shy smile. "You are pretty damn good at the tall tales, Tess. I believed everything you told me about the childhood you never had."

"Me, too!" Samantha exclaimed. "You really are a talented…um…"

"Liar?" Tess supplied.

"I was going to say 'actress.'" Samantha giggled. "But, okay, *liar* works."

"Liar, liar, pants on fire," Jenna said in a squeaky schoolyard voice, and that was it. All the massive heartache and guilt turned into hysterical giggles that erupted from Tess with a snort that had them all laughing. Tess felt a floating in her limbs and muscles, the deepest, most profound relief that her friends loved her, that they didn't care who she'd been or that she'd lied. For the first time ever she could sit here with them, totally at ease, because now they knew who she really was.

A faint hope glimmered that there might be a better way to be than the tense, manufactured shell she'd become. And that she might be on her way to finding it.

THEY'D BEEN DECORATING since 7:00 a.m. Tess had set the alarm for six, determined to make up for the time they'd lost during her enormous meltdown. She'd made cappuccinos, run to the bakery down the street for pastries and then tempted her sleepy friends out of bed with them. It hadn't been easy, especially after the movie marathon they'd insisted on last night. A string of the most ridiculous comedies Jenna could find, which, despite the emotion of the day, had gotten Tess laughing.

And now she was on a ladder borrowed from one of the building maintenance workers, attaching blue paper baby booties to her ceiling. "You know," she said to Samantha, who'd insisted on helping with her own shower and was tying little blue ribbons on the party favors, "you need to get knocked up again right away. When I went shopping the other day I couldn't believe how cute all those little girl clothes were. I mean, no offense to the young gentleman you're carrying, but the boy clothes were so boring!"

"Maybe *you* should have a baby," Samantha said softly.

"Uh…been there, done that, and it was a disaster."

"But that was years ago, and you were a kid yourself."

Tess thought about the little clothes she'd picked out for Samantha's baby, how sweet they were, how tiny. How they'd inspired this strange maternal tug that was so unfamiliar she'd barely recognized it. "I'll just be the honorary auntie who spoils your kids. I'm not exactly a good candidate for reproducing. I'm jobless, guyless and all I really know about parenting is what *not* to do!" The booties were up and she started back down the ladder.

"That's not true, Tess," Samantha countered. "You can get any job you want, once word gets out that you're free. And you'd be an amazing mom. You've taken care of Jenna and me for years."

"Yeah, remember that night after Jeff and I broke up and you took me to Mack's Place and made me try all of your favorite kinds of Scotch?" Jenna asked.

Tess laughed. "Getting you drunk in a bar isn't exactly a good indicator of parenting potential."

"But you talked to me the whole time, remember? About having confidence and not needing men to make me whole? In fact, I remember you saying something about them having one real use, which could, at times, be taken care of by a small mechanical device."

A shocked yelp of laughter from Samantha had them all laughing. "How did I miss this outing?" she asked.

"You fell for a rancher and moved off to the middle of nowhere," Tess said.

"You're in love with a rancher, too," Samantha retorted.

"We're not talking about that. Unfortunately, I didn't find one like Jenna's, who prefers the city and cooks amazing food. Or one who actually likes me."

"Tess, it's obvious you miss Slaid," Jenna said gently.

"I do," she admitted. "But he fell in love with who he *thought* I was. Once he found out who I really am, he changed his mind. So I'll just have to get over it." She paused, taking a deep breath, looking for some humor to carry her through. "Plus, I barely survived a month in Benson, and I just saw the weather report—it's snowing a ton there now. Even if I decide to try to see him again, I have to wait at least six months for it to thaw out there."

"Oh, admit it, you miss wearing that parka. You know it looked fabulous on you," Samantha teased. "And from all the town gossip I heard, you were pretty happy to spend a fair amount of time out in the cold as long as you were with Slaid."

Tess glanced at her closet, where her parka hung. She remembered that first day when Slaid had chosen it for her and her chest felt funny, as though her skin was on too tight. "I'll pull it out on foggy San Francisco mornings," she said. "Anyway, Slaid wants nothing to do with me. He made that very clear."

"I think that's his pride talking," Samantha said gently. "And yours."

"Well, pride's about all I have left right now." Tess was pretty sure she'd exceeded her capacity for self-disclosure, *and* for thinking about Slaid and all that she couldn't have. "Let's go in the kitchen and you can make sure I have all the serving dishes organized. The caterers will drop off the food in about an hour."

CHAPTER TWENTY-SEVEN

SLAID RUBBED HIS eyes and reached for the coffee cup on his desk. It was empty—how had he gone through an entire pot already? The screen on his computer blurred and he rubbed his eyes again. One more of these email interviews and he was done. He was officially resigning from his week-long gig as the nation's most green mayor. He'd done interview after interview explaining that it wasn't just him, that it was a group effort that made the town solar powered. But the media evidently didn't appreciate a collective effort. A *New York Times* reporter had headlined her article The Sun King which had made him feel plenty stupid. Especially when the city council had laughingly presented him with a crown at their meeting earlier this evening.

He needed a PR person. Someone like Tess. But Tess was gone. Long gone. She'd left without saying goodbye and he was sure she'd never be back.

His cell phone buzzed and Slaid grabbed it, hoping it was Tess. But it was his sister, Mara, letting him know she'd just pulled up outside the town hall with Devin, who'd been having dinner and doing homework at her house while Slaid worked late.

Gratefully he shut down his computer, shoved some notes into his briefcase and headed out the door. He glanced at his phone once more before shoving it in his pocket. Nothing. He didn't know why he had any hope that Tess would call. He'd been such a jerk to her, she probably wanted nothing to do with him.

He'd been hurt that there'd been lies between them. He'd had enough of that with Jeannette. Hell, his ex-wife had let him think everything was fine between them when all the while she'd been planning her move to Florida.

But Tess hadn't told lies to hurt him. Or to conceal anything he had the right to know. He'd been in the wrong that last day in his office. So wrong that he knew he'd probably never get her back even if he called and begged her forgiveness.

But deep down he knew it wasn't just about being forgiven. He had some soul searching to do. It was clear that he had a problem with judging others. He'd convinced Tess that it was safe to open up to him, and when she finally did, he'd judged her. Now that he'd had some time to think, he'd realized that he'd had no right to.

He had no idea what it would be like to grow up like she did: unloved, uncared for and forced to make it through the world alone at such a young age. No wonder she'd picked a new name and constructed fantasy parents and a fantasy childhood. Because who would want to constantly revisit those real memories?

He pulled the big town hall doors shut behind him and walked over to where Mara was parked. Devin barely responded to Slaid's greeting. He slammed the car door, gave a brief wave to his aunt and walked over to Slaid's parked truck, waiting with crossed arms for Slaid to open the passenger door. It was eight o'clock at night and cold enough that the air prickled his skin and in the streetlight Slaid could see Devin's breath exhaling in white puffs. But he let his son tough it out in the cold air for a few moments. It seemed like he needed to cool off.

He went to the driver's side of Mara's SUV, and she rolled down the window.

"How is he?"

"Still grumpy. What did that woman do to him? He only met her a few times and he's acting almost as bad as when Jeannette left."

"They just really clicked. I guess he took it personally when she went back to the city."

"You have to talk to him, Slaid. He barely ate dinner, and I made my famous chicken potpie."

The stab of jealousy must have shown on Slaid's face because Mara laughed. "Don't worry, I saved you some." She handed him a plastic container and he clutched it passionately to his chest. Mara giggled again.

"Hey, don't laugh, this is precious stuff. Thanks for passing some along."

"Now go fix things with that son of yours. And double-check his homework. He did it, but his heart wasn't in it."

"Thanks, sis."

Slaid walked to the car and unlocked the doors.

"Jeez, Dad," Devin said as he clambered into the cold cab. "Thanks for letting me freeze."

"Seems as though you survived. You barely even said goodbye to Aunt Mara. I get that you're mad at me right now, but please don't take it out on her."

Devin looked straight ahead and Slaid started the engine. He knew his son was thinking his words through.

"It's your fault Tess didn't say goodbye, Dad. You led that rally, you destroyed her whole meeting. You totally humiliated her. You could have at least given her a chance to present her side."

His son's words stung, especially because he'd been thinking the same thing. Logically, he knew he hadn't done anything wrong. He'd protected his town, like he'd told Tess he would. But he should have found a way to protect her, as well.

"I warned her about the solar project, but I admit, I totally lost control of the protest. It got bigger than any of us expected."

"She could at least call, or text." Devin's voice was glum and, worse, resigned. He was used to not hearing from the women he bonded with, and it broke Slaid's heart. Especially because *he* was responsible for Devin's pain this time. He'd pushed Tess away. His close-minded judgment was why she'd left town without a word.

"Don't take it personally. She's mad at me, son, but she's got no reason to be mad at you. You two hit it off. Just give her time to cool down. I know she'll want to hear all about how you did on that essay."

He glanced over and saw Devin's brief smile. He'd earned an A on his essay, a miracle for a kid who usually kept his writing very brief and very sloppy.

"Did you two have a big fight?"

"Yes, we did. We were on opposite sides of the windmill conflict. And I was upset…" He didn't finish his sentence. He couldn't explain to his kid why he'd been furious. That he'd finally opened his heart to someone and couldn't handle finding out she wasn't perfect.

"Then you should apologize. Isn't that what you're always telling me to do?"

It was such a simple idea, but better than any he'd had. "You know what? You're right. I do owe her an apology. A big one."

He just hoped she'd listen. He was in love with her. He'd been drawn to her beauty but fallen for her dry humor, her silliness, her bravado and the softness in her eyes when she helped Devin. Knowing her quirks made her more beautiful to him than ever. Could accepting her imperfections do the same?

She'd have to accept plenty in him. He knew now that he came with way more flaws than he'd realized.

He wanted her in his life, forever. Right now it seemed impossible, but two years ago, when she'd disappeared from his hotel room, finding her had seemed impossible. Then she'd walked into his office in Benson and made him believe in all kinds of possibilities.

He couldn't let her walk out of his life again. He needed to figure out how to convince her that he was no longer the idiot who'd pushed her away, or the jerk who kept judging her. He had to show her that he was the man who would always believe in her, who loved her for who she really was, if he hoped to find a way to get her back.

TESS FLOPPED DOWN on the couch next to Samantha. "I can't believe I'm about to do this."

"Eat a slice of cake and drink some champagne? I think you can handle the calories. I've barely seen you eat anything since I got here."

"But the cake is blue!" Tess eyed it suspiciously.

"It's boy cake!" Jenna sat down next to her. "It's really good. And the coloring is all natural."

"Natural? There's nothing naturally blue in nature," Tess said. "Except blueberries, I guess." She took a bite of the strange blue creation anyway.

"Oh, my gosh, it's delicious," she blurted out with a mouthful of crumbs.

Samantha giggled. "I think the guests thought so, too. There's not that much left. Thank you so much, you two, for an amazing baby shower. I had so much fun." She patted her round belly. "I think this guy did, too. I think he's dancing in there."

"Can I feel?" Jenna jumped up from her place on the other side of Tess and went to sit by Samantha. She put her palm on her friend's belly and a huge smile lit up her face. "I can feel him! Come on, Tess, put your hand here."

Tess reluctantly lifted her hand and let Jenna guide it. At first she didn't feel anything, but then something pressed against her palm, and moved along it. "He's swimming!" she exclaimed. Samantha smiled in pride and Jenna added her hand alongside Tess.

"He's got moves," Jenna said. "Maybe he'll be a dancer."

"Jack's convinced he'll be the next horse whisperer, Slaid thinks he'll be mayor of Benson someday and you..." She broke off. "Sorry, Tess, I shouldn't have mentioned Slaid."

"How is he?" she asked quietly.

"He's been busy with all the media attention," Samantha said. "Mostly he seems kind of distracted and sad, I think."

"I never said goodbye," Tess confessed.

"You didn't call him?"

"What's the point? He made it clear that he thinks I'm horrible. Even if he didn't, he's there, I'm here, end of story."

"You don't have to be here. You got fired, remember? And I've already told you, with the baby coming, I need help with my company. As in, I need you to take over."

"I can't go back to Benson. It's freezing, and everyone hates me."

"No one hates you!" Samantha sat up and looked at her with outrage in her green eyes. "Everyone knows you were just there to do a job. And everyone saw how happy Slaid and Devin were with you. No one hates you." She grinned suddenly. "Well, maybe some of the single ladies who had a thing for Slaid hate you...but other than that, I really don't think you'd have a problem."

"I do have a problem. I told Slaid about my past and he kicked me out of his life. Just like that."

"Well, whatever he did, I think he regrets it," Samantha said.

"Plus, you're making things right," Jenna said. "You read the letters, and now you're going to get in touch with your son and his adoptive parents. Right?"

"Am I?" Tess asked. "Because honestly, I don't know if I can. I'm not exactly known for my courage when it comes to my personal life."

"You have more courage than anyone I know," Jenna told her. "Look what you went through as a

kid. And look where you got yourself!" She gestured around the apartment. "This place. Paid off.
A great career. Well, a great career until last week,
I guess. But anyway…"

"But I don't feel like I have any courage. I just
want to hide in here and eat a lot of blue cake.
Maybe we're born with a finite supply of courage
and I've used up mine."

"It just needs replenishing," Jenna assured her.

Samantha stood up and took the plate of blue
cake crumbs out of Tess's hand. Jenna, following
some invisible agreement between them, stood up,
too, and took the champagne glass out of her other.
Both her friends extended a hand and pulled her
off the couch. "Mack's Place," Jenna said.

"Greasy fish and chips for dinner and as much
Scotch as you desire," Samantha added.

Tess tried to imagine leaving the cocoon of her
apartment and couldn't. Between her misery over
the letters and life in general and the baby shower,
she hadn't been outside in thirty-six hours. She
could easily imagine curling up on her couch for
at least thirty-six more.

Samantha's phone beeped and she picked it up.
Her mouth tilted up in a smug smile as she read
the text.

"It must be Jack," Jenna said. "Look at that
smile."

Samantha just shook her head once and walked
away from them, texting rapidly as she went. Then

she turned back and her green eyes sparkled. "Okay, let's get you dressed, Tess—in something gorgeous. It's time to go find your missing courage."

CHAPTER TWENTY-EIGHT

"WEE JENNA!" MACK'S voice boomed across the bar as they pushed through the door. "And beautiful Tess. My darling, have you come back here just to break my heart?" Mack's thick Scottish accent put a musical note into everything he said. His gray hair was combed neatly into place as always, his white oxford button-down straining a bit over his ample belly. Tess ran over and reached across the bar for their customary hug. Mack was her favorite man to flirt with—a happily married grandfather, totally safe and hilarious. Tess felt better already, just seeing him.

"Mack, how have you been?"

"Destitute since you left." He clutched his heart in mock agony. "Are you back for good now?"

"Here to stay."

"My life is worth living again."

Tess laughed at his outrageousness.

He looked at Tess's skintight black dress and raised an eyebrow, all grandfather now. "And you're wearing that outfit because…"

"It's supposed to make me feel brave. Things haven't exactly been going my way."

"Well, young lady, I think you might've gotten *courage* mixed up with *encourage*."

"That might not be so bad…" Tess raised an eyebrow and Mack laughed.

"I've missed ya, Tess."

"So what do you recommend tonight?" She glanced back at Jenna. "It's going to take more than my fabulous outfit to buck me up."

Mack reached for his top shelf, where he kept the best stuff. "Try a nip of this, darlin'." He poured two fingers of amber liquid into a glass for her, and another for Jenna. "A twenty-five-year-old Bowmore. Can't tell you where I got it…" He gave an outrageous wink. "But if this doesn't make ya feel larger than life, I don't know what will."

He poured himself a tiny splash as well, and they clinked glasses. "And where's that Samantha tonight? Wee Jenna here told me she was coming to the city this weekend. I've got a gift here for the baby, from Mrs. Mack."

"She's changing back at her apartment," Tess said. Samantha lived in Benson full-time, but she'd never given up her San Francisco apartment. She joked that the price of housing had gone so high, if she sold it she'd never be able to buy it back again. But Tess knew it was because her friend wanted to keep a connection to her life in the city. "She should be here any minute."

As if on cue the door opened and Samantha came in, looking adorable in a long black maternity top, leggings and ballet flats.

"It's the mother-to-be!" called Mack, and he came around the side of the bar to embrace Samantha. "Look at you!"

But Tess wasn't looking at Samantha anymore. She was looking at the man who'd come through the door behind her—the man who seemed to fill the room with his broad shoulders and strong presence. Slaid, minus the cowboy hat, wore a black leather jacket and jeans that fit like sin. His eyes were locked on hers as he walked slowly toward her.

Tess grabbed her glass and took a gulp, praying that the rare Bowmore really did have the magical powers that Mack promised it did. "Why are you here?" She gasped.

He stopped a few feet away from where she leaned on the bar. "To see you again."

"I mean…" She faltered. "How did you find me?"

"Samantha."

Tess looked at her friend, who was talking with Mack, pretending not to watch Tess and Slaid anxiously out of the corner of her eye.

"Tess, I owe you so much…" He swallowed hard and looked around the bar, seeming to notice his surroundings for the first time. "Can we sit down for a moment?" he asked.

"Sure." Heart pounding, she led him to the old scarred table by the window, the one she and her friends called the conference table. Far away enough from the bar for privacy, yet still close enough for people watching.

They sat across from each other, and Tess silently commanded her slamming pulse to settle down. Slaid reached across for her hands. She cautiously reached back, and he easily enfolded hers with his. "I need to apologize."

"For what?" she asked.

"There's so much. For not realizing what a circus that town meeting was going to become. I'm the mayor, I should anticipate that kind of thing. It got bigger and crazier than I'd imagined."

"You were a part of it, Slaid. You were Don Quixote attacking the windmills."

"I planned that back when the parade was supposed to be a small march. We were parading to *attract* media attention. I didn't know we'd be drowning in it. I had no idea that so many people from out of town would join in. Or that there'd be dead bird puppets and all that. But I should have seen it coming… I wasn't paying close enough attention."

"Apparently I wasn't, either. And I got fired because of it."

"I'm sorry. I didn't know." He looked at her closely. "Are you sorry?"

"I'm not sure," she answered truthfully.

"You're amazing at your work. You'll find something better. Hell, I'll be a reference. I've been on the receiving end of your skills!"

She had to laugh at that. "I just might take you up on it."

"Tess, I reacted so badly when you told me about your past. Honestly, I'm ashamed to think of it. I didn't even try to see things from your point of view or consider the enormous courage it took for you to tell me everything. I just judged—again. It's a part of my character I'm not proud of. I was raised conservatively, taught that there's just one right way to be. And I pressured you to be that way. I will try my hardest not to do it ever again."

"That would be nice," she said weakly.

"I think about you all the time. About us—you, me and Devin. I feel as though we're meant to be together."

"Look, I know you. You're the Eagle Scout. You want to do good in the world, help people. I won't be your charity project. I don't want your pity. Or anyone else's."

"Is that why you've never dated?"

"What's the point? As soon as I started dating someone, the guy would want to know my life story, and I could either lie or have them look at me all sorrowfully, like you're doing now." She pulled her hands from his and took a sip of her Scotch.

"It's not pity, Tess."

"Then what is it? Because you sure didn't look at me like this before I told you about my past."

"I guess it's sadness. I love you, and I'm sad that the most amazing person I've ever met went through such hard times. It doesn't make me pity you. It makes me admire you even more."

"What's to admire about being a pregnant teenager living in a group home?"

"Because you are no longer that pregnant teenager. You overcame insane amounts of hardship and what must have been a really lonely and scary childhood and became this gorgeous, successful person who I want to spend all my time with."

It was hard to absorb his words. Her glass was empty. She stared at it blankly and Slaid rose. "I'll get you another. I could use one myself." And she knew he was really just giving her a moment to take in what he'd said. He loved her. She loved him.

Slaid came back with a very large glass of Scotch for each of them. Tess looked at it, astonished. "Mack said it looked as if we could each use a stiff one," he explained.

"Mack might be trying to give us alcohol poisoning."

"Well, he did mention something about being jealous, and that I'd better treat you right or I'd have to answer to him."

Tess burst out laughing at the idea of Mack trying to have it out with Slaid. It was sweet and silly all at once. She looked past Slaid and raised her glass to Mack, who was at the bar polishing glasses and keeping an eye on them. He raised a sparkling glass in response.

"So you don't hold it against me?" she asked.

Slaid froze with the glass midway to his lips. "Hold what against you?"

"That I gave my baby up for adoption, and that I never stayed in touch."

"I know what it's like to love a child. I can't imagine the pain of saying goodbye to one. I'd like to think I'd try to be there for my kid, but how do I know what I'd do? I've never been in your shoes." Then he smiled. "Thank goodness, because I don't think I could walk in heels."

Tess smiled back. "Well, I'm going to try to get in touch with him. With Adam. My son."

There was relief and joy in Slaid's smile. "I'll be there for you, through it all, if you'll let me."

"I'd like that."

"I'd like to be there for you every day." He took her glass away and held her hand. "Please come back to Benson and stay with us. We miss you."

"How can I go back to the scene of my very recent public humiliation? I'm pretty sure everyone hates me."

"They like you. You heard Betty at the football game. They just didn't like what you were selling."

"But what would I do there?"

"Learn to ride. Work with Samantha. Take up the hobbies you've never had a chance to try because you've been too busy working so hard all your life. Have babies with me—"

"Easy there, cowboy!" But the image of Slaid holding their tiny baby crept into her mind and took hold. She took another sip of her drink.

"The snow's been coming down all week," Slaid said.

"See? Another reason why this could never work."

"You were excited about the first snowfall! Have you ever skied, sledded, tried snowboarding, made a snow angel?"

"No," Tess said dubiously. "But if you think you'll convince me that lying down in ice-cold snow and waving my arms around is a good idea, I think Mack's addled your brain with that Scotch."

"We'll bundle you up really warm and you'll love it."

Tess looked down at her glass. Courage. She'd asked for courage and her girlfriends had brought her here, and Mack had poured her a couple glasses of it. Now was the time to gather it up and use it. "Two weeks," she said. "I'll commit to a two-week visit."

Slaid was out of his seat and had her out of hers in seconds, hugging her, lifting her off her feet, swinging her around and nearly taking out a couple of Mack's other patrons in the process. He set her down and kissed her, sending her senses reeling.

"What's going on?" Jenna called. Her voice, coming through the haze of Slaid's kisses, sounded as though it was miles away. "Slaid, did you propose?"

He looked up, and Tess watched the way humor sparkled in his eyes. "I got two weeks! She's staying with me for two weeks. Drinks for everyone, on me!"

AFTERWORD

CHRISTMAS LIGHTS GLOWED around the roofline of Slaid's house. Through the window, Tess saw Devin curled up on the couch, reading a book. It was dusk, and she'd stayed out longer than she'd meant to, mesmerized by the way her skis slid over the snow in the now-familiar rhythm of cross-country skiing.

Her two weeks had turned into a month. Thanksgiving had come and gone and now it would be Christmas soon. One more family holiday she'd always avoided. One more family event she now looked forward to. Family. She still couldn't believe she had one, but she really felt like she did. And she'd never been happier.

Slaid opened the back door as she skied up. "Hey, there. I was starting to worry." He stepped out and helped her put her poles and skis against the side of the house. Once inside, he gave her a steaming cup of cocoa.

"Thank you." She kissed him on the cheek and took a sip.

"Your cheeks are all pink. You're beautiful."

"It was so nice out there. Peaceful. It was hard

to get myself to turn back." When she'd first come to Benson the quiet had scared her. Now she liked being alone with her thoughts, because most of them were happy ones these days.

"Did you fix the railing?" When she'd left for her ski, Slaid had been out repairing things in the barn. In her four weeks here, she'd discovered that winter on a ranch involved a lot of fixing things.

"Yep. Feels good to finally get it done. I love having you here, Tess, but you're a distraction. I haven't checked much off my to-do list these past four weeks."

"Yes, but you've checked a lot off mine." Tess lowered her voice, making sure Devin wouldn't overhear, in case he was nearby. "Let's see, there's sex, and more sex, and teaching me to ski, and then…sex…"

Slaid silenced her with a kiss that promised he'd keep working on her to-do list later that evening. Then he went to the stove to stir the soup they'd made together earlier in the afternoon.

Tess sipped her cocoa and looked out the window as the last light left the sky. The past few weeks had been amazing, and despite what she'd just said to Slaid, it hadn't *all* been sex and skiing. She'd also spent time just hanging out with Devin and Slaid, and she'd visited Samantha frequently. Her friend was due any day now.

She was also getting to know Samantha's business. It looked as if Tess would be taking over all the public relations accounts Samantha had established in the year since she'd moved to Benson. Samantha intended to be a full-time mommy for at least the first year of her little boy's life.

And Tess had finally written to Adam's parents and thanked them for the years of letters. With their permission, she'd written to Adam, too, and now there was a plan afoot for all of them to meet in Los Angeles this summer. Slaid and Devin were going with her to Disneyland, and there, in the happiest place on earth, they'd meet up with Adam and his family. Both boys were excited for the trip and had connected via email. They'd found common ground in being adopted and in having spent years wondering about their birth mothers.

Of course Devin was still wondering, and Tess worried that maybe he always would. His birth mother had several more years on her prison sentence, and his letters were always returned unopened.

"Either you find your reflection in that window as beautiful as I do, or you're deep in thought. You've been staring out there for a while."

"I was thinking about everything. You, Devin, Samantha, Adam... So much has fallen into place for me this past month."

"It's because you're happy here," Slaid said, turning her to face him. He kissed her lightly. "It's because the three of us are a family." He kissed her again while she relished his words. "And because you and I are amazing together."

A small shiver went over her as his mouth closed on her neck and worked its way down to her shoulder and back up to her ear. "If we get any more amazing we'll have to send Devin to bed early." She laughed.

"Rain check?" he asked hopefully.

"Snow check," she corrected. "Definitely."

And suddenly Tess knew it was the perfect time for the surprise she'd been planning for the past week, with Devin's help. She still couldn't believe she was brave enough to do what she was about to do.

She went into the living room, where Devin was curled on the couch with a book. "Remember what we talked about the other day?" she asked him in a low voice.

His face lit up. "The Plan?" he whispered.

"Do you still have the ring?"

"Of course! It's in my sock drawer."

"And you still think this is a good idea?" She'd asked his permission to marry his dad. Devin had dealt with too much relationship upheaval—Tess wanted him to have a say in this next part of his future. To her huge relief, he'd been ecstatic about the idea and had been walking around ever since with a huge, mischievous smile on his face. It had been making Slaid crazy trying to figure out what his son was up to.

"Yeah, of course! I'll go get the ring."

He bounded off the couch and ran to his room, returning with the small velvet box. "I can't believe I'm doing this," Tess whispered. She put the box under the tree. "Okay, now go sit on the couch and act normal."

Devin's grin was Cheshire-cat huge. He hopped back on the couch, holding his book up in front of his face at an awkward angle. He didn't look the slightest bit normal.

Tess went back into the kitchen and kissed Slaid on the cheek. "Hey, by the way," she said casually. "There's something under the Christmas tree for you. An early present."

"Really? Santa showed up today?" Slaid looked excited, and it struck Tess suddenly that this holiday thing was kind of new for him, too. As a single dad, he probably wasn't used to surprises under the tree.

"Go check it out." Her heart was pounding—she was far more nervous than she thought she'd be.

Slaid went into the living room and Tess followed. Devin looked up from his book. "Tess said I have an early present," Slaid said, walking toward the tree they'd decorated together. Her first Christmas tree—she couldn't get enough of its sweet pine scent and its twinkling lights. "Tess, does Devin get one, too?"

"Sort of," Devin answered.

Tess watched Devin, looking for signs of worry

or doubt, but there was none. He caught her looking and gave her a thumbs-up.

Slaid stood up, holding the small box, and shook it.

"Careful!" Tess and Devin said in unison.

Slaid looked from one to the other. "Is this what you two have been giggling about all week?" he asked.

"No…" they both said at once, in the same falsely innocent voice.

"Huh." Slaid looked at them warily. "Should I be worried?"

"Just open it, Dad!" Devin gave up all pretext of reading and set down his book. Tess walked over to the couch and put her hand on Devin's shoulder. "Don't be nervous," he whispered, so loudly that Slaid gave them another questioning look.

He carefully untied the bow, then opened the lid of the box and pulled out sparkly gold tissue paper. Then his eyes got wide as he took out the navy blue velvet ring box.

"Um…" He looked at Tess, obviously mystified.

"Go!" Devin said.

Tess took the ring box out of Slaid's hand and sank to one knee, just like she'd practiced with Devin. She opened the lid with shaking hands to reveal the plain platinum band, and looked up at Slaid. She had to concentrate to remember what it was she'd planned to say.

"Slaid? I didn't think that love was possible for

me. I didn't think that family was possible. But now that I've found you, and Devin, and love, I've found my family. And my home. I love you so much. Will you marry me?"

Slaid looked down at her, and his eyes were wet with emotion. He glanced at Devin.

"She already asked me, Dad. I said yes."

Slaid's laughter rang out. "Well, I'm glad, Dev. Because I'm going to say yes, too. Although I want you to know, Tess, that I would have asked you. Ages ago. But I didn't want to pressure you…"

"So is that a yes?"

"You bet it is." He took a step forward and knelt down with her. "Tess Cole, will you marry me? Will you be a family with me and Devin and let us love you forever?"

She was home. After a lifelong journey, she'd finally come home. She threw her arms around Slaid's neck, kissing him and laughing at the same time. "Yes! I'll marry you, Slaid." She kissed him once more and then stood, pulled him up with her and held her arms out to Devin. He came over and she pulled him in for a hug. Then Slaid pulled them both close, wrapping them in his strong arms, and they stood there for a moment, and all Tess could think was that they were hers. *Her family.* And she loved them so much.

And then Devin's muffled voice emerged from between them. "Hey, I'm getting squished down here." And they all burst out laughing. She and

Slaid let go and Devin stepped back and said, "Gross. Way too much love stuff, you guys." But his smile told a different story.

* * * * *

LARGER-PRINT BOOKS!

HARLEQUIN *Presents*

PASSION GUARANTEED SEDUCTION

GET 2 FREE LARGER-PRINT
NOVELS PLUS 2 FREE GIFTS!